The Starstone

Grace Chetwin

THE
STARSTONE

FROM
Tales of Gom
IN THE
LEGENDS OF ULM

j

c. 1

1989

(*Bradbury Press* · *New York*

Bradbury Press
An Affiliate of Macmillan, Inc.
866 Third Avenue, New York, N.Y. 10022
Collier Macmillan Canada, Inc.

Printed and bound in the United States of America
First Edition
10 9 8 7 6 5 4 3 2 1

The text of this book is set in 12 point Garamond No. 3.
The illustrations are rendered in pen-and-ink.
The map of Ulm is based on the one Carrick the tinker gave Gom.
The view of Folgan's mountain house
is based on one drawn from Gom's recollection.
The view of Sundborg is based on Lady Vala's diagram.

Library of Congress Cataloging-in-Publication Data

Chetwin, Grace.
The starstone : from tales of Gom in the legends of Ulm /
by Grace Chetwin.—1st ed.
Summary: Apprenticed to a wizard, Gom begins to learn how to use
the powers that help destroy the evil Katak and recover the lost
emerald Seal. Sequel to "The Riddle & the Rune."
ISBN 0-02-718315-7
{1. Fantasy.} I. Title.
PZ7.C42555St 1989
{Fic}—dc19   88-30249   CIP   AC

Series – 6-28-10 P∩R

For Briony
With love

GREAT

RINGING
VALLEY

DUNDERFOSSE

T H E   W I L D S

SUNDOR
Sundborg

S O U T H E R N

KRUGK

HIGH VARGUE

Quend

Green Vale

Bragget-on-the-Edge

LONG VALLEY

Lake Langoth

Pen'langoth

SHORE

Chapter One

GOM LAY on his back, listening. He was not alone. He could feel the other presence probing the darkness, searching. . . . A speck of light sparked above his head. He blinked and looked again. The light flared, then condensed to form a ghostly skull that floated, hollow sockets fixed upon him.

"Katak!"

As Gom spoke the name, cold touched his fingertips, crawled through his hand, and up his arm. Katak's deathsleep! He reached for his wizard mother's rune to ward it off—not there, of course. Move, Gom urged himself. Move, while you can, before you freeze entirely! He tried to sit up, but couldn't. He tried to call out, but his lips were clamped. Fear rushed through, a burst of hot panic unlocking his paralysis. . . .

Gom sat up in bed, his heart pounding. He raised his eyes apprehensively to the darkness above. Nothing. Yet moments before, that pale skull, the form in which the alien shape-changer usually appeared, had hovered over him, and its evil cold had crawled up his arm, and into his chest, toward his heart.

Katak: Spohr: shape-changer. *Here?*

Gom raised his left hand, felt its icy coldness.

His eyes adjusting to the night dark, Gom looked about the walls of his tiny bedchamber, thinking of the deep place under the Sound, where he and the sea creature Ganash had trapped Katak and shut him away with the Spohr's own seal-spell. Had Katak somehow gotten free of the kundalara and found Gom out?

Agh! Gom crossed his arms over his chest, rubbing his ribs in brisk dismissal. Hadn't Harga reassured him that Katak would stay safely put? And hadn't Ganash guaranteed it? This had been but a nightmare. Hadn't his last waking thought been of the Spohr? As for the numbed hand—Gom leaned down, felt the floor. There! His arm had been dangling over the side of his cot; his fingers resting on the icy flagstone. But, yet . . . Gom hugged himself again, rocking back and forth. Those dark sockets, that empty stare . . .

Down in the cavern under the Northern Sound, as Gom had crouched in the protective coils of Ganash's tail, Katak's cold had stolen over the pair of them. And had it not been for Harga's rune, they might be there still.

Fear increased. Freed, would Katak really seek him out? That other time, Katak had sought the rune that Gom's mother, Harga the Brown, had left with him on the day of his birth. But Harga had it back, so that couldn't draw the evil one.

Gom wasn't entirely comforted.

He reached up to the bedrail for the belt his wizard mother had given him, and opened the pouch. His fingers encountered a small silver ring. More than ring: it was key, a magic key to Harga's domain. Nudging it aside, Gom took out a pendant, a small crystal with a tiny gold flake embedded within it—another gift from Harga at their parting. This crystal was nowhere near as powerful as her rune, for that stone had accumulated so much magic over many years. But Katak might yet come after it. The Spohr sought gems of all kinds, whether invested with magic or not, hadn't Ganash said?

"If Katak is after magic, why does he want your treasure?"

"Because . . . from precious gold and silver and priceless gemstones is much magic made. . . ."

Katak was going to need a great deal of magical power to fulfill his aim on Ulm. Ah! Gom shook his head. He was giving himself far too much importance! There were many gemstones in the world of much greater value than Gom's crystal! Precious jewels belonging to the rich; runestones belonging to the Hierarchy. Katak would be far more interested in them, Gom told himself, but he was still not reassured. What if the Spohr sought revenge for Gom's shutting him away? It might be wise to keep that dream in mind.

A bang on the door made him jump. "Ho, boy! Only one hour to dawn and there's much to do before then! Up, up and stir yourself!"

Folgan.

Gom stuffed the crystal back in his pouch, not daring to wear it in the wizard's company, then he tumbled out of bed, and pulled on his clothes. His new wizard master was calling him out to begin the first official day of his apprenticeship. Gom slipped through into the kitchen to find the man fully dressed and waiting.

At the sight of the wizard standing there in a clean gray gown, with long gray locks and beard neatly brushed, Gom felt crumpled and shabby, even scruffy. He was aware of his own travelworn shirt and breeches, his dusty boots, hastily tied. He had not washed as yet, of course, and his dark brown hair stuck out in clumps all over. He pulled himself up to his full height—which was not much—raked his tangled mop back with his fingers, and faced his new master square on.

"Humph. Asleep, eh? On your first night here?"

"No, sir. I wasn't," Gom began, but Folgan was off and running through a well-worn homily that he wasn't about to change on Gom's account.

"In my day, apprentices never slept the first night. They were excited, eager to start work." Folgan pulled on his beard, looked down at Gom from under his brows. "But times have changed, and things aren't as they used to be. Oh, well." He thrust a sheet of paper under Gom's nose. "Your list of early chores. Hurry, or we'll be eating our breakfast at dinner!"

"But—" Gom stared down, dismayed. "I—I can't read, sir."

"Can't—" The wizard frowned. "Harga the Brown's son, unable to read?"

Gom opened his mouth to protest, closed it again. Harga had not had chance to teach him anything, but he couldn't say so, couldn't say a word about his mother's business, not to this man—not to anyone.

"Makes me wonder, boy, why she was so anxious to get rid of you, to foist you onto some other mage. Oh, well, I suppose now you're here, you might as well get on." Folgan raised the list to read it out. "Remember each thing, for I'll say it only once: first you'll feed and let out the horses. Then fetch up logs from the pile by the door and water from the spring down the mountainside. You might clean yourself up while you're at it—you look a disgrace! After you come back, you'll stir the fire and make breakfast—and be quick about it. When it's ready, you'll summon me from my workroom with this." The wizard reached down a small brass bell from the mantelshelf.

At mention of the wizard's workroom, Gom's interest perked up. "Where do I find the workroom, sir?"

"You don't, boy." Folgan shook the bell. "Just stand in the doorway there and ring the thing. I'll hear, I assure you. Now get moving, the day's already half gone."

It was still not yet light when Gom carried fresh hay into the horses' warm cave. Stormfleet greeted him sleepily. "How goes it?"

"Oh, wonderful," Gom grumbled. "Folgan is all kindness, don't you know?" He thought with longing of The Jolly Fisherman back in Pen'langoth. Of Essie the landlady, who would now be bustling about the kitchen, preparing breakfast for her customers. Of his friend Carrick the master tinker lying in the attic room he'd shared with Gom: a low, comfortable chamber with wide view of the lake. Gom had felt so welcome there.

"Never mind," Stormfleet said. "Better than nothing. Just think: if you hadn't been so quick-witted, you'd not be anywhere."

True. Gom patted the cito's flank gratefully. "You'll be all right?"

Stormfleet tossed his mane. "Right as rain," he said. "Hevron says we have the run of the place. When Folgan's not traveling, we may come and go as we please. As soon as it's light, Hevron is going to show me around."

"Oh, really," Gom said. "I'm very happy for you."

"You don't look it."

Gom wasn't, much. Not fair, that he should be penned up while Stormfleet roamed the mountainside at will! And yet—that was a bit selfish. And perhaps unwise. Back in Pen'langoth, when the shoe had been on the other foot, Stormfleet had gotten very restless cooped up in Essie's stable. If the wild colt had not found his brief stay in that inn stall to his liking, how was he going to take a seven-year stint in this lonely mountain hole? Still. "You're born of the plains. You don't like this kind of territory, remember?"

"Ah," Stormfleet said. "That was then. I'm a seasoned traveler now."

"Seasoned traveler, indeed." Gom was not impressed. "Only yesterday, while we were climbing up here, you almost fell in a couple of places. In fact, that last time I thought you'd refuse to move another step."

"I was tired," Stormfleet said. "That's all."

"No, that's not all." Gom ran his hand over Stormfleet's sagging spine, sadly remembering the once wide and slippery back, the black glossy coat, long legs, and telltale silver ringmark on the brow. Who would guess that this sorry-looking old nag, with his knock-knees, dull gray coat, and yellowed rheumy eyes, was that proud, immortal cito? Such was the disguise Harga the Brown had laid on Stormfleet at the cito's own request, a disguise to protect him from those who sought him, especially the Yul Kinta. Although Stormfleet could move better than one might think, he still lacked his real strength and grace and balance. Dangerous, for Stormfleet to roam those tricky slopes in his present state.

Stormfleet arched his neck. "I can see exactly what you're thinking, Gom Gobblechuck. Rest assured I'll watch my step."

"Please do," Gom said, and made to say more, but bit his tongue. His friend, wild and proud, and a cito into the bargain, didn't take kindly to advice and admonitions.

"You're a regular bag of fret, aren't you?" Hevron blew gently on Gom's cheek. "I promise you I'll watch where

Stormfleet sets his hooves. I'm not about to lose welcome company. And anyway," the roan added, "a cito is immortal, is it not?"

Gom looked from Hevron to Stormfleet in alarm. "Immortality's not proof against a broken neck, Hevron!"

"Oh, don't fuss so!" Stormfleet stamped a foot. "I'll be fine!"

"If you must worry"—Hevron butted Gom's shoulder—"look to yourself: get back upstairs, before my master comes to fetch you!"

Gom put his arms about Stormfleet's neck. "Enjoy yourself," he murmured. Turning about, he took up some three, four logs, and hauled them inside, all the way up to the kitchen, his thoughts churning. What if Stormfleet should get stuck? What if he should fall? Gom almost ran back down to beg the colt to reconsider. But there'd be no point. *Seven years!* Stormfleet had to learn to go afield—and Gom must let him!

Folgan was grumpy at breakfast, and in no mood for talk. But when he'd finished his toast and tea, and filled a fat, black briar from a baccy barrel on the mantelshelf, and lit it with a taper from the fire, the wizard did show Gom the rest of the house.

It reminded Gom of Harga's, for both were hollowed out under stone. In both, the front hall was the lowest level and the workshop, the top. But in between, Harga's living space ran horizontally under a lake island bluff, making three levels in all; while Folgan's chambers were stacked one above the other almost vertically under granite rock face for full four. From Folgan's entrance hall, way above—one hundred or more steps above—was the kitchen. Gom's tiny room, a converted larder, lay back

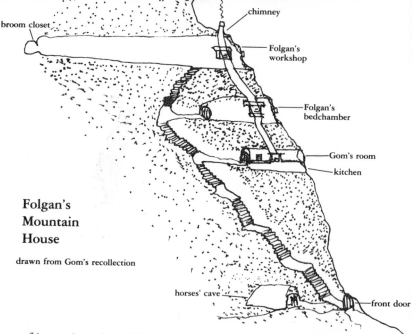

broom closet

chimney

Folgan's
workshop

Folgan's
bedchamber

Gom's room

kitchen

**Folgan's
Mountain
House**

drawn from Gom's recollection

horses' cave

front door

of it on the other side of the chimney. Above the kitchen,
up another flight of steep, uneven steps, was Folgan's
bedchamber. In it was a wide four-poster bed that Gom
was to make each day, and a washstand with a wide blue
bowl that Gom was to fill every morning with hot water.
Beside that stood a highdaddy crammed with clothes that
Gom was to keep washed and darned for Folgan.

Over that chamber was the top and final level: Folgan's
workshop, but Gom did not see it that day. It was barred
by a stout oak door across the bottom stair—which would
remain barred, Folgan said, until Gom had mastered his
letters and numbers. Gom tried not to let that bother
him. After all, if he worked hard, it shouldn't take long,
a week or two, perhaps. Then Folgan would have to let
him up that stair to begin his real work at last.

All morning, Gom obeyed Folgan's orders faithfully.
For elevenses, he made a hot vegetable broth with buttered crusts toasted at the hearth. And he set a table fit

for the Lake Lord himself. But if Folgan was pleased, he didn't say so. The wizard only complained that the broth was not salty enough, and that the toast was soggy.

Not true! Gom took a slice and snapped it in half. Really, the man's eyes were everywhere looking for complaint! Gom washed the dishes fast, eager for his first writing lesson. But he spent the afternoon washing the dirty clothes from Folgan's traveling pack, with no sign of letter or number. Gom tried not to mind. After all, the wizard had been away from home for several weeks. He must have some catching up to do.

That night, Gom lay in his cot, looking through his narrow window. The deep sky was salted with stars. But he'd not find the one where Harga was. The Seven Realms were strung like a bright necklace across the far side of Ulm, over the southern seas. Gom took the crystal from his pouch.

If any time the stone should flash, close your hand about it, and you'll stand once more by the crystal stair. Alamar. *If you should be asleep, or otherwise engaged, the gold flake will call you with a waking dream. . . .*

Mother.

If only the crystal would summon him to her! Any moment, perhaps the very next one, she might call him to meet her, face to face. Not for real, though. Gom sighed. Only *alamar.* Only his mind would travel, while his body remained locked in deep unconsciousness in Folgan's mountain house. And yet it would be better than nothing, as, alamar, he climbed the glassy stair to speak with her in the bright beam of the Tamarith, wondrous pillar of living crystal, shining starstone of enormous power.

Loneliness settled over him, cold as the air in his room.

When, Mother? When?

It could be long. Whole days on Ulm were as moments among the stars, though Harga couldn't explain why. Yawning, Gom stowed away his crystal and lay down on his narrow cot. It certainly was firm! He thought of his friend Mat—*former* friend Mat. He pictured Mat lying in idle comfort in Bokar Riffik's house, having an easy time at Gom's expense. The last time he'd seen Mat, Gom had been on his way to meet his new master, Bokar Riffik. Mat had tricked Gom, sending him away from the meeting on an errand. By the time Gom had finally returned, Bokar Riffik had gone—with Mat in Gom's place. And Gom had been left for Mat's intended master, Folgan. Just wait until he met Mat again—Gom would tell him a thing or two! Gom turned over, dismissing Mat from his thoughts. His mind drifted. He took to thinking of the dream he'd had the night before, of the death's-head shining in the dark.

Katak. *Spohr.* Evil entity from an alien star.

Gom grew apprehensive now. When he fell asleep, would the skull reappear? The very idea jolted him wide awake. He opened his eyes, saw the solid shape of his staff leaning against the foot rail, the outlines of the mountain creatures coiling up around the stock, the little wooden sparrow poised on top as though to fly. His father, Stig, had carved it as walking stick just before he died. Gom's staff now, it had been with him on all his travels, comforted him, given him courage, and saved him from many a disaster. Like that first time, when, only days out of Windy Mountain, Katak had attacked him in the shape of a skull-bird. The staff had saved Gom's life. His face softening, he recalled lying down to sleep in the bear cave. Then, the sparrow had magically come to life, had spoken with Harga's voice. Back in the Dunderfosse, Gom had offered to give his mother the staff as a memento of Stig, but to his great relief, she had declined. Keep it, she'd said. It will make a fine wizard's staff one day. *Harga.* If only they could meet now. She'd reassure him. And he'd tell her in turn, Don't worry about me. I'm with Folgan, as you wanted—(no need to say how that had come about)—and I'm working to become the wizard we need me to be, a match for Katak, for sure.

Agh, Gom looked upward defiantly. A dream, that's all it had been. An ordinary nightmare. So . . . He lowered his gaze. How come he still felt uneasy? Gom tossed and tossed about, but couldn't shake the fear. What if Katak had gotten out of his northern prison somehow?

The idea had been for Harga to teach Gom magic, make him a wizard like her so that together they could guard against the Spohr, keep Katak from destroying Ulm. But Harga had been drawn away against her will, and Gom was left alone without any magic, without the least idea what to do should he come face to face with Katak. He could see himself now, standing by the crystal stair, the death's-head hovering before him—on the very threshold of the star-gate: *what would he do?* Gom shook his head into the pillow. In his mind's eye, he saw Ulm, itself a small bright star in the sky. And he saw himself racing to catch it before it fell into the reach of Katak's grasp.

Chapter Two

NEXT MORNING, the fears of the night behind him, Gom worked eagerly through his chores, thinking about the lesson he would have that day. But to his dismay, he saw no sign of letter or number—or of Folgan, either, once breakfast was over. Until further notice, the wizard announced, filling a smelly after-breakfast pipe, Gom was to leave all Folgan's meals by the workroom door, ringing the handbell to signal their arrival.

Downstairs, Gom's mood was dampened further. Stormfleet was back, full of news. On the mountain's far side, the cito informed him, grassy slopes falling down into a marshy valley promised good grazing come warm weather. As his friend talked, Gom thought wistfully of all the wonderful company that would be out there: deer and fox, muskrat and badger, harrier and waterfowl. Company he would surely miss, for there was nothing and no one up on this barren side, save an occasional high eagle. Oh, well, Gom tried to console himself, perhaps soon Folgan would give him an hour or two to roam abroad.

But as summer passed into early fall, Gom was allowed to go no farther than it took to forage for firewood. Outside Folgan's stone dwelling, the sun sank lower on the horizon, and the days dwindled. Way below, where conifer gave place to oak and ash, leaves flared then fell, and clumps of bare, round trees filled the hollows like puffs of smoky cloud.

Gom labored on without complaint, though it was often hard to endure the loneliness, and lack of human warmth. But many times, just as he was about to despair, Folgan would appear for supper, and afterward linger by the fire, smoking his malodorous pipe. On these rare evenings, the wizard's face would soften, his sharp old eyes would spark with life, and he would tell Gom tales of past wizardry: strange adventures; perilous, even funny. And as the wizard spoke, Gom would watch the aged face all seamed with lines and folds between wiry cowlick and long, gray beard, hoping that maybe the man was beginning to like him—and not just so that the workshop door might open up at last. For Gom was growing fond of the wizard, finding in the old man a certain crusty charm despite the distance and the coldness. But that fondness was not without reservation. From time to time Folgan would throw a tantrum, or commit an act so grossly unfair that Gom would retreat, hurt, re-solving to keep his distance. But the next minute, the wizard would be all over him, throwing him into con-fusion once more.

"I don't understand," Gom complained to Hevron, "why he tells me stories one day as if he were my uncle, and the next he treats me like dirt. You can never be sure where you are with him, or how he will treat you. And those stories—they're always about how folk try to outwit him, or trick him, and how he gets even in the end."

Hevron nodded slowly. "So you're catching on at last, lad," he said. "You know, I've been around mages since

I left the Vargue. They're all bitten by pride and ambition—saving one or two, like your mother. And Folgan is one of the worst. Because he's second-in-command, you see."

Gom frowned. "I don't understand."

"No more should you." Hevron dipped his head. "Mecrim Thurgeril—he's Grand Archimage, number one in the Hierarchy—and Folgan went through their apprenticeships together. Great friends, they were, but close rivals even so, them being the cleverest of their time. They say Folgan had the edge on Maister Thurgeril, but Thurgeril didn't mind, for he was more easygoing than Folgan. As time went on, and they became wizards, Folgan let his ambition get the upper hand. Over the years he got so jealous of his rank and reputation that he forgot what his job was supposed to be about. When time came to elect a new Grand Archimage, do you know, the Hierarchy overlooked Folgan for all his cleverness, and chose Maister Thurgeril instead.

"Folgan's never gotten over it. It still gnaws him, like a canker. And because of this, in spite of his genius, he'll never be great. He still can't see how his very ambition prevented him from succeeding. Pity, for they say he used to be quite charming. The times you're talking about, when he comes and sits with you—that's the old Folgan poking through. But not for long. Sooner or later the bitterness is back, and then—watch out! I've seen him often enough myself, taking it out on apprentices, even other wizards lower in the Hierarchy. Short of a miracle, the old man will never change, never know peace. Listen, young Gom, never, never, *ever* question him, or show him up in front of others. It will be the end of you."

"No danger there," Gom said thoughtfully. "If he's as great as you say. Besides, the way things are going, I'll be lucky if I even learn to read!"

Armed with Hevron's warning, Gom held on through Folgan's moods and sudden changes, watching, wary of saying the wrong thing. But sometimes, the old man's moods proved too much to bear. One afternoon, at the end of his tether, Gom clumped up to the wizard's workroom door, pumped and primed to pound it with his fists and demand his proper due. But when he got up there, hot and out of breath, he simply stood, looking at the stout wooden barrier, aware in the silence of the thudding of his heart. He took out his crystal uncertainly, almost hearing Harga's voice. *And when Folgan opens that door, just what will you say? And just what do you suppose he'll answer? And after he dismisses you, how will you then become a wizard as you promised?*

Gom leaned his back against the door, consumed with frustration—and curiosity. What was up there, really? He could see his mother's domain so clearly: piles of books lying in perilous stacks against blue-washed walls; benches scattered haphazardly down the length of a curving chamber—all cluttered with various jars and bottles and boxes, some occupied, some empty. Gemstones, prime source of powerful magic, had lain in careless heaps everywhere, and dust had coated everything.

Gom knelt, put his eye to the keyhole. Nothing, only steps going up into dark. He put his ear against the lock. Way above, he thought he heard the whine of Wind, and something bubbling in a pot. He put his nose to the tiny hole. Something stale and sour hung in the air. Gom sniffed, caught a whiff that pricked his nose.

He was going to sneeze!

In a panic, Gom turned and ran, along the passage and down the stair, his resolution gone. Halfway to the kitchen the sneeze overtook him, then another, and another. His eyes streaming, he ran all the way downstairs and out the door to breathe in cold, clear air.

From overhead came the creak of a window opening, then, "What are you doing, boy? Get in and make the tea!" The window banged shut again.

Gom tipped his head back, gazing up. One would never dream there was a four-story dwelling there in the mountainside. The windows looked no more than natural cracks in the rock face, while the door was deeply hidden inside a narrow recess. The only sign of human life was the neat pile of logs he'd stacked by the front step. Gom glanced up toward the workroom window. That Folgan! Gom could scarely stir a step without his knowing. Had the wizard heard him sneezing? Guessed that Gom had been spying through his lock?

Leaping to the woodpile, Gom pulled out a log. In his earnestness, he knocked out a wedge and sent the timber rolling down the slope. Now look what he'd done! Hours of work destroyed in an instant! With a sigh, Gom scrambled to retrieve the logs and stack them up again. Tea would be late, and Folgan would be waiting, he told himself. But when at last Gom scurried up the steps, his arms full of wood, the kitchen was empty, no sign that the wizard had been down—save for one thing: in the middle of the kitchen table lay a slate slab, and beside it, a chunk of chalk.

Gom dropped the logs, and weighed the chalk on his palm. He slid the slate toward him and began to mark it with short, bright strokes. Then he made longer, lighter ones; loops and curves, until there was no room for more. Gom cleaned off the tangle with his sleeve, then began to make circles, crosses, and some of the figures he'd seen on the signpost along the Pen'langoth Road, as near as he could remember them.

Teatime! Gom put the slate down with a snap. What was he thinking of, with the kettle not filled, and the fire not stirred, and the pot not warmed! He scurried about, putting things to rights, then, seizing the toasting fork, he jabbed up a thick slice of wheaten bread, Folgan's favorite. By the time he took up the tray and rang the bell to summon the wizard, the delicious smell of buttered toast pervaded the house.

After tea, Folgan suddenly appeared. If the wizard had noticed that his tray had been late, he did not complain. He went straight to the slate on the table, and took it up, scanning the mess of lines and whorls crowding its surface. Then he nodded slowly. "Mmm. You have a good eye." The wizard took up the chalk, and, scrubbing the slate clean, drew a sign on it. "That is an *A*. Here." He shoved the chalk at Gom. "Copy this, now. Come on, I haven't got all day! No, not with the left hand. With the right!" he snapped, as Gom took the chalk and began to draw.

Gom obeyed, but his right hand felt awkward. So almost without thinking, he shifted the chalk back and executed the sign perfectly first time.

"Other hand, other hand!"

"But why, when I work quite well with this one?" Gom said, and winced, remembering Hevron's warning.

"Why, you say?" Folgan threw up his hands. "I might

ask the same. Why, why, *why,* of all the boys in Ulm did I have to be saddled with the son of Harga the Brown! Why not a regular boy, who doesn't have to be contrary like his mother? Get on! We've four more letters to learn today—and five numbers, too."

Gom got on, so fast that Folgan gave him ten letters more, and the numbers up to twenty. From then on, Folgan taught Gom for a couple of hours every afternoon, and in only days, Gom was making whole words, and could add, subtract, and recite his multiplication tables entire.

But still the man did not let him upstairs. The snows were coming soon, the wizard said. On top of all his other chores, Gom must spend time building up the woodpile to last through the freeze. Such a prevaricating, annoying, impossible old man, Gom thought, his breath coming in stiff short bursts in the chill fall air. Surely no other apprentice had put up with him this long! As he was shoring up the pile, he came across a piece of old wild cherry—brought up from below by some former apprentice, no doubt. It was a good piece, full of knobs and knots, the sort his father had liked to carve during the deep winter months. Gom stacked it with a few other promising logs in the horses' stall. Come long nights with Folgan alone in his workroom, Gom would now have something of his own to do down by the kitchen hearth.

The days passed. Outside, the first snows fell and the slopes became too treacherous to climb. No one went afield. Gom and Stormfleet alike grew restive and quite short on humor. "He's never going to let me up," Gom grumbled one night, as he banked up the horses' stove and raked in fresh hay. "It's not just on account of what you said, Hevron. It goes deeper than that. I am the son of Harga the Brown. He still thinks I might be spying for my mother. He has no intention of ever showing me his magic. I give up!"

"Congratulations." Stormfleet swished his tail. "And just what will you do now?" He jerked his head toward the snowlocked slopes outside.

Hevron struck a front hoof on the stony floor. "Stormfleet said that you'd be the one apprentice to come through."

"Come through!" Gom cried. "How can I come through if I don't learn anything? My mother said he was a fair man, that he'd teach me well. But you were right, and she was wrong. However hard I work, he'll never accept me. The man's a bully and a cheat. He's bitter, distrustful; mean, and unfair."

The chestnut roan shook out his mane and blew through his flat dish nose. "How naive! Haven't you thought that some unfairness could be to your good? There's more than magic to be taught here. I'd say he's grounding you."

"Grounding?" Gom's brows went up.

Hevron thrust his head so close that Gom could smell his warm, grassy breath. "Life, my young friend, is tough. It dishes out mean shocks. And if it didn't, there'd be no call for wizards. They come into their own in the bad times, when folk are up against it. Now how can a wizard thrive in the perilous times if he can't stay on his feet, hrrrrmph?" Hevron raised his head and shook out his mane. "Folgan is the hardest master in all Ulm. And the best. Survive him, and you'll be a wizard indeed!"

He would? Gom eyed Hevron doubtfully. "He might at least explain."

Hevron snorted.

"Wizards don't explain themselves, least of all to their apprentices! Furthermore, as you yourself just said, you're Harga's son. Perhaps he'll never trust you entirely. Would you, in his place?"

Gom's anger faded. Hevron was right. "If only there was something I could do," he murmured, "to win him over."

Hevron looked at him sideways. "You like him, don't you, really? And it hurts, the way he keeps his distance. Well, who knows, you might find his heart, and if you do, he'll give you all he has. But if not, only be patient. Even if he never takes to you, you are his apprentice so sooner or later he's bound to let you up there—though I'd guess later: after the first fern crook unfurls—and you have passed more tests."

"*More tests?*"

"If you're lucky. The next one should be an errand. He'll send you out to find a stone, or twig, or leaf, but he won't tell you where or how far to go. Count your blessings. Half the past lot never got this far."

"What happened to them?"

"They either gave up, or got lost, or worse."

Gom patted Hevron's flank. "Thank you," he said. "How can I repay you?"

"Brrrrh, just keep going. The longer you stay, the longer I have Stormfleet's company. So I'll help you all I can, you have only to ask."

The next morning, as Folgan filled his pipe, the wizard exclaimed, "Look at that! My best briar, and now there's a crack in it!" He rummaged along the mantelshelf, found another pipe, a small corncob with a straight stem. "Not half as good," he grumbled, and went out, still grumbling, his voice trailing away up the stairs.

Gom watched after him thoughtfully. Perhaps there was a way he could please the wizard, after all. On his next trip outside, Gom fetched up the cherrywood log and set it in the hearth to dry. Then that night, after supper, when Folgan had gone back upstairs, Gom took out his pocketknife and set to work to make his master a new pipe. First, he picked the knot to form the bowl, then he cut it from the log and began to hollow it out —no easy task, cherry being such a hard wood, especially a piece as old and seasoned as this. All through the evening, and for several after that, Gom labored by the fire, thinking how pleased the wizard would be, how at last he'd have to recognize Gom's good faith. Gom shaped the bowl deep and wide, with a fat curly stem to fit it, just like the old briar. Then for good measure, he carved the whole with suns and moons and stars. When he had finished, he polished it, and oiled it, then he showed it to the horses.

"Ffffrrr," Hevron said. "That is a true wizard's pipe. And to tell the truth, in all the years I've had him for master I've never seen the like. What will you do now?"

"I'll put it on his supper tray," Gom said, gratified at Hevron's praise. After he had done so, he waited by the kitchen door for Folgan's footsteps on the stair. Surely, any moment now, the wizard would come hurrying down to thank him for his thoughtfulness, and praise his workmanship. But the wizard never came. Yet when Gom fetched the empty tray down, the pipe was gone.

The next day, after breakfast, Folgan took out the new pipe and filled it with great deliberation. "Where did you find this, boy?" He threw Gom a narrow glance.

Gom felt the heat rushing to his face. "I made it, sir."

"Made it. Mmmm." Folgan turned the pipe about, examining it minutely. "Your father was a woodcutter, you said. Good trade, that, for a young man." The wizard stood, and stretched, and went upstairs.

Gom watched after him, glumly. After all that work, not one breath of thanks! And far from pleasing the wizard, he'd given the man ideas. *Good trade, that, for a young man.* Why, Folgan was as much as telling him he'd be better employed following his father's calling! Unhappily, Gom took himself off to fetch firewood—but when he returned, he found the slate gone off the kitchen dresser, and in its place a pile of parchment sheets, a bundle of quills, and a jar of dark brown ink!

By winter's end, Gom had mastered the quill, and could recite all his computation tables. He even knew the square root table by rote. Folgan was pleased with him, Gom was sure of it. Many times, he caught a certain glint in the wizard's eye, and once or twice, a quick nod of approval, there and gone in a blink. And so the wizard should be pleased, for Gom worked in every spare moment he got. For extra practice, Gom copied all these tables in neat, straight columns onto parchment, until he had covered so many loose leaves that he sewed them together to make a book, which he stored under his bed. Thus Gom compiled his first wizard's records, even though he was nowhere a mage as yet. But it was useful practice, the makings of a valuable habit. Harga had already told him how wizards scribed their own annals, and kept them jealously, sharing them with no one, not even their peers. When Folgan began to teach Gom the names of certain stones and quartzes by word of mouth only, Gom repeated them over and over, writing them out after he'd taken his candle to bed. Name after name Folgan taught him: sheet after sheet of parchment Gom used up—and fair to say, as fast as Gom did so, the wizard set out fresh sheets, without comment.

Yet while Gom's records grew, and the heap of rough-made books under his cot, still he did not climb the workroom stair.

The piebald snow receded. Bare limbs were showing delicate shades of yellow and green when Folgan gave Gom his first lesson on the Herbal Primer, in the kitchen, this time with slate and chalk. Beginning at aconite, the wizard drew leaf and seed and flower, root and tuber. He listed color, and size, the place where it grew, what heavenly body governed it; its virtues and its properties. Gom leaned over the kitchen table, watching the lines form on the slate, his face getting all red with eagerness. He knew all about aconite, *wolf's-bane*, as Stig had called it. He could almost hear his father's voice over the wizard's recital.

There's all different kinds of wolf's-bane on the Mountain, son, and you must not go near them, save one that, if you treat it right, will prove a friend. "Healer's wolf's-bane," your mother called it. It grows farther down the Mountain, below the hut. I'll show you when it flowers come early summer. What do you use it for? Well, Gom, if you should happen to eat poisonous leaf or bark, it might well save your life. But use only the shoot, as I'll show you, and with proper respect, as your mother taught me. A good friend, she called it, but a deadly enemy . . .

Oh, yes. He knew aconite, all right. In his excitement he almost blurted it out. But, somehow, he didn't. Better, he cautioned himself, remembering Hevron's advice, not to be so knowing. Better to think first and speak after. Besides, if he didn't let on what he already knew, he'd seem to be learning all that quicker! And . . . what if he didn't know as much as he thought?

Nodding to himself, he held his tongue.

Well that he did, for he soon discovered there were many herbs of which he'd never heard, ones that Harga had not taught to Stig. From aconite, they moved to agaric, all-heal, and alkanet. Then from adder's-tongue through to agrimony, past ale-hoof to betony, briony, and bi-foil. Each night in bed, Gom drew pictures and wrote out the notes as he remembered them, and each day he learned more; of cotton-thistle and dove; dodder of thyme, and dragon, and fig-wort, and flag. Then, one rainy afternoon, instead of giving Gom instruction, the wizard met him in a rush. "Lungwort! I need lungwort! Go fetch me some—by dark!"

Lungwort? Folgan hadn't taught him that yet. What was he going to do? He pulled on his coat, grabbed his staff, and ran downstairs.

"Lungwort." Hevron nodded. "Lungwort, you say? By dark? And you haven't yet learned it? Truly, my master is a hard man. Luckily I know it, and where he gets it. Follow me."

Gom looked doubtfully out across the slippery, rain-swept slopes. "That's good of you. Will you be all right in this wet?"

"I must. I have an interest in your success, remember? Come Stormfleet. Let's take him by Crooked Path."

Stormfleet nuzzled Gom's elbow. "You're in luck. We'll have you there and back well before dark. The way is tricky, but tread where I tread and mind yourself, and you'll be fine."

"Tread where I tread—" Gom began, but Stormfleet had already moved out in Hevron's wake. Tread where I tread, indeed, Gom grumbled to himself, gripping his staff and starting after. That, to a mountain boy!

The rain came down harder. In no time, Gom's hair was plastered to his face, his clothes were soaked, and his boots, squelching loudly, chafed his ankles. But in less than half an hour, they were down and around the mountain, coming out onto grassy spaces dotted with clumps of oak and beech. Hevron led Gom to the nearest oak and arched his neck. "That's lungwort, and this is exactly where Folgan comes for it."

Gom tilted his head back, gazing up into the high branches, at what looked like black swellings showing against the sky. Why, it was moss, patches of moss, dark and dead-looking at this time of year, but he couldn't help that. He slung his staff, shinned up the tree trunk, and, bracing himself in a fork, scraped off a patch. He was just replacing his knife at his belt, when, with a blinding flash, a loud crack split the air.

The horses shied. "Lightning!" Stormfleet neighed. "Come down from there!"

Stuffing the moss in his pocket, Gom leapt, staggered a pace or two, then raced into the open after his friends. There came a second flash, then a loud bang that startled him although he'd been prepared for it. Out of the corner of his eye he caught sight of a small speck high in the sky, tossing like a leaf in the wind. He narrowed his eyes, gazing up. Not an eagle. What, then? Uneasy suddenly, Gom thought back to an earlier time, another speck wheeling over him. . . . He stiffened. *Katak, in the form of skull-bird!* He unslung his staff, held it at the ready.

"Stormfleet, look!"

As Gom cried out, the speck wheeled, flapped its wings into the wind, then dove toward the place where Gom stood. "Run!" he shouted to the horses, but before they could move, the creature was thrown up in a wide arc by the wind's force. Then again it plummeted, almost to the treeline, where its wings opened and once more began to flutter.

Gom dashed water from his eyes. Too small for Katak, he could see that now. The narrow V of the wings said hawk, a marsh hawk—harrier, from the flick of white by the tail. There came another flash, then the loud crack of thunder, just as the bird touched the treetops. In that same moment, a tall beech cracked, then toppled.

"Ke-ke-ke-ke!" came a faint and muffled cry. A harrier, in distress.

Gom began to run.

"Come back!" Stormfleet tried to cut him off. "It's still lightning!"

"Keep clear, Gom!" warned Hevron.

Gom dove back into the trees, fighting his way toward the fallen beech through brambles and around scattered boulders. "Where are you!"

The bird called again, and there, to the left, was a mass of twisted, splintered trunk and limb. The cry, loud and urgent, came from somewhere underneath. "Help me! Help me!"

Falling to his knees, Gom crawled under the tangled mess, poking about with his staff. "Where? Call again!"

"I'm in a hole! And, oh, I'm afraid! It's so dark!"

Gom looked back over his shoulder to the two horses still standing out in the open. "A marsh hawk's trapped under this tree. Can you shift it?"

Warily, they picked their way toward him. Hevron poked his nose under the tangle, sniffing at the fallen trunk part-buried in a mess of loam and moss and leaf mold. "I can't get any farther in."

Gom leaned forward. "Try."

Carefully, the horse edged closer, until, coming up against splintered branches, he recoiled. "It's no use."

"But you must do something!" Gom cried.

"Well, we can't raise the thing directly, but Stormfleet and I could drag it aside—if we had some rope."

Rope! Gom looked about. All around, the trees were hung with last year's vine. "Take courage," he called to the bird. "We'll have you free!" He hauled down armloads of the creeper, and twisted it into twin lengths. Then, looping them under the tree trunk, he slipped them around the horses, halter fashion. "Ready?" he said.

The horses nodded, pawing the ground to test it.

"Then heave away!"

Hevron and Stormfleet heaved. At first, nothing seemed to happen, but just as Gom went to help, the great trunk shifted. With a squawk and a noisy flutter, the red-brown bird rose from its prison and shot off without a please or thank you.

Gom watched it go. Male fledgling? Or a full-grown hen?

"Manners," Hevron remarked, as it dwindled into the distance.

Stormfleet tossed his head. "It's wild."

"And frightened," Gom added, slinging his staff and freeing the horses from their creeper harnesses. "I'm only glad we could save its life." He looked up. The sky had darkened appreciably. "Come on," he said, patting his bulging pocket. "I've to get this back by dark!"

Chapter Three

THE NEXT morning, when Gom went to fetch up water from the spring, he was startled by a flurry of wings.

"Good day." The harrier landed on a branch above him.

Gom smiled. "Good day. You're feeling better?"

The bird flew ahead a little way, then settled again, waiting. "You are Gom. Your friends back there told me."

With a nod, Gom walked on. "And you? Who are you?"

"Keke. I lived down in the marshes. I nested many seasons there. Right now, I need food." It rose up in a rush of feathers, and flew off.

Gom watched it go. Nested *many* seasons? A full-grown harrier, and, therefore, female. *Keke.* A sudden creature, and strange. On his way back indoors, Gom looked in on the horses. "You saw the bird, then."

"Yes," Stormfleet said.

"She came to find you," said Hevron.

"She did? I wonder why." Not to thank him, evidently.

"Wild creatures don't have to give reasons," Stormfleet said.

"Even when they have them," Hevron snorted.

"Which she did."

"Oh?"

The two horses exchanged glances. "Brrr-rrrr." Storm-fleet blew out his lips. "She's a widow."

"I see," said Gom, but he didn't, really. Like certain other birds—geese, and swans, and eagles; kestrels, redstarts, and loons—harriers paired once, for life. When one mate died, the survivor lived out its days alone, even in the midst of the flock. Sad, for such a bird to sit by every year, watching its fellows nesting and rearing young. Sad, but, "What has that to do with me?"

Hevron bared his teeth. "She's come to live by you."

"*By me!* But—harriers don't live on mountains."

"Neither do wild horses of the Vargue," Stormfleet said, and, taking up a mouthful of breakfast hay, he began to chomp it with great noise.

Outside, Gom gazed skyward. Was the little marsh hawk serious? Did she really intend to stay up here? Or was it just a passing impulse? The rest of the day, Gom watched out for her; went to bed disappointed.

But next morning, Keke was by the front door. "It's clearing nicely," she said. She followed him down to the creek, splashed herself while he bathed and filled Folgan's pail, scolding him nonstop. "Bright and early spring as we're having," she said. "Every young unbonded creature is already busy seeking a mate and a nesting place. But you, instead of preening yourself and strutting for the hens, you shut yourself away up here with a bag of old, dried bones. Why?"

Gom bent over the water, looking down at his reflection, taking his time. Preening and strutting, indeed. No amount of preening would ever make a peacock out of him. Long face and chin, bent nose, dark, deep-set eyes with sharp, shrewd look that put folk on their mettle. The whole surrounded with a shock of straight brown hair that stuck out in all directions no matter how often he combed it. He sighed down at his reflection. The image of Harga, everybody said. And yet these features looked so well on her! But her son: too plain, too clever, with a look old beyond his years. No hen for him. Why, he was not free even to think of such things. He straightened up, saw Keke still waiting for his answer. "I have to," he said. "I have important work to do."

"Keh!" she retorted. "Important work, my tail feathers! What work can be more important than building a nest and having young? You're not as clever as I thought."

At that moment, Gom was inclined to agree with her. He picked up Folgan's water pail, and started back to the house.

"It would be nice," Keke said, fluttering after him with a fair display of effort, "to ride your shoulder. All this sparrow-hopping tires me out."

Gom nodded gravely. "I'll see what I can do."

Later that morning, Gom took an old saddle from back of the horses' cave, and cut it up to make a shoulder pad and a simple gauntlet so that Keke could come to his hand or ride his shoulder as he went about his chores.

Still she didn't thank him. "You must be glad to have me," she said. "You look as though you could use some cheerful company."

Gom laughed aloud. "Stormfleet and Hevron are the best friends a body could wish for. Though," he added hastily, "it is good to have you too, and I hope you'll stay. But won't you miss your folk?"

"I might. But it's going to be much more lively up here. And think—in time when you travel I'll get to meet other kin—we're spread around the world, you know: wherever there's fenland—that's marsh. There's just one clan I'd not visit, one place I'd not see—you neither, if you have sense."

"And what place is that?"

Keke's feathers fluffed out until she looked quite big and fierce. "Sundor. It's a bad place, full of men with knives and bows to hunt a body down. Why my cousins persist in nesting there, I can't begin to guess, when there are so many better places to live."

"I agree with you, Keke. My mother has told me about that fen. There's a mountain in the middle of it, I believe." It was marked on the map Carrick had given him, and on Harga's globe. A hollow mountain, a low peak beneath which evil King Galt ruled his band of thieves and murderers.

"Mountain!" Keke ruffled her feathers. "Mountains are high and noble. Sundborg is more an abscess in a running sore! And yet," she went on, "they say it was fair once, when old King Gorfid ruled. It's a wonder any creature lives in that poisonous waste. Don't ever go there."

"My mother warned me to steer clear." Gom stroked Keke's feathers smooth. "So don't worry: *We'll* not go near that place."

Buds swelled on the trees, and burst, veiling the valleys below with pale green lace. One year since he'd left Windy Mountain to seek his mother, since he'd been set upon by Katak, skull-bird, and had fallen down the Bluff. One year almost to the day since Hort and Mudge had nursed him back to health, since he had met with Zamul, the conjuror, and Carrick, master tinker.

Eight months since he'd come into this place and still no sign of spell!

"Patience," Hevron said. "How many more times must we have this out? As you are Harga's son, Folgan is slow to trust you."

"But not to use my services," Gom grumbled. That night, after he'd recorded all that he had learned that day, he took a clean sheet of parchment, and began to write: *More than one half year since I began my apprenticeship, and still Folgan has not let me into his workroom. I'll bet Mat is having a better time of it with Bokar Riffik! Not fair, to be used as a skivvy and to be kept from my rightful due. How much longer, before I can get on with things? And in spite of my friends downstairs, I am so lonely. I wish I could see Harga . . .*

Gom paused, pen upraised. Better not say where she is. Not that Folgan was likely to come in and spy on his private writings, but even so. Harga had told him expressly not ever to speak of it in any way.

. . . and Carrick, and Essie. I wish I could spend one, just one evening in The Jolly Fisherman. Carrick will be on his way there right now, down from Green Vale and Deeping Valley, down along Long Valley for his spell in Pen'langoth market.

Sighing, Gom set down his quill, thinking of the great and bustling city, of Lake Langoth, and Scandibar, its island citadel. Of the wide avenues, the narrow winding streets down by the fishing quarter. Of the inn, and Essie. And Brody Leggat. *Every young unbonded creature seeks its nesting partner . . .* He'd put all thought of her from his mind, but looking back now he remembered the night in Essie's parlor when Brody had brought him the dish of sweetmeats: she, clearly wanting his favor; he, much too caught up in finding a master to pay her much attention. Idly, he drew Brody's face, the round cheeks that flushed in the space of a breath; short nose, dark eyes with the hint of a smile. Seeing what he had done, he hastily scribbled it out. Six years and more, until he saw her again—unless Folgan went there sometime on business. Maybe, if the old man did, and took Gom along, Gom could slip away to see his friends—and Brody. On that hopeful thought, Gom put his writing things away and lay down to sleep.

At last, as the first spring leaves turned to deeper green, Folgan called Gom up the workroom stairs. His heart going at a clip, Gom climbed, trying to look—to *be* calm. The wizard had finally decided to accept him!

Gom stepped out under a high, vaulted roof, looking eagerly about, mindful of his mother's dusty clutter. The lamplit workroom stretched back under hollow rock, as Harga's had. There, the resemblance ended. Instead of Harga's lucky chaos, here was stringent order and cleanliness. Whatever stones the wizard possessed were stored away somewhere. His books, sentinels of knowledge with gilded spines, stood to attention on neat shelves running the length of one wall. Benches ran down the room in tidy ranks, standing four square. Most were clean and bare save for center racks of flasks and jars, each filled to tidy levels with powders, and crystals, and liquids. Two benches only showed any sign of present use. On one, a lamp burned with a blue flame. Over the flame sat an earthen bowl from which vapor trailed up to the cavernous roof. Beside it stood a heavy jar stoppered with a stout cork bung. Around the jar stood glass bottles, and various dishes and tools, and tubes and flasks of the strangest shapes. On a second bench nearby sat a large black box, padlocked.

"Now," Folgan said, leading Gom down the room, and pointing to the big glass jar, "this is a carboy. See those brown dregs in the bottom? Don't sniff them or you'll get your nose burned off. And don't get the stuff on your hands, unless you want to lose your skin." The wizard picked up a short fat stick with a round blunt end and wagged it in Gom's face. "This is a pestle, and that, a mortar." He tapped the pestle on the rim of a thick clay mixing bowl encrusted in stinking paste, half-dried.

Gom turned in distaste to the mixture bubbling on the blue flame, wondering what spell was forming there. "What's that?"

"That," Folgan said, frowning, "is a crucible—a bowl for smelting metals." A small red clay bowl, scratched with many signs; thinner than the mortar, its curving sides smoke-blackened from the flame beneath it.

"I mean what's that inside?" Gom said. The wizard had deliberately misunderstood.

Folgan sighed. "Ractite. Ha! You're none the wiser, are you? It's a rare ore, boy, that ordinary folk have never heard of. Now, that's enough. You're not here today to bother me with noisy questions." The wizard, pointing, picking up, continued to name names until Gom knew every article on the bench. "And now, boy," Folgan said, "you'll get busy washing, and scouring, and polishing, and restoring these things to their proper racks, here, and here, and here." The old man gestured about the benches. "Then you shall dust all the bench-tops, every one, save . . ." He went over to the bench with the black box. ". . . this one. If you touch this box, I'll know—and you'll be sorry! Come." He led Gom to a small, dark alcove down the far end of the chamber. At the sight of the brushes and mops and brooms inside, Gom's spirits fell. "These tools you know, so now—to work!"

Fuming silently, Gom obeyed. Yet soon he took to thinking, ractite. A rare ore. Used for making magic of some kind. He had never heard of it. And likely would not again for a while. He ran his duster over the spotless benches, thinking with longing back to Harga's cobwebbed confusion. Such a mystical air of serendipity had been in that place. The feeling that marvelous accidents might happen to surprise even Harga herself. Not so here. Folgan would know, Gom bet, if a single thing were out of order, or happened out of place. Gom worked on, repeating *ractite* over and over silently to remember until he could write it down that night.

When Gom was done washing up, Folgan had him sweeping and tidying needlessly until teatime. At last, Gom climbed into bed, spent. He'd been so glad to enter the wizard's workroom at last. And now?

He wrote with savage strokes into his journal. *I have twice the washing up and cleaning as before. And that crucible! The dregs of molten ractite had set inside, and were quite impossible to clean off—as Folgan must have known! He is a hard man, and an unforgiving master. No wonder the others never stayed! There were still traces of the ractite left in the bottom of the pot when Folgan sent me down to make tea. Not daring to say anything, I have hidden the dirty crucible at the bottom of the clean pile until tomorrow, when I shall finish scouring it first chance I get.* And so he meant to, but the next day, Folgan kept him so busy running around that he never got a chance, and after that, the thing completely slipped his mind.

* * *

For many days thereafter, Gom cleaned and scoured and polished Folgan's utensils. Once, he had his ears boxed for leaving a scruple of powder in a bowl and spoiling a spell. Once, he almost had his ears boxed for cleaning only too well. On that morning, Folgan had three spells in the making all at once, on three separate benches. He had Gom clean up one bench, then the second. As soon as the third spell was completed, Gom, thinking to please Folgan by jumping to without being asked, took up a damp cloth to sweep some black grains off the benchtop.

As he reached out, he had a glimpse of the wizard whirling about. "No, don't—" Folgan cried. Cloth touched sand with a hiss and a puff of smoke. As Gom's knees buckled, he felt the wizard's hand close over his nose and mouth, then the next thing he knew, he was lying at the foot of the workroom stair, the wizard wafting a handkerchief over him. "Foolish boy." Folgan raised a hand to box his ears, lowered it again. "I suppose you don't know any better," he muttered. "Wait here."

The wizard went downstairs. Gom closed his eyes. The floor was very cold, but he couldn't move. He didn't hear the wizard come back, only felt a hand lifting his head, and a cup set to his lips.

"Here, drink, boy. You'll be better in a moment. If not, you'll have to lie. I'm not up to carrying you down any more stairs."

"What happened?" Gom asked weakly.

"You put wet to agarax, that's what, you foolish lad. Dream-sand, as we wizards call it. The smoke of but one grain breathed in deep will put a grown man to sleep for full three days! Lucky I dragged you clear in time. Now

I'm shut out of my own workroom for the rest of the day, until the fumes have cleared, and me with but one crack of a window. Two of my most difficult spells are spoiled! Next time, wait until I tell you to do something, hear?"

Wrong if I do, and wrong if I don't, Gom grumbled under his breath. There is no pleasing the man! *Agarax: dream-sand,* he wrote that night. *Such strong magic stuff it is, without need of any spell. He wouldn't tell me where one finds it, but 'tis rare, and regular folk don't even know of it. This evening, when Folgan had me up there cleaning things away, I swept the rest of the grains into a DRY cloth, which I have hidden under my bed. Tomorrow, I shall carve a little box to keep them in. Since they are not magic in themselves, and since Folgan had discarded them, I feel free to keep them by me. Never know when they might be of use. . . .*

Much as Gom hated his workroom chores, by handling those endless mortars and crucibles and tools—cleaning and polishing them, fetching them out and putting them back, Gom soon came to know them all, all, that is, save the black box that stood alone. Day by day, as Gom worked around it, his curiosity increased. Its magic must be powerful indeed, and very secret. Many times he fancied that he heard it humming, but he never dared put his ear to the box, or feel for vibrations, not even when Folgan, back turned, was bent over some bench, seemingly absorbed in his spellmaking. It wasn't worth the risk.

Spring passed into early summer, but still Gom saw nothing of spells and their making, only their aftermath. *Yet I hold on,* he wrote in his journal, *with Stormfleet's help, and Hevron's, and Keke's wicked humor.* He stopped, smiling at the memory of the little bird that morning, running up and down before the front door, flapping her wings ildly, pecking the ground in a mock panic, shrieking,

"Faster, boy, faster,
or a box on the ears from your master!"

Then, slowly, so gradually that Gom did not notice exactly how it came about, he was finally assisting Folgan to mix his spells: holding this mortar still, that book open at the proper page while the wizard ground and mixed; steadying the crucible while the wizard shook in powder or colored droplet that sent clouds of smoke up into the dark. At last Folgan let him use the tools he'd cleaned so long: to grind rock and horn and root; to extract oils from the plants whose virtues Folgan had taught him; to concoct, decoct, and distill; to work with a crucible over the small blue flame, first with Folgan, then all by himself while the wizard hovered at his elbow. Soon he was making simple remedies: lotion to quell the traveling sickness, ointment for sores that would not heal; fizz for headaches, and unguent for a raspy chest so pungent that Gom's hands smelled of it for days afterward.

Then one day, after Gom had gone down to make tea, there came a loud crash, and, running upstairs to see, he found Folgan lying at the top of the workroom stair, eyes shut, blood trickling down his cheek and mingling with his beard. Gom knelt beside him. He must have fallen, there was a cut on the edge of the old man's cheekbone. He scrambled up, fetched a cloth and a bowl of cold water. He bathed the cut, but the bleeding would not stop.

He looked around. The staunching ointment. Gom had helped make it. He knew exactly in which rack it was stored. He looked down uncertainly. Was the wizard really unconscious? Or was this some trick to test—what? His resourcefulness? His blind obedience to the rule forbidding apprentices from applying their master's remedies? Another drop of blood welled from the wizard's cut and rolled down his cheek.

Wrong if he did, wrong if he didn't! Gom ran down the chamber, took the ointment pot, and applied a liberal smear to the cut. The blood stopped flowing instantly. He cleaned the skin around the cut, then fetched the smelling pot and stuck it under Folgan's nose. The wizard's lids fluttered open. He seemed dazed at first, then he lit on Gom. "Boy! What's this? What—" He put a hand to his cheek, wincing.

The hand came away smeared with ointment. The wizard looked at it blankly. Then he saw the bloodied cloth. "I remember now. I tripped, I think. Going too fast for myself. Well, don't stand there! Help me up!"

Gom helped Folgan downstairs and into bed. Then he brought the old man's supper tray.

"You—you used my remedies," the wizard said sharply. "What else did you do whilst I was lying there, eh?"

Gom opened his mouth to protest, shut it again, remembering Hevron's words. Even so, the ingratitude!

The old man reached out and gripped Gom's arm. "Once a wizard, always a wizard, boy. Don't mind me. You are a good lad, a tribute to your mother. It's lucky you were here. We lost Cosgard the Old some years back, very same way. Fell fourteen flights down his tower. Couldn't call anybody, of course. Found him a skeleton, bones picked clean by crows. Now, if you don't mind, take this key and lock the workroom door, and bring it back straightway. I've had enough for today."

There is no fathoming a wizard's mind, Gom wrote that night. *One of the greatest mages in all Ulm, and he thinks in some ways like a simpleton! If I had not been there, who knows when Folgan would have woken up—if he'd have woken up, so much blood he'd have lost. He himself owned as much. And yet he had me lock his workroom against myself, lest I steal his precious secrets! Truly, the man has no sense of gratitude.*

So Gom thought, but the next afternoon, instead of having Gom help with spells, and doing his regular chores, Folgan took him aside. "You have done well," the wizard said. "You have learned a deal of simple magery. But much of this is merely apothecary work. Now you shall begin to learn of subtler arts and practices, of how a wizard comes by certain magic properties—and how he stores them in rod and rune, so that, in the field, he might call on them in a fingersnap. How do we do it, you well may ask."

The wizard paused, gazing intently into Gom's face.

Gom thought back to his mother's rune, the lifetime's magic stored therein. He'd never seen her staff. Did she have one? Or was rune enough for her? Magic stored . . . His heart beat faster. Folgan was about to open some door to him, a door of some real worth at last. "How, sir?"

"The answer's here." The wizard jabbed a bony finger against his grizzled temple. "Here's where it's done, boy. In here. Aha! But don't think I'm handing you some quick and easy trick. The practice is simple, as you'll now see—but it takes years, *years* to master it! Come."

The wizard led Gom halfway down the chamber, where he stopped, pointing down. There, on the stone floor, was a small, blue mat laid in a circle of pebbles, smooth and shiny. "Here, step over those stones—careful not to touch them! Now, sit. Cross your legs, that's right. Now, hands on knees, close your eyes, and picture an apple, a big green apple, on a twig. Got it?"

Gom shifted his ankles a bit, set his hands as bidden, and pictured a large green apple hanging in the darkness before his eyes.

"Right, now stay still and watch that apple until I come and tell you to stop. I warn you: let it slip, and you'll have a bellyache worse than if you'd eaten it, understand? No! Don't answer, just keep your eyes shut!"

Gom listened to the sound of the wizard's boots receding over the workroom floor. This was the secret of a wizard's awesome power? Picturing unripe apples? How? He dared not ask. But—Gom thought of the pebbles all about him—perhaps he could work it out for himself. Perhaps the wizard put a spell on him through the ring of stones, perhaps— He sucked in his breath as pain, sharp and fierce, gripped his belly, pain remembered from his early forays into Maister Craw's orchard. He had lost the apple, was picturing the pebbles instead! Quickly, he brought the apple back, and the pain faded. How had Folgan done that? Where was the spell? In the ring of stones, obviously. Why wasn't he supposed to touch them? He pictured Folgan placing them, chanting over them. Again, pain struck, goading Gom back to the apple. Truly, he could not believe it was so hard to hold his mind on one thing!

Gom stared at his green apple doggedly. If he didn't want to feel that pain again, he'd better keep it there, steady and bright. Minutes passed. The sight of the apple began to make him hungry. He wondered how long before Folgan let him go downstairs to make tea. He'd baked fresh bread that morning, with extra honey and a handful of raisins, his favorite with— The gripes were back, doubling him over. The apple—quick! With an effort, Gom straightened up, brought the apple image back into focus, and the pain receded, reluctantly this time, it seemed to Gom. Oh, but his middle was aching now, as from a bout of colic. He remembered Stig, bending over him, spoon in hand. *Two of these, son, and you'll feel better. It's a remedy your mother*— Gom caught himself just in time. He fixed his mind grimly on the apple, sick by now of the sight of it. Again and again, his mind wandered out, and each time the pain brought it back. How long before Folgan came to release him?

Random images crossed his mind. Of his sister Hilsa, of Hort and Mudge back in Green Vale. Of Carrick, head bent over a big, round pot. And Essie, smiling. Of Ganash, green scales glowing brightly—sign of his well-being.

And of Katak.

The apple swelled, swamping Gom's inner sight with green light. Then it vanished, but no pain griped him. Strange, thought Gom. The green light still remained, reminding him of Ganash. Even as he thought that, the light began to waver, as though under water. A glint of red shot through the cool green watery light, like—Gom tried unsuccessfully to push the thought away—the Spohr's sealstone, gleaming in its crevice above the mouth of Katak's prison. Yes, the sealstone: it was! Had Gom slipped somehow into a waking dream? Was this a sign, a warning? If so, of what? Fear drew Gom's mind to a point. *From the depths of his dark prison hole, did the Spohr seek him out?*

Cold brushed Gom's face, not Sessery's light breath; no, not the playful drafts of deep underground, but something else. He took a step, resisting, toward the cold—Katak's pull! "No, no!" he cried. "I won't come to you! Let me go! Let me go!"

"There, there," a voice said. "I've let you go. You're all right, boy."

Folgan's voice, oddly gentle and reassuring.

Gom opened his eyes, found himself lying on the floor, the pebbles scattered about. In his head was a sort of buzz, the old, familiar feeling of a waking dream's aftermath. He tried to sit up, fell back again, dazed.

"Here, hold on." The wizard pulled him up, helped him to a stool, and brought a cup of water. "You went deep, that's for sure. And so quick! I've never seen the like. But, then, you're Harga's son, I mustn't let myself forget." Folgan frowned. "What did you see? More than an apple, I'd say. It'd take more than a green apple to get you shouting at the top of your voice."

Gom looked up, found the old man's eyes sharp upon him. What had he shouted? He couldn't recall. What had he seen? Green light, and the red glow of Katak's seal under water. "Water," he murmured.

"Water? You've got it in your hand!" Folgan cried. "Why, I think the sitting's turned your head. But if you'd be a wizard, you'll just have to get used to it." He stood stiffly. "Come on, up you get. And go and make the tea. You've had enough for today. But tomorrow afternoon, and every afternoon from now on, you'll sit an hour or two inside that ring and perform your mental exercises."

"Why?"

"Because"—Folgan frowned—"while a wizard makes magic with things, he works it with his *mind*. A strong mind. You don't climb stairs with flabby legs, do you? Tcha," he said to himself, "the questions these boys do ask!"

Gom went slowly down to the kitchen. A waking dream, for sure. He ought to know, he'd had them often enough in the past. But . . . He leaned his face against the wall and closed his eyes. In the past, they'd happened seemingly at random, in the middle of quite everyday affairs. This one, and he'd bet on it, had been brought on by the green apple, by his sitting down and drawing his mind to a point. But what had triggered it? Gom shuddered. Not any of those good, kind people he'd been daydreaming about. No, it had been the Spohr.

And the vision? It had been of the cavern under Great Krugk, of Katak's prison cave. Why? He thought back over others in the past. Those waking dreams had warned him of things to come—both good and ill. Of finding gold under Windy Mountain. Of meeting Mandrik. Of Katak's pursuit. And now? That green and wavery light: it had reminded him of his friend Ganash, who had lighted the deep spaces with the glow of his scales. Ganash had saved his life, had helped him shut the Spohr away. And Ganash had promised to guard Katak's dark hole and never let him escape. In the vision, the seal had still been lit, the cave mouth, sealed. Had that vision, therefore, come to tell him not to worry, to reassure him that all was well?

Gom fervently hoped so!

Chapter Four

THE NEXT afternoon, as Gom sat in the circle of stones, Folgan told him to imagine a pin. If Gom let it go, it would prick him, the wizard said. Gom pictured the pin, held it steady. This time, to his surprise, it was easier. After a while, he found he could let his mind wander and hold the pin steady, both at once. His legs went stiff, his arms lost feeling. But so what? Many a time he'd sat thus, for hours at a stretch, just to catch the flash of sun on a dragonfly's wing, or the first crack of a hatching egg.

A sudden worry struck him. Would sitting trigger another vision? And could it be of Katak? He shivered at the memory of the cold and the sealstone's glow. Courage, he told himself. He'd never had the same vision twice. So if this practice did bring on another vision, it would be of something else. Gom waited for his mind to settle.

But it wouldn't.

How could he be sure he'd not see Katak again? That thought pulled him sharply all the way back up to the everyday world. He became aware of his surroundings, of Folgan's quiet movements down the room. Gom had a sudden urge to get up, run down and out, away from all chance of being in that green place again. But he couldn't. So he sat in dread, braced for the cold and the hateful red light. Yet when the waking dream did come, he saw only pearly clouds and rainbows; raindrops glistening in sunshine; and water falling, from a great height. Gom sighed, deeply relieved, thinking that this was just the sort of vision he'd have hoped for!

As he sat in the peace of that dreamy light, he began to think. Sitting brought on waking dreams, he was sure of that now. Only in the ring of stones? Or could he sit and bring one on anywhere?

If so, could he also choose what it would show him? Like this peace, this calm, this pearly light like the haze about the crystal stair. It soothed him. Was it his doing? If so, then sitting held no fears for him. All he had to do was focus on that haze and not think of Katak in any way.

Katak!

Fool! Now you've done it! Gom told himself. He tried to pull back his thought, but the pearly haze vanished into wavery green radiance, and the sealstone gleamed once more. Almost as though that place had been waiting for him, Gom thought, feeling himself being drawn toward it as before. With all the strength of his will he fought that pull, but it was too strong. Dragging his feet, Gom stumbled, caught the toe of his boot on the floor. Down he went, full length. He winced, waiting for the impact, but to his horror, he passed right through the floor, and down into cold and dark, leaving the green radiance behind. He tried to turn, to pull himself back up, in vain. The cold grew sharper, until it seemed to burn. He fell deeper, slowly, by degrees, through granite bedrock, until his flesh went numb, and he felt nothing.

Gom opened his eyes onto late afternoon light. Still sitting, then, within Folgan's ring of stones, feeling cold and stiff as new leather. For full three hours he had sat thus, Folgan told him, looking quite bemused. And now it was time for Gom to go downstairs to make tea. Gom obeyed, preoccupied with his vision. Despite his fear, his mind had slipped and he'd brought on the very thing which he had dreaded! The same vision—twice! The same? Not quite. Gom shuddered. Oh, that cold! Katak's cold? Or only the chill of deep water? Frowning, Gom recalled how he'd been drawn forward again, how he had then tripped and fallen. And he felt again the terror of his falling. . . .

What had it all meant? Had it been a warning of what might happen if he went that way again? Or something else? Perhaps . . . he should go back into that vision to see. Gom shook his head vehemently. No! He would not, could not ever bring that place back of his own free will. The next afternoon, and every afternoon thereafter in that magic circle, he wrapped himself in pearly light and resolutely kept from thought of Katak and his prison cave.

Folgan seemed pleased with Gom's progress in the ring of stones, for the most part. But there were some days when the old man's behavior was cranky beyond Gom's understanding. On these afternoons, the better Gom sat, the crosser the wizard became. "I might as well have messed things up, the way he carries on," Gom grumbled down below.

"He's envious, that's what," Keke said maliciously. "He can't stand the sight of you sitting easy as breathing, when it likely took him years!"

"Keke could be right," Hevron said. "But only partly.

As he is a good teacher, he believes in hard training. He likely fears you're not getting it as tough as you ought."

"Blah!" Keke retorted. "You would defend your master. Take my advice, Gom, and keep your own counsel. Stop making it look so easy, or you've an enemy there."

Gom looked from one to the other, undecided.

"Won't hurt to heed them both," Stormfleet said in his ear. "Some clever folk can be quite petty on a purely human level. Whatever comes easy, don't let on. Pretend to put the effort in, and don't tell him anything."

Gom heeded their advice, watching himself more carefully than ever, taking care not to get above himself, doing things by the book. As the days lengthened into midsummer, he was performing all kinds of fancy tricks in his mind, juggling three or even more ideas all at once, without suffering a slip. But never, never would he go back down into that northern cave.

As the year turned, Folgan began to teach Gom how to extract ore from rock; the properties of metals, and their uses. At last Gom learned of the rare ractite's principal purpose: to boost the heat of certain admixtures to flashpoint. But this dangerous measure was never entrusted to Gom. Folgan gave Gom only the common ores to work with, safe ones, such as smeddum. "It's in mologrite, a stone found everywhere, as you must know. Why"—the wizard waved his arm about—"there are seams of it running through these very walls. Smeddum is a most useful metal, Gom. Magnetic, like iron, only stronger. See." Folgan held up a small jar of tiny metal filings, and taking a four-inch nail, he stroked it against the jar. Then he held it a few inches from the jar, and let go. To Gom's amazement, instead of falling to the floor, the nail flew from Folgan's hand, hit the glass vessel with a click—and stayed there! The wizard repeated the measure half a dozen more times until the jar bristled with nails like a startled hedgehog. Then he swept off the nails and dropped them onto the bench, where they lay in a lump, still stuck together.

Folgan reached into a cupboard under the bench, pulled out a small piece of sparkling black rock. "Mologrite. Soon, I'll show you how to get the smeddum out and cast it. But first, watch." The wizard stroked the mologrite with the jar of smeddum filings, then he set jar and rock on the bench, side by side. The moment Folgan let go, rock and jar slid toward each other, colliding with a smack.

"Skies!"

Folgan looked pleased at Gom's reaction. "It even works on ore still in the stone. And not only to attract it. See what happens when you hold the rock the other way." The wizard turned the rock around, and handed it to Gom. "You try. Make them touch."

Gom took rock and jar in his hands, and slid them toward each other. They were almost touching when he felt them recoil, as though an invisible barrier were between them, a soft barrier, like a cushion. He tried harder, but no effort would bring those objects together.

"When they repel, we call it reverse polarity, Gom," Folgan said. "Now turn the rock again."

Gom turned the rock around to the way Folgan had first had it, and there! They joined instantly.

"Hmmm," Folgan said. "A useful metal. Very."

"For what?" Gom ventured to ask.

"Oh, many purposes. The simplest one is finding more smeddum. Come, I'll show you." Folgan disengaged the filings jar from the rock and led Gom over to the wall.

"As I just said, there are mologrite strata in these walls. Let's see . . ." The wizard rubbed the jar up and down the rock wall in long, light strokes. Then suddenly, his hand moved on, but the jar stayed behind, halfway up the wall. "See, boy, see?" the old man cried triumphantly. "Mologrite, and the smeddum found it out. Look, there it is, only a thin vein, but the smeddum flew to it as sparks up a chimney." Folgan pulled the jar from the wall. "Now to extract smeddum for yourself."

First the wizard had Gom set a pail of cold water beside the bench. "To cool the whole thing down," he said. "When you're done." Now Gom was to heat the rock and extract the smeddum: a simple enough process for a beginner, the mologrite being soft, and the smeddum having a low melting point.

"A crucible, boy, hurry! Fetch yourself a crucible, I'm waiting!"

Gom recognized the warning signs. The wizard was growing impatient: his geniality, fading fast. Gom reached for a crucible, tipping the pile in his haste. He righted it again and hurried back to the bench while the wizard stood watching, arms folded. As Gom set the crucible on the flame, he caught sight of gray metal specks inside. In his shock, he almost dropped it. The dirty ractite bowl! He'd quite forgotten it. One glance at the wizard's face and he dismissed all thought of owning up. He set the dirty crucible on the flame and put in the stone, thinking of another time when he'd spoiled a spell with a pot not fully cleaned. He broke out in a sweat. The purpose of ractite was to heat certain mixtures to flashpoint. What would happen when it mixed with another ore? Gom leaned down anxiously.

The mologrite was warming up!

To his relief just then, Folgan went out. But for how long? Gom looked toward the door. He must be quick: fetch another clean pot and set it up with a fresh lump of molognite. Gom knelt down, opened the cupboard door. Yes, there, another rock, just like the one he'd ruined. He set it on the benchtop, then ran to fetch a clean crucible. He was on his way back when there came a bright flash and a puff of smoke from the bench. Skies! He'd left the old crucible still heating on the flame! Gom leapt to take it off, then doused the thing in a hiss and a cloud of steam. He glanced around the chamber. Where to hide this disaster until he could smuggle it out? His eyes lit on the alcove in the far end wall. His broom hole!

Gom fished the crucible from the pail. An alloy of ractite and smeddum had formed inside the crucible—a hard, black mass. At the sight of it he really began to panic. Folgan would be back any minute—and the new setup was not even on the flame! Quickly, Gom dropped his disaster onto the bench next to the molognite, and reached for the clean crucible. Old pot and new rock shot together, colliding with a crack. The bowl broke, but the fragments stayed in place, fixed to the mass within. Gom prised and tugged to pull the two apart, but they seemed fused together.

Oh, oh, oh, what to do! Frantically, he seized the whole conglomeration in both hands and ran down the chamber. He reached the alcove, bent to set his load behind a pail, but it flew from his hand, and crashed against the back wall—in plain sight! Gom tugged and pulled, but the lump wouldn't budge. He braced his foot against the wall, and tried again. Nothing happened. He needed a lever, a wedge of some kind, but there wasn't time to find one now. As a last resort, Gom hung his jacket over rock and pot, and arranged his brooms in front of it. Then he ran back, knelt down, and seizing up a third piece of mologrite, threw it into the clean crucible, and set them on the flame, his heart pounding, his breath coming in gasps.

"What? Not even started? What have you been doing!"

The wizard stood behind him, frowning. Gom had not heard him come in. How long had the man been standing there? Gom strove to calm himself. Folgan didn't guess, or he'd surely have had more to say than that! He closed his eyes and prayed that the old man would not notice two more rocks were gone from his cupboard, and that he'd not go down the chamber until Gom had somehow managed to prise his day's disaster off the wall.

For the rest of that session, Gom was kept so busy that he had no time to brood. But at last he was able to prise the mess off the wall—chipping a mallet, breaking a stone wedge in the effort—and smuggle it out under his jacket. What was he to do with the thing? Best to bury the whole sorry failure as far as possible from Folgan's house. Meanwhile, he would hide it in the horses' stall.

Stormfleet sniffed the thing suspiciously. "What on Ulm is that?"

"An accident." Gom eyed the mess in disgust. "I was supposed to extract smeddum from a piece of mologrite, but some ractite got mixed in, and, well, that is the result."

"Words, words. Tell us what that means," Hevron said.

Gom explained more fully how he'd been supposed to produce one thing and had accidentally come up with quite something else.

"So now that rock and the bowl won't come apart." Stormfleet nudged the lumpy mass with his nose. "It really is quite firm."

"You say you've made a mess?" Hevron spoke up. "I'd say you've done quite the opposite."

Gom frowned. "The opposite? How can you say such a —" He broke off, realizing the truth of Hevron's words. Far from making a disaster, he'd come upon a great discovery. The smeddum's powers were multiplied at least one hundredfold with ractite added! "So I have!" he cried.

"So tell Folgan what happened, he'll be pleased," Hevron suggested.

"And then again," Keke said, "he might not."

"Not?"

Stormfleet agreed. "He might not like his assistant discovering something he doesn't know himself."

"Oh, he'll know of it, surely. But, come to think, he might not like my finding out about the ractite before he's ready to teach me," Gom said. "In fact, he'd more likely scold me for breaking a crucible—*dirty* crucible— than praise me for finding out something on my own. Thanks for the warning."

And so he said nothing to Folgan of his accident. Instead, he wrote that night how he'd made a great discovery entirely on his own, and purely by accident. *All on account of a dirty crucible—and I'll bet that's how magic was made in the beginning: through things bumping together by chance. And I'll bet it happens in my mother's workshop all the time. That's why she's the greatest wizard in all Ulm, and Folgan is not. . . .*

The weeks passed, the autumn days grew shorter. One morning, as Gom was helping Folgan with a spell, holding a delicate glass bubble while the wizard dripped in a distillation of ground feverfew, there came a high whine that made Gom almost drop the whole thing. He turned his head. The sound was coming from the black box.

"Tcha!" Folgan turned down the flame in annoyance, shot Gom a warning look. "You drop that, and you ruin eight hours hard work!" The wizard shuffled over to the box, snapped open the padlock, and raised the lid. A bluish glare lit the wizard's face, giving him a demon look. "Yes?" Folgan reached into the box, did something Gom couldn't see.

A voice came from inside; low, and indistinct. Gom held quite still, straining to hear. He craned his neck, caught a glimpse of flashing crystal and wire coil. This contraption was like Harga's crystal sphere, except that hers had had no need of all that wire.

The bubble was tipping. Gom righted it with a jerk, just as Folgan snapped the box lid down and clapped the padlock shut. "Forget that. Go pack me a bag to last four days, and saddle my horse. I leave in half an hour."

"I don't know that black box, or anything inside the house. But I can tell you he's been summoned on a professional call," Hevron said, as Gom saddled him up. "By rights, he should be taking you. It must be urgent business, and secret, to be leaving you behind. Never mind," Hevron added, as Gom slipped the bridle on, "I'll tell you all about it when we return."

Folgan locked the workroom door with a flourish. Keep the place clean and tidy, he warned Gom, and stay away from the workroom door. If Gom should even peep through the keyhole, he'd know, the old man said, and rode away.

Gom watched horse and rider recede down the mountain trail. After all this time, he thought ruefully, Folgan still didn't trust him.

Gom made the most of the wizard's absence, turning it into a welcome holiday. He roamed the mountain with Stormfleet, allowing the cito to show him Hevron's special paths and byways, while Keke rode his shoulder, making endless commentary. On the third day, Gom went down to explore the marshes, Keke puffing out her feathers before the harrier flock.

"Keke!" came cries on every hand. "Where have you been!"

"Up the mountain," she cried proudly. "I am as the eagle now."

"The eagle!" First they looked shocked, then they laughed. "Oh, my!" they scoffed. "How we give ourself airs! How inflated we become, in human company."

"Pay them no mind," Gom said. "One day you'll show them, and they'll choke back their words!"

Oh, such a good time they had, going out all day for the first four. After that, they did not wander so far, expecting the wizard at any time. But by the sixth day, Gom was watching down the mountain constantly. His curiosity grew. What had the wizard gone to do? What magic had he performed? Would Hevron know of it?

Gom spent the seventh day sitting by the front stoop, while Keke kept lookout below. By dusk, Folgan still had not come. Four more hours, Gom waited, then he went to bed.

The next morning, Folgan was up in his workroom, as though he'd never been away, and he spoke not one word of his errand.

Gom ran down to the stable.

"There's been terrible trouble," the roan said. "We rode to Bokar Riffik's house. Someone tried to steal the wizard's stone."

Mat! Gom stood quite still.

"My first thought was that tall, weedy fellow, the one who stole Riffik from you. My, you described him well. He really didn't look as though he'd have the gumption, and that's his cleverness—you were right. I'll bet he'd have taken it if he could. But he didn't. There was a man. Riffik caught him climbing through a back window, and locked him up. But when the wizard tried to make the man say how he'd managed to find the house, break the boundary spell, and get inside, he wouldn't say. Well, Riffik set a seal-spell on him and summoned Folgan." The horse blew through his nose. "But do you know, by the time we arrived—*the man had gone!*"

"Gone?"

Hevron nodded. "He'd actually broken Riffik's seal-spell and taken off. Now Riffik isn't the best of wizards, but even so. They're in a tizzy, I can tell you, trying to explain how a common thief could crack a wizard's bonds."

Gom's skin began to tingle. "How did the man look, did Riffik say?"

"Like nothing much, save for one thing. It seems that on his chest was a tattoo—"

"Tattoo?"

"— of a death's-head: a human skull."

Chapter Five

"SKULL!" GOM turned to Stormfleet. "Another Zamul! This is Katak's work!"

"Zamul?" Hevron's ears pricked. "Katak?"

"Zamul was a foolish man; Katak, his master—one who'd destroy this world. He's loose, I knew it! Oh, what am I to do?"

"Brrr. Sounds like wizard's work. Go tell Folgan."

"I can't do that."

Keke flew in. "Why not?"

Gom shook his head.

"Tell them," Stormfleet urged. "As you told me."

And got himself a good friend into the bargain. Gom sat down on a barrel. "You're right," he said. He began to speak, of the Seven Realms spanning Ulm's southern skies. Of Bayon, the First Realm, with its wondrous column of living crystal: the Tamarith-awr-Bayon, the Prime Tamarith from which all others derived. He spoke of the Spinrathe—starfolk; of Jastra, lord of Bayon and overlord of all the Realms. Of Lord Karlvod of Maluc, the Fifth Realm. Of how, coveting Jastra's seat, Karlvod had broken the peace among the starfolk, sowing strife and mistrust, dividing the peoples into factions, and stirring the factions to war.

"Why?" Hevron asked.

"Each Realm has a Tamarith—offshoot of the Prime Tamarith—whereby the Spinrathe pass from world to world. These they call 'star-gates.' Karlvod seeks control of them, especially the Prime Tamarith, for he'd usurp Jastra, not as overlord, but absolute ruler: emperor of all the Realms. By the time Jastra learned of Karlvod's aim, to change commonwealth to empire, the Fourth Realm had fallen into chaos and the gate to the Third Realm was under siege."

"But how did Karlvod get so far without being found out?"

"He's still not found out!" Gom cried. "Many folk won't believe Jastra. In fact, some even think Jastra's at the bottom of it all. That's how bad things are!"

"Why? Why can't they see that it's Karlvod?" Keke cried.

"Because of Karlvod's cunning. In fact, many folk think him a victim as much as themselves."

"He must be cunning as a fox, to cause such commotion without a trace. Fox, or bird on the wing. How does he do it?"

Bird on the wing . . . Katak, skull-bird: Keke was on the mark. "Karlvod discovered three beings on Maluc; creatures called Spohr."

"Go on."

"Having no true form of their own, they can take the shape of anyone or anything. They can be solid flesh and bone, insubstantial as smoke. They are slow, but still they are deadly, for they can enter the minds of others and bend them to Karlvod's will—while he is worlds away."

"These Spohr: Katak is one?"

"Yes."

"What's he doing here?"

"Karlvod sent him."

Keke fixed her golden eye on Gom. "Why? What for?"

"When Jastra learned that Karlvod sought the Prime Tamarith, he broke the star-gate link between Bayon and the Second Realm, and so made the Tamarith safe, for the time being. But so that Bayon was not entirely cut off, he installed a secret star-gate here on Ulm, connecting the First and Second Realms. Karlvod found out, and sent Katak to find it," Gom said. "To take it, and open it from here."

"Where is this gate?" Hevron demanded.

"Beyond the High Vargue, where even the wild horses do not run."

"Sad," Keke said. "But folk will fight, even among the stars. However, the Spinrathen quarrel is not ours. And this gate is far from the paths of Ulm folk. So let the foreigners fight it out, as long as they don't hurt us."

Gom shook his head. "It's not that simple, Keke. Katak is master at stirring up strife. As his fellow-Spohr sow the seeds of war in the Realms, so will Katak among us if it will help his main purpose."

"But that would be terrible!"

"Terrible—but not the worst. Jastra so made the Ulm star-gate that, if breached by hostile force, it will destroy itself—and all Ulm with it!"

"Destroy—*all Ulm?*" Hevron reared. "This Jastra is evil as Karlvod!"

"So I thought at first. But Harga says there were no living beings on Ulm when Jastra built the gate."

"Well, there are now," the roan cried. "The Spinrathen lord must come and change that seal-spell."

"He can't. It's irreversible."

In the silence, Keke shook out her feathers. "Then Katak is the crux," she said briskly. "He's the one to stop—and you're the one to stop him!"

"I thought I had!" Gom cried. He told how he and Ganash the kundalara had tricked Katak under the Sound, sealing the Spohr in a cave with his own seal-spell. "But still he works his evil. Even from there he reaches into the minds of foolish, greedy men, and bends them to his bidding."

"Which is?"

"To bring him a gemstone, preferably one that already has magic, with which to break his seal-spell and free himself."

"I said this was wizard's work!" Hevron cried. "If you can't do anything, what about your mother?"

"She's not here—that's why I am with Folgan." He told now how Harga had traveled the star-gate to join Jastra against Karlvod's advance.

"She left Ulm?" Hevron pawed the ground. "Things must indeed be bad up there."

Gom nodded. "Jastra was desperate. She didn't want to go. I saw her once, alamar, when I was in Pen'langoth. She said—she said—" Gom's voice failed him.

"What about you, Mother? How is it?"

"I'm on the Third Realm. They're holding the line before the Fourth Realm star-gate, but it's slipping. I've been over there, and, oh, Gom . . . the Fourth Realm boils with hate and blood feud among the ruling houses. If we can't stop them, then Karlvod will have the gate, and move one Realm closer to Bayon. . . ."

"If neither of you can do anything for Ulm, you must go to the Hierarchy," Hevron was saying.

"No!" Gom cried.

"Why not?"

Gom looked away, thinking of Harga's written word. *I only can defend Ulm from destruction. And yet this charge is too great for me alone. But to whom can I turn? Only Tolasin, and he is old . . . I myself could have a child, a special child as I would bear by the right man . . . a secret child, left to grow under the protection and influence of gentle father and native soil, and of my own precious magic runestone . . . and under the stone's enchantment, the child shall grow slowly and slowly, like heart of oak, not counting the years as others . . .* All this Harga had read him from her chronicle, saying that only Gom would serve as Ulm's defender — but not *why.*

"I don't know," he said. "Yet no mage can know of the star-gate, by Harga's command." Gom's voice rose. "As she works to protect us up there, so I shall work to defend the crystal stair."

"Crystal stair?" Keke hopped about full circle. "Stairs and star-gates. What more wonders are there?"

"The star-gate floats in a hall high above the eastern plain." Gom stood up. "You reach it by a crystal stair so fine that you can scarcely see it. I myself have climbed that sky bridge alamar and stood beneath the Tamarith. It is a wondrous thing."

"Wondrous?" Keke said. "Deadly, don't you mean?"

"So," Hevron broke in. "Harga has trusted the fate of Ulm to you. Say, if Katak stood on that stair today, what would you do?"

"I have no idea."

"Don't listen to him, Hevron," Stormfleet said. "Gom would know exactly what to do. He always does, in a pinch, whatever he says!"

Gom looked at his friend gratefully.

"Well," Hevron said. "Your mother did seem to think you capable, and I suppose she knows what she's doing. Pity you can't reach her now and tell her about this tattooed man."

"And the other one who tried to take Tolasin's ring," Stormfleet said.

Gom nodded, grimly. Back in Pen'langoth, the old wizard Tolasin had shown Gom a snuffbox with a death's-head embossed on its lid—taken from a man who'd tried to rob him of his cabuchon ring in the Wilds. *My rune-stone, boy. The repository of much of my life's work. He demanded it by name—before he died.* . . . Katak must have sent that man to take Tolasin's magic ring, just as he'd sent Zamul after Harga's rune. And this third and latest ruffian after Riffik's. How many more were at Katak's bidding? And how long before one succeeded? "I must cut them off," Gom murmured. "But how, without losing my place here?"

"What would you do, anyway?" Hevron lifted his nose out of the oat pail.

"Why, I'd—I'd—" Gom broke off. He didn't know. Even with Harga's rune, he'd never have succeeded in trapping Katak had he not taken the Spohr by surprise. And even from his prison cave Katak had wormed his way into Gom's mind, and would have turned him but for Ganash.

"Ganash!" Gom smacked his fist into his palm. "I must see Ganash!"

Stormfleet tossed his mane and pawed the rocky floor. "I'll take you to him gladly, but perhaps there is a way to tell Ganash of all this—and still keep your place with Folgan." The cito turned his eye on Keke, still perched on the oat barrel. "Suppose someone else took Ganash your message: someone who could go faster than you, there and back in no time at all?"

Gom followed his gaze. *"Keke?"*

She bobbed up and down excitedly. "I'll go at once!"

"But—" Gom looked from horse to hawk. "You've never flown that far!"

"True. But that's not to say I can't."

Gom eyed her doubtfully. She was so small. Her wings, while powerful, were not conditioned for long flight. Yet many of her kind migrated every season, long distances from north to south and back again. She was a determined creature, Gom had seen that. And her sense of direction was faultless. However . . . "What if anything should happen to you, Keke?"

"It won't." She spread her wings impatiently. "Just tell me where to go and what to say, and I'll be off. Look," she went on, "I'll be careful. And I'll be back before you know it. Now, how do I call this kundalara, and what do I say?"

Gom went through the rest of the day in a haze of anxiety. He dropped a bowl, spoiled three spells, and was dismissed to the kitchen in disgrace. After he had gone to bed, he looked out his window. Where was Keke now? On what high ledge did she roost? Was she safe? How far until she reached Great Krugk and the tiny island near Ganash's underwater home? Fly due north, Gom had told her, until you smell something like the tang of the marsh only much stranger and stronger, filling the air. That is the smell of Great Krugk, arm of the Northern Sea cutting the glaciers asunder. Follow its eastern shore, he'd said, and you will come to a tiny island like a wizard's conical hat.

And then? Ganash had given Gom a jeweled horn at their parting. One blast on that, the kundalara had said, and I'll hear it wherever I am. Gom had hidden it up on the cliffs overlooking the island, and marked the place with cunning signs, but Keke couldn't use that! So Keke would have to spread word to every creature in sight that she sought Ganash urgently, on Gom Gobblechuck's behalf.

Gom fell asleep worrying, and awoke full of anxiety.

Folgan, still rattled, worked him so hard that day, that Gom could not dwell on his worry for long. Today, the wizard declared, Gom was to help repair Folgan's water rod, magic tool for restoring wells run dry. Folgan fetched out a tall stick, like Gom's own walking staff, but with a forked end. It looked to Gom much like the divining rod Gaffer Gudgeon had used to find fresh springs for Maister Craw below Windy Mountain. But that had been a plain forked hazel stick. Folgan's rod was so old Gom could not begin to guess what wood it was—or once had been. Its length was carved with many symbols, and ringed with thin bands of silver alloy. And the forks were alloy-capped, one tip worn and much corroded.

"You shall now learn how to anneal metal, boy," the wizard announced. "That is, how to heat and cool it gradually so as to soften it. This way, we can beat it out to whatever thickness or shape we need it for. Now: pay attention to what I do."

I already know that word, and how to apply it, thought Gom, watching the wizard light the flame. But, remembering Hevron's advice, he held his tongue.

All morning, Gom helped mix new alloy, then cast it, and beat it into a thin, flat sheet. As he helped, he thought of his friend, Carrick the master tinker. Gom had helped the tinker a great deal, cutting patches while Carrick hammered them to fit the curve of kettle and pot. Gom watched the wizard beating out the alloy on the bench and making heavy weather of it, too. Fast as he beat one area smooth, another seemed to shrivel into pits and pocks. The wizard was allowing the metal to cool too fast, it seemed to Gom. And the hammer head seemed to be the wrong shape. Yet still Gom held his tongue until he could no longer bear it.

"Excuse me," he said. He explained hesitantly how Carrick had gone about the same work, he a master tinker and specializing in those things. He told how Carrick had annealed the metal, closely controlling its temperature while he beat it into its proper shape with the tool best fitted for the task—a tool different from the one Folgan was using. Folgan's eyes narrowed as Gom spoke, and then opened wide. Gom's heart sank. Hevron had warned him not to speak! Well, now it was too late.

When Gom had done, the wizard turned the hammer over thoughtfully, rubbing his forefinger over its bulbous end. "Mmmm. I've heard of that Carrick. He is well regarded." Folgan looked up. "Tell me, how does this hammer differ from his?"

Gom took it, weighed it in his hand. "The head of Carrick's is flatter, sir." That was a start.

"It is?" Folgan took back the tool and, after a moment's deep thought, he went off down the chamber, beckoning Gom after him. The wizard uncovered a grindstone set upon a treadle and bade Gom work it with his foot. While Gom obeyed, Folgan ground the hammer head flat.

"Like that, boy?" Folgan held it up.

Gom eyed it narrowly. The angle was not quite true.

"If you'll allow me," he said politely. He put the head to the grindstone, and peddled away. Then he inspected it again. Could be better, but he dared not take off any more. Half ground away, the head even now was not as well balanced as Carrick's flat tap hammer, but . . . it might work.

"Well?"

Gom handed the hammer back. "That's it, I think, sir."

"Think, think? What kind of guarantee is that?" Folgan went back down the chamber grumbling. He took up the half-beaten alloy sheet. "Show me," he said, "how your tinker friend anneals his tin."

Gom, proud that Carrick could teach this wizard a thing or two, took up the sheet, heated it over the blue flame, then demonstrated how to hammer a little, and reheat, and hammer again, until a smooth patch was beaten out.

"Mmmmm," Folgan said. "Move aside, boy. I shall finish now." The wizard took the hammer and set to work. Truth to tell, Folgan did not do so well as Gom. Under his hand, the hammer left slight ridges on one side, and the man knew it. But he only looked up, eyeing Gom from under his brows. "You say you worked with this tinker. Then let's see how good you are. I want two caps cut and shaped to fit those tips. Get to it!"

By midafternoon, Gom had the caps perfectly in place, ready to be invested with the proper spells.

"You've done well, Gom Gobblechuck," Folgan conceded. "Here, stand by."

Gom flushed with pleasure. The wizard was going to chant the water-spell in front of him. But he didn't have time to think, how fine, for the wizard began to recite straightaway. Gom repeated the chant silently, committing it to memory, hoping to keep it sharp until he could write it out that night.

As Gom went down to make the tea, a hawk's loud call sent him racing to the window. Keke back already? There, a high and distant speck. It wheeled closer, flew overhead. Not Keke. One of her kin, on some local errand. Gom turned away. He must not be so anxious. There was nothing he could do. He could not even guess how long she'd be gone. He could only wait, and watch.

The next day passed, and the next. And the next.

Gom scanned the skies constantly for sign of Keke, hoping that at any moment she'd appear with good news from Ganash. But one week went by, and she still did not return.

"The north is far," Stormfleet said. "Give her time."

On the eighth morning after her departure, Folgan summoned Gom early. "Saddle the horses, and pack our bags. Hurry," he snapped, as Gom still stood there. "We leave in half an hour!"

Half an hour!

"And bring your best clothes. We're off to a wedding."

"A wedding?"

"The Lake Lord's sister-in-law is being married to the Lord Urolf." The wizard laughed. "How foolish you look, standing there, boy. Close your mouth. Don't worry, you're not invited. In fact, you'll remain below stairs for the duration. Now, go, for we have many villages to stop by on the way to Pen'langoth."

Gom ran downstairs. Pen'langoth! All this time he'd pined to go, and now? The day that Urolf had captured Gom, the Yul Kinta lord had been on his way to

Pen'langoth from his woodland domain, Aelyth-Kinta-lyn, to ask for the Lady Leana's hand. And now here was this grand wedding. Gom burst into the horses' stall. All those people! Why, everybody who was anybody would be there: lords, ladies, kings, and princes—and Yul Kinta!

Hevron looked up from the oat pail. "Now what's up?"

"We're called to a grand wedding, that's what. But I won't go, I *can't!*"

Stormfleet twitched his tail. "Don't tell me—it's Urolf's."

"Ha," said Hevron. *"That* wedding. There was much talk about Lord Urolf and the Lady Leana back in Pen'langoth. Many folk were against the idea of immortal Yul Kinta marrying human. They said it wasn't right to mix the blood. By your scowl I see that you agree."

"Not at all," Gom said. "I believe such an alliance can work only to Ulm's greater good. I'm happy for Urolf and his bride: I wish them well."

"Yet you'd rather not go to see them wed," Hevron replied smartly.

Gom hauled down Hevron's saddle and slung it across the roan's broad back. "You don't understand. The place will be swarming with Yul Kinta. The moment they set eyes on me, I'll be in irons!"

Stormfleet snickered. "You surely will."

"It's not funny!" Gom fastened Hevron's girth strap grimly.

"What's not funny?" the roan demanded. "If there is some joke here, I'm missing the point."

"Stormfleet was promised to Urolf, remember?" Gom said shortly. "Lord Urolf and I have already met on that account. He sees me again, I'll spend the rest of my life in a cell."

"Not necessarily. If this wedding is to be the big affair that you claim, there'll be crowds of people. Who's going to notice you?"

That was a point. Gom bit his lip. "What about Keke?"

"We'll leave her word to follow," Hevron reassured him. "Folgan will no doubt take his regular route down Long Valley, which is simple enough to follow. The villages where he'll visit all lie along the mountain tracks, she'll catch us up easy."

Gom buckled Stormfleet's saddle—a Yul Kinta saddle—and adjusted the stirrups. "Very well. You give word out, while I run inside and pack."

Folgan led Gom at a fair pace through the ranges, to reach their first village by nightfall. The moment word of their arrival was out, folk flocked to meet them, clamoring for Folgan's services, especially to fix their well, for the summer had been dry, and the water table ran low. Gom stood by proudly while Folgan wielded the shining tips of his divining rod where drying grass was turning yellow and brown, until the cry came: "It runs!" Everyone crowded to peer into the well, exclaiming with joy. Folgan had not only found water, but had pulled it to its proper place.

Gom followed on the wizard's heels, watching his way with people. They knew him, they feared him, but— they seemed to like him, and to trust him. Gom watched the old wizard pick up a crying child and comfort her. She had a running sore, her mother said tearfully. From a spider bite, which had resisted all the herb wife's remedies.

Gom listened eagerly. The very salve he'd applied to

Folgan's cut. The wizard, turning about, commanded Gom to fetch it from the wizard's pack. No one paid him any note as he fetched out the salve and handed it over. My ointment, he thought, made at Folgan's direction. Gom had the formula in his journal—in his head, even. He could make up a batch right there, on the spot.

Folgan applied the remedy, leaving the herb wife to bind up the sore. Then he filled a tiny pot with salve and handed it over in return for five golden guineas. A lot of money, Gom thought, watching the mother's face. More than it was worth, more than she could comfortably afford. Folgan didn't need it. But, the wizard had told him, the higher the fee, the more they respected you. Gom put the salve back, thinking. One day, he'd be stopping aches and pains, healing hurts, and filling empty wells. But only for what folk could pay.

Eight whole days they journeyed—no sign of Keke. On the ninth day, they reached the first inn on the valley floor, where Folgan went inside to take a handle of ale, giving Gom leave for an hour or so. Gom took Stormfleet on a gallop, much to Hevron's disgust. They had scarcely left the village behind when Stormfleet pricked his ears and looked up. High above them, a speck approached, weaving erratically.

"Keke!"

The wings spread wide, and the bird came straight at them, overshot, and sank below a gentle rise. When they reached her, she was lying still, a small brown speck in the waving grasses. Gom lifted her between his hands. She felt limp and heavy as death. "Keke?"

On her right leg something glistened. Gom turned her over, the better to see. It was a band, a silver band, and on it was inscribed a human skull.

Chapter Six

"IS SHE dead?" Stormfleet backed off a way.

Gom touched the bird's breast, felt the small heart pumping, and warmth within.

"No. Not dead."

"What then?"

"I don't know." Was she under Katak's evil sway? Gom looked closely at the silver band. A ring, made for human finger, a large human finger. The metal was soft, thank goodness. Whoever had put it on Keke had pinched it to fit, then folded the excess around the leg a second time. Slipping his nail under the overlap, Gom prised it up gingerly, carefully opened out the circle, then slid it off Keke's leg. There, Gom thought, if evil tainted that ring, Keke was now free of its influence. He set the thing onto the grass, and, picking up the hawk again, cradled her in his cupped hands.

But still the harrier didn't stir.

Stormfleet leaned down. "Will she be all right?"

"We'll soon know, I hope." Gom stroked her feathers, willing her back to wakefulness, until at last Keke opened her eyes, struggling to stand. "Put me down," she said weakly, "if you value your skin."

Gom set her on the grass, and sat beside her. "How are you?"

"Exhausted, that's for sure."

Gom held up the ring. "Who put this on your leg?"

"Why, Ganash, of course." Keke spread her wings stiffly, fluttered them a bit to stretch them out, then folded them back into her sides.

"Ganash?"

"When I got to the island, I . . . I . . ." Keke's eyes closed again.

"Keke," Gom said. Then, louder, "Keke! Oh, bother the bird!"

"Don't be so ungracious," Stormfleet said. "Come on, time we were back. Folgan will be after your hide."

Gom looked up, saw how far the sun had moved across the sky. The cito was right. He slipped Keke inside his jacket, then stood, looking down at the ring winking among the grasses.

"What are you waiting for?" Stormfleet said impatiently.

"I'm wondering about that ring."

"Bring it. It must be harmless now, or Ganash would never have placed it on Keke's leg."

That made sense. Gom retrieved it, pressed it flat, stowed it in his pouch, and leapt astride the cito's back.

The moment they returned, Folgan ordered Gom to pack. Time to leave for the next village, the wizard said, to be there by nightfall. When they were ready, Gom hoisted Keke in his open bag as casually as he could. But the move didn't get past Folgan.

"What, boy?" The wizard peered in. "Taken up hawking now? Where did you find it?"

"Over the fields a way, sir," Gom said.

"Did you now?" The wizard prodded the harrier, then hastily withdrew his hand. "What's the matter with it, anyway?"

"She seems to be exhausted."

"Hmmmph." The old man climbed onto Hevron's back. "Well, if you would bring it, keep it away from me. I don't like the look of those claws."

They rode on.

Keke was still asleep as they reached their stop, and Gom was forced to leave her with the horses. It was hours before he dared slip down to their stall to see how she was.

He found Keke perched on the water pail, drinking thirstily. She had flown from Folgan's house nonstop, she said, passing through every village they'd visited on the way. Before that, she'd raced from the north with news from Ganash.

Gom's eyes shone at the mention of his ancient friend. "How was he? What did he have to say? How did things turn out?"

"Give me breath!" Keke hopped full circle on her perch. "I told Ganash exactly what you said. I scarce had the words out of my mouth before swish! he was gone! I waited days for further sign of him. Then suddenly, he was back, in a tidal wave that sent water halfway up the cliffs clear across the Krugk! He said to tell you the sealstone glows, so Katak could not have come out. That he has sealed the main cavern with stones, both entrances, flooding the place, right to the roof. And the whole is set about with kundalara spells. No man will be down there visiting Katak now."

Gom listened intently, remembering his waking dreams in Folgan's workroom. He hadn't been able to decide whether they came as warning or reassurance. Now it seemed they'd served as both. The green radiance: hadn't it reminded him at the time of the light from

Ganash's scales? Was that what he'd seen, then?—the main cavern, just-filled with Ganash's floodwaters? He recalled the sealstone's red light shining through the water, sign that the Spohr was still within his small side cave. And now confirmed by Ganash's own word. Yes, a reassurance that all was well. And Gom's falling through the floor? *That* had been the warning—to stay well clear!

"So here we are," Hevron said. "It's a good thing you sent Keke, Gom. You know for sure now that Katak can't get out—nor can men go to him. He's fixed for good!"

"Mmmm." Gom wasn't entirely persuaded. "What news of Katak, did Ganash say?" Not drowned, for sure. The creature could live indefinitely in water.

"The Spohr gave Ganash no sign. But not to worry. Katak was likely too angry to speak! Ganash sends his best wishes, to both you and your mother, and hopes that you'll visit someday. Until then, he promises to watch that place, which he calls the Isle of Lorne."

Gom nodded, satisfied, relieved. He fished in his pockets, pulled out the ring. It was fairly mangled now, yet the skull-lines were still plain. "And this, Keke?"

Keke shook out her feathers, took a sip from the pail, raised her head, and swallowed. "There was a man. A big man, bigger than you."

"I'm still a youth, and not so large at that."

"He came to the island, he went under the cliffs while Ganash was down there, I watched him go."

Gom nodded. He knew that entrance to the cave under the island. He'd used it himself. "And then?"

"Ganash didn't say. But the man never came back up, and when the kundalara reappeared, he said he wanted you to have that thing as a token of his good faith. He fitted it to my leg to save my beak." Keke cocked her head. "Ganash divested it of its evil power. He said to tell you that it now is only what it seems: a trinket, memento of the cavern's sealing."

Gom turned the ring over in his hand. The kundalara collected treasure. In fact, he was a bit of a miser. It was some measure of his regard that he had let this go. "Thank you, Keke. I shall keep it well."

"Don't thank me. Thank Ganash. As for me, I'm fair feathered, and tomorrow, so I hear, we go on to Pen'langoth!" She cocked her head at him. "Why? Why does the proud Yul Kinta lord go all the way to Pen'langoth to wed his bride? Why not the other way around?"

"I can answer that," Hevron said. "Urolf would not have crowds of mortals trampling his greenwoods."

"More than that," Gom added. "Aelyth-Kintalyn is a closed and secret place, like the Dunderfosse. Urolf would not have its whereabouts known to so many people. Why, the Yul Kinta take even honored guests in blindfolded."

"Ke-ke-ke, well I'm not complaining. There'll be so much to see in the Lakelands. Good night." The harrier flew off into the rafters.

Gom watched her settle herself to sleep. He looked down at the silver ring. *Another man . . .* Too soon for Bokar Riffik's thief. The worry leapt back. Ganash may have cut off Katak's cave, but that didn't stop the Spohr from reaching into men's thoughts and bending them to his bidding. Would the evil one find a way at last for them to free him from his deep cave? Those men, seeking out runes and gemstones for Katak: how many, and where? "Oh!"

"What is it?" Stormfleet said.

"The wedding. There'll be so much finery: gold and silver, and precious gems. And a grand convening of wizards with their runestones, all the makings for magic met in one place, and not in secret as at the Covenance, but out in the public eye. There is great peril in this."

"With Katak's cave shut off?"

"Don't count on anything where the Spohr's concerned." Danger would be stalking the lake city, danger greater than any so far, and he not a wizard by a long chalk. No magic stored in stone or staff. And only the beginnings of mind power. He pressed his hands to his brow. All he had were his everyday wits, and—he patted his pocket—a few grains of dream-sand to take a would-be robber unawares. . . .

Bidding his friends good night, Gom went to bed. He lay in the dark, unable to sleep. *Only the beginnings of mind power . . .*

Not good enough!

A wizard born, Harga had called him.

Gom sat up guiltily. He had gifts beyond the normal human scope, that he knew. He could bring on a waking dream by sitting anywhere, not just inside Folgan's ring of stones, of that he was sure, even though he'd never tried. And he could also determine what the vision was to be about. Should he not sit and wish for a vision to tell him where Katak's thought was directed? Gom shuddered. He had felt Katak's probing before, had suffered the Spohr's touch. Nothing would induce him to send his thought that way, for fear Katak might sense him. Like a small creature, he'd be, poking his head from the tall grasses, easy prey for fox or weasel. No, he'd bide his time, put his other gifts to use. Safer to learn the writing, and numbers; to collect the lore of rock and leaf and root: build up his mage's powers.

Safer, but for how long could he afford to shirk from acknowledging his gift, from learning how to use it? A mage born, Harga had said. Her long-lived tool. . . . He crossed his legs. Face it, he should start now, tonight. Sit and think of Harga. He took out his crystal, laid it in his palm. All these months he'd waited for it to summon him back to the crystal stair. Perhaps—perhaps he had the power to make it work—at will. He looked down. He must now try to use his mind the way Folgan had shown him, and try to go there of his own accord.

He closed his eyes—then opened them again. The risk! One mistake, and the Spohr might sense him, find him out. He closed his hand about the crystal. Coward. He'd not reach Harga with his belly to the ground! He composed himself again, pictured his crystal, swinging slowly by its chain, flashing as it caught the light, back and forth, back and forth. Minutes passed, and still he sat steadfastly keeping the movement of his crystal before him. Then, all at once, the familiar buzz began in his head.

Keeping his mind calm as he could, Gom sent out the thought: *Harga, call your son!*

Nothing happened. He heard his breath, sounding like another's, and the blood pulsing in his ears. He shrank his vision to a point and called again.

The crystal flared in his inner sight. To his great relief, there came no watery light, but the lovely pearly haze as in his practice visions. He looked about curiously. *Harga?* He listened. Nothing. Only the misty light, just like the light around the crystal stair. And, as in that place also, no wind, no sound of any living thing. He began to grow uneasy. *Harga! Harga! Can you hear?*

Out of the mist Gom detected movement: a shadow, a dark smudge.

Gom drew in his breath. "Harga?"

Slowly, it emerged, a tall shape—an armored warrior: visor down, pale green plume waving at its helmet's crest. The armor was dusty, and dull from much use. Yet on the breastplate shone a golden emblem; a hind, rearing like a stag, and sporting a horn on her brow. Even as Gom noted all this, the figure slowly raised the visor with a steely gauntlet, and unseen eyes silently appraised him from the shadow beneath.

Gom stood his ground. "Who are you?"

The figure made no move.

"Are you from my mother?"

Still no response.

Gom grew bolder. "Why you? I called upon my mother!"

Out of the hollow metal mask came a voice, deep and resonant. "Harga cannot come. Speak to me instead."

"Nay! Where is she?" Gom cried. "She has not come to harm?"

"She's too far to heed you. Speak, and I will take your message to her."

Gom hesitated. "How can I be sure?"

"Young man," the voice took on an urgent note. "Speak—and fast." The outlines of the armor began to shimmer. "Your mind is wavering. Quick, before you lose the link!"

Gom steadied his mind, and the figure came back into focus. "Give me proof that you are not Karlvod's tool."

The figure sighed. "I see you have her stubborn will. You who are of the sparrow and the bear: your mother has spoken much of you. She loves you more than anything, I think. If she could, I know she'd be here, but as I said, she's too far down the line."

Gom's hand went to the belt Harga had given him. He fingered the two creatures forming the pillars of its buckle: sparrow, for Harga; bear, for Stig. "And you, where are you? How did you hear my call?"

Another sigh. "It would take long, and time is short. Whatever is your message, say it now."

Gom obeyed, telling of his fears. How, even though Ganash had flooded Katak's cave, men still likely did the Spohr's work. "I'm afraid he'll break free before I'm ready." Gom waited, sensing the stranger's keen scrutiny.

At last the warrior spoke. "Not strong enough, not ready? You reached across the void and plucked me, even from the battlefield." The warrior walked from Gom a little way, head down in thought.

Gom watched the stranger, puzzled. Void? Battlefield? Was this man up in the stars, then? Had Gom reached with his thought *even beyond the star-gate?*

The warrior came back again. "You know of the starstone?"

"Starstone?"

"I see the answer's no." The warrior folded his arms. "Jastra has a starstone, a crystal seed plucked from the very heart of the Tamarith-awr-Bayon. He keeps this starstone for you, against the hour when you must take it up against the Spohr. In the First Realm he has it, and I know where."

Gom's lips parted. He remembered Jastra at their

meeting, the Spinrathen lord's crystal browband, big as a thrush's egg. "What is this starstone like, what will it do?"

"How should I know? I'm not the mage. Probably enhance whatever power you possess, I'd say. Jastra said you were not ready, but I think you are. Anyway, you have to be. Listen, I'll fetch that stone soon as I can . . ." The figure began to melt at the edges, the voice faded in and out. ". . . pass the line . . . reach the gate . . . only hold on . . ."

"Wait!" Gom shouted, rallying. "Come back!" But all was mist. Then the mist faded, leaving Gom in the dark of his room.

He was still sitting cross-legged, stiff with cold. Had he shouted out aloud? Gom held quite still for a minute or so, listening for sound of the wizard stirring next door. Then he slumped over, exhausted. Oh, how could he have lost that link! With great effort, he straightened, closed his eyes again, and willed himself back into the mist, willed the armored warrior to stand once more before him. But though he sat thus for another hour or more, he got only leg cramps and an aching neck. Frustrated, Gom slid under the covers and curled up. That warrior! A Spinrathe, for sure. . . . *you reached across the void and touched me, even on the battlefield* . . . In calling on Harga, he had somehow reached to the stars, and touched the mind of the alien! But how, and why that one? Had not Harga told Gom that those people had lost their magical powers? Could it be that the warrior still retained some? If so, what great good luck that Gom should chance upon him, with Harga being too far to hear. The warrior was friend, Gom would swear. A man of his word? Only hold on, the warrior had told him. But for how long? It could be years. He lay back on his pillow. What choice had he but do as the warrior said: watch, and wait.

Gom's eyes gleamed. A starstone—set aside for him! A starstone—seed, the warrior had called it, from the heart of the Prime Tamarith itself!

. . . Jastra said you were not ready . . .

Jastra was probably right. Why, the danger of possessing that thing now! Gom drifted toward sleep. His mother's face came into view, dark eyes full of concern. Then the warrior stood before him, pale green plume slowly waving in some distant wind. *. . . . Jastra says you are not ready, but you are. You have to be . . .*

Gom turned over. Katak was subtle, and cunning beyond measure. He'd given Ganash no sign that he was there. What if he had been too busy? What if the Spohr even now worked to break out of his cave somehow? Gom tossed onto his other side. He was wearing himself out with fear.

Three days after, they came in sight of Pen'langoth. Within hours, they were traveling the crowded thoroughfares toward Scandibar, the Lake Lord's island citadel. By now, Keke rode Gom's shoulder in plain sight, chattering nonstop, missing nothing.

"Why, it's so close to the shore!" she exclaimed excitedly. "You could almost reach over and touch it!"

"And risk a broken neck," Hevron remarked, looking down over the cliff edge to the narrow wedge of water between island and shore.

The citadel was truly an impressive sight. Boat-shaped,

like the island on which it was built, it was surrounded by high walls, quite secure from the shore. There were two ways into Scandibar. The first, was by the Lake Lord's private drawbridge at the far end of the island; a narrow entrance, lowered only when it was in use. The second, was by the wide public drawbridge leading from the main city square. This remained open—though guarded—night and day, the portcullis, up.

Gom followed Folgan toward the portcullis arch, noting the tall sentries standing to attention, pikes cocked, watching all who would go in and out. The last time Gom had come to Pen'langoth, Leochtor's soldiers had combed the entire city for him on Urolf's behalf. As they passed under the portcullis, Gom sat up straight, braced for trouble. But no one gave him a second glance as wizard was recognized and greeted with great ceremony, and conducted inside under the Grand Portal. Gom was left with the horses.

A knot of youths stood about the stable door. As Gom led the horses over, they turned toward him.

"Who are you?"

"What's your name, half-pint?"

"Who're you with?"

Gom drew himself up. "My name is Gom Gobblechuck. I come with Folgan."

They looked at one another, then eyed him up and down in awe. "Folgan!"

"And still going?" one muttered.

"How do you do it?" said another.

"You haven't said your names," Gom reminded them.

A red-headed boy spoke up: medium high, Gom came to his shoulder. "I'm Afen, I come with Mecrim Thurgeril."

Gom nodded. The Grand Archimage. "What's he like?"

Afen shrugged. "He's a hard master, but kinder than yours!"

Everybody laughed nervously.

Gom turned to Afen's neighbor, a stocky lad with sallow face and bright gold hair. "And you?"

"Hilleray. I am bound to Blifil Bludge."

More laughter, this time not nervous at all.

"An easy time he has of it," Afen said. "His master is lazy as a pudding. He gets the others to do his work."

A third lad peeled himself from the wall. The one who had called Gom half-pint. Big as a barn, and strong, beard already sprouting, yet he smiled affably enough. "Dingle, at your service," he said, making a fancy bow. "I'm for Potra, so I mind my manners, not like these bumpkins."

A fourth looked up: a girl; freckled, plump, friendly, with wide open grin. "Zobe, at your service. Don't mind them. I'm with Maister Mathery."

Gom looked beyond, wondering if Mat were anywhere around. As if in answer, a figure emerged from the stable shadows. "Gom! My dear chap! My old *friend!*" Mat strolled out into the sunshine.

Gom ignored the outstretched hand. "Good day," he said, stiffly, remembering their last encounter. He turned back to the others. "Nice to meet you. See you all later," he said, then went on, aware of Mat's injured stare. He walked the horses through the stable door, toward a groom's beckoning arm. Outside, a murmur came, then Mat's voice, raised in reply. What was Mat saying? Gom hated to think.

"In here, lad, in here." The groom held open a double stall door. "My, that's a fine roan. Maister Folgan's, as I recall." The man looked Stormfleet over in mock disbelief. "And that—"

Keke stretched her wings to their full extent, and opened her hooked beak wide.

"—is yours, I take it?" The groom backed off, his eye on the bird. Keke fluttered noisily to perch, not too far, above his head. Without another word, the groom helped Gom take off the horses' tack and hang it up. "I got to go," he said at last, setting down the horses' water pail. "You'll manage your bags all right, lad?" He nodded to the gear lying by the stall door. "There's a guard waiting outside to show you to Folgan's quarters. It's a bit of a fuss, walking them great halls, but don't let it scairt you. After that, you're out of it, below stairs with the rest of us low types." Smiling reassurance, the groom took himself off.

Gom turned to his friends. "Will you be comfortable for a while?"

"Fine," Stormfleet assured him. "Go, before Folgan comes looking for his things. We'll keep ourselves good company."

The guard, in helmet and plumes, stood waiting, pike upraised, putting Gom for a startled moment in mind of the Spinrathen warrior. The soldier saluted solemnly, and gestured Gom to walk beside him. An odd couple they must look: the tall escort striding with long and measured tread, and he, Gom, his staff slung across his back, the two heavy packs in either hand, going almost at a trot to keep up. The stable yard was now quiet and empty: Mat and the rest were gone.

* * *

That night, Folgan was to attend a banquet in honor of the bride and groom. The wizard would not require anything until the morrow, he said. In the meantime, Gom was to stay in the servants' quarters, be seen and not heard, and otherwise behave himself.

"If you please, sir, may I go into the city?"

Folgan frowned. "Indeed, you may not. All apprentices are confined to Scandibar."

"But—" Gom looked at the old man in dismay. "I mean no mischief, sir. I only wish to visit old friends. It would be quite harmless."

The wizard's eyes narrowed. He was growing annoyed. For a moment, Gom thought the wizard would dismiss him summarily, but then the old man bade him sit. He took out his cherrywood, rammed tobacco shreds into the bowl. "My boy, thieves are abroad, bold men who'd steal not only gold or purse but the very power that a wizard wields. If you or one of the other boys should fall into those men's hands, there's no telling what harm may result. If once word that Folgan's apprentice is loose out there, these men would find you, and—well, who knows, you'd be lucky to get off with your life."

Thieves? Bold men? This was bad news indeed. That Folgan was aware of this new danger gave Gom some comfort. But not much. None of the wizards could begin to guess its full extent. Perhaps he should stay in the citadel, as the wizard said. And yet—he badly wanted to see Essie and Carrick, just once. "Sir," he said. "Who'll know me, or that I'm off Scandibar, if no one tells?"

"Silence, boy!" Folgan stood up angrily. He made to

say more, then his eyes grew sharp. "You wouldn't be sneaking off to see your mother?"

"Why, n-no, sir. I swear. There are friends, down in the fisherman's quarter. I'd be quite safe there."

"Hmmm." Folgan stroked his beard. "Listen, you have worked reasonably well, better than most of the idiots it has been my lot to bear. Promise me this: that you'll not reveal yourself to those friends of yours, that you'll not speak to anyone—*anyone,* friend or stranger. If you promise me this, then you may go out until the midnight hour. Well?"

Not speak? Not reveal himself? But that was grossly unfair! What would be the point of going! Gom stood up, minded to refuse the wizard's offer.

"It's not just your neck. In allowing you even this much, I go against the ruling of the Hierarchy, young man. Well? Do you swear?"

Folgan was being inordinately kind, Gom realized. Taking a risk to offer him even this much. Gom thought of Essie in her parlor, and Carrick on the settle by the fire. If he refused the offer, he'd not see his friends for another six years. Surely just to glimpse them, even if he might not let them know that he was there. . . .

He nodded slowly. "I swear, sir."

"Very well, boy. But be back by midnight, you hear?"

Gom heard, and, taking up his staff and pack, he fled.

The waiting guard led him down a series of high and hollow halls, then along a passage toward a staircase leading down. They were almost there, when a voice called behind them.

"Gom? Gom Gobblechuck?" Gom turned. "Gom Gobblechuck it is! By all that's strange and marvelous —whatever are you doing here!"

Chapter Seven

EYRWARL! UROLF'S younger brother.

"What in Ulm's name brings you here?" The Yul Kinta pulled up, taking in the tall guard. "I hope you're not—that my brother hasn't—"

"I am apprenticed to Folgan," Gom said quickly. He watched with no small satisfaction the shock in Feyrwarl's face.

"Well, well." The Yul Kinta nodded. "And Folgan's here for the wedding." Feyrwarl turned to the guard. "Trouble yourself no further," he said, taking up Gom's pack. "I myself shall take the boy to his place. I know the way."

The guard saluted, clicked his heels, and marched off.

Feyrwarl stood looking Gom up and down. "Wizard's apprentice now, are we? Well, that surely follows, you being Harga's son. But why not to your mother—nay, I mustn't ask, and you won't answer. So: you got Folgan. Hmmm. Difficult, I imagine," he said thoughtfully, then snapped his fingers. "Haha! I see it now: you were on your way to find a master when we—ah, bumped into you last year." Feyrwarl looked back up the hall. "Well, I needn't tell you to watch out this time. There are those who'd gain favor with Urolf, and even up a score or two, remember?"

Gom remembered. Thrulvar, Urolf's right-hand man, who'd captured Gom. And the jailor—Luthar, a burly, surly sort, against not only Gom but all humans—even the one his master was to marry. "Is Luthar below stairs?"

Feyrwarl shook his head. "All our folk have places up above, even such as that one. Friend—" The Yul Kinta looked sidewise. "Keep your head down, watch out by the stables, and with luck, you'll get by." He walked on, smiling. "There is one who'd wish to see you, though."

"The Lady Vala?"

"Is unaccountably fond of you. Perhaps, who knows, we three shall meet in some small space quite soon."

"That would be fine," Gom said, and meant it. The Lady Vala had shed tears for Harga, had protected Gom from Urolf, and helped Gom escape at great risk to herself. Yes, he'd be right glad to see her.

"Ah," said Feyrwarl, slowing. They had reached a narrow, curving stair, leading down into darker levels. "Here, I'll lead the way. Watch how you go. These steps are crumbly. His Honor the Lord High Chamberlain, bless his elevated nose, is not so much concerned about appearances downstairs."

After supper, Gom slipped out to the stables.

"How is it? Leochtor's halls are very grand I hear. Are there many people? How is your pallet? Why do you bring your gear out here? You're not going anywhere. Did they feed you enough at board?" Keke was waiting to greet him, although it was past her bedtime.

"I sleep in a dormitory." Gom set his pack and staff by the back wall. "A cot in a line of cots. With the other apprentices. I'd leave nothing of value down there."

"Hrrr!" Stormfleet snorted. "Mat, I take it."

Gom nodded. "He's holding court downstairs. You'd

think him a fully fledged mage the way he talks, and the rest hang on his every word!"

"So you're avoiding him?" Hevron said. "That's why you're here?"

"Yes, and no." Gom turned back to the cito. "Stormfleet, we're going to visit The Jolly Fisherman—"

"Aaahh," Stormfleet said. "Essie's oats."

"—but we can't show ourselves, and we must be back by midnight."

"Oh." Stormfleet nuzzled his arm. "You must be disappointed."

"Aye. Will you come?"

"Gladly. You might need fast heels. There's talk in the air. The wedding brings its own troubles, strangers who give the Lake Lord's men a run for their money. There has been more thievery and unruliness than usual these past weeks, so they say."

"I wish you'd stay put," Keke said. "But if you must go, I'll ride your shoulder."

Gom smiled. "Thanks, Keke, but an owl might serve me better at this hour. I'll take care, I promise, and Stormfleet will watch out for us both."

"Huh." Keke ruffled her feathers. "I still say you'd be better employed around here. There are some fine young hens about, if you follow me, and they all seem to be doing their courtship dances around the stables. But if I can't change your mind, good night." She flew up into the dark.

Gom slung his staff and led Stormfleet out across the yard and over the drawbridge. "Be sure to be back by midnight, young fellermelad," the gate sergeant said. "I have orders from Folgan not to let you in a minute after."

He had? Shocked, Gom climbed onto Stormfleet's back

and crossed the wide drawbridge to the city square. That Folgan—just as Gom had begun to hope the wizard was grown fond of him at last! Truly, it might never do to take the man for granted!

Gom looked up the grand avenue, his mood lifting. The last time, he'd been forced to ride that thoroughfare as a sort of comic mascot before Urolf's procession. "It was a fair good rout, was it not?" Stormfleet snickered. Gom smiled. At Stormfleet's signal, the Yul Kinta horses had unseated Urolf, setting off a tidal wave of chaos while Gom and Stormfleet had escaped into the crowds, unseen.

They turned from that broad, straight way, treading instead the steep and twisting streets down toward Lakeside and the fishing quarter. There were folk about still, out for an evening stroll in the mild fall air. Gom looked around constantly, alert for sign of trouble.

The sun sank, the light faded from the sky, and the streets were quite dark as they reached the fisherman's quarter. Rounding the last corner, Gom saw the inn sign swinging over the front porch lantern to his right, halfway down the hill. "Wait for me here?" he said, dismounting.

"I shall. Be careful, Gom Gobblechuck. If you need me—call."

Gom went on down the cobbled road. Below him, at the bottom of the steep hill, lay the marketplace; the stalls empty, the aisles deserted.

Reaching the inn, he slipped under the back entry arch and through into the yard. It hadn't changed a whit in the one year's space. The sweet smell of hay wafted from the open stable doors, and mingled with the lingering scents of supper. Memories flooded in. Of Stormfleet standing, a sorry sight: knock-kneed, bent-backed, head down by that very wall in broad daylight, and beside him in blessed ignorance, Jofor, the solahinn chief, demanding his cito's return. Of Essie, wooden spoon upraised, fending him off.

. . . listen here, solahinn man. Touch one hair of this boy's head and you'll not be welcome in this inn, nor nowhere else in Lakeside no more—now get you off to your plain!

Gom darted across the yard, and peered around the open inn door. A woman's loud laugh came over the general hubbub. Essie! Full figure encased in bright gold satin, hair upswept, she carried a loaded tray across the hall from kitchen to parlor. Homesickness washed through him. And longing. Why, *why* could he not just slip through and— Gom sighed. He'd given his word.

He walked back out, crept along by the front wall until he reached the parlor windows. Maybe, if he didn't get too close, he'd catch a glimpse of those familiar faces, Essie's, Carrick's, Brody's, without anybody seeing.

The room was crowded, and noisy as ever. He could not see the other side where the hearth was, could not see— A slight parting of the crowd and there was Carrick, leaning back against the settle. He looked tired. In the market he never got a minute's rest, for he was so good that many folk disdained the other tinkers, saving their pots for him. This year, he hadn't Gom to help him. Gom's eyes moved on. Was Brody still here? Yes, by that far nook! Pretty as ever, Gom saw, but . . . different. Older, with her hair piled on top of her head, giving her neck a long, graceful look. Why, Gom realized with a shock. She was a girl no longer, but a woman.

An arm reached out, pulled Brody down and, laughing, she landed with a bump in a fisherman's lap. "Hey!"

came a voice. "Let your missus alone for one hour more, Willy! We're waiting for our beer!"

Missus? Gom pressed his face to the window. At that moment, Essie turned her head. "Gom!" Her tray crashed to the floor.

Gom leapt back. She mustn't find him, she mustn't! A touch on his hand brought him about. The cito's muzzle.

"Quick!" Gom leapt up on Stormfleet's back. "Essie's seen me!"

They galloped uphill, rounding the corner as figures erupted into the street. "Gom?" he thought he heard Essie's call, then they were gone. Fool! he chid himself, as Stormfleet sped back through darkened streets. What good had come of it! Serve him right if they got back late! They rushed on, until, almost at the citadel, Gom heard a loud cry ring out from a side alley. Partway along, two figures struggled under a street lantern. Suddenly, one cried out, then went down. The other set off, away from Gom, going at a clip.

Gom dismounted and, taking his staff in hand, ran to the man and knelt beside him. The man was heavy; big, and broadshouldered, like his attacker. Gom felt the man's wrist. The blood ran fast, but strong enough. At Gom's touch, the man looked up in a daze, struggling to speak. His hand went to his belt. "Stop . . . thief," he murmured, then fell back.

Gom set the man's head down gently, then scrambled up. The thief had taken the man's pouch? Well, Gom must try to get it back, though not, he thought, remembering the thief's great size, by regular means. He slung his staff and reached into his pocket.

"Gom! Take care! This might be no ordinary thief!"

Gom held up his box of dream-sand. "Stormfleet, wait here, and don't follow me!" He took off after the thief, his boots slipping on the cobbles.

At the sound of approaching feet, the thief looked over his shoulder. "Hey up." To Gom's surprise, the man turned back toward him.

Gom stood his ground, hand tight about his sand box. The thief was *big!*

"Well, lookee here, if we ain't got ourselves a hero." Laughing, the man held out his hands. "Well, come on, then. Ain't you going to arrest me, in the name of Leochtor?" He reached out farther to grab Gom. Holding his breath, Gom picked out a grain of sand, spat on it, and flicked it in the robber's face.

Then he ran.

Behind him came a hiss and a cry. Then silence. A faint whiff overtook him, but it was only the harmless aftermath as the spent fumes scattered on the wind. Gom knelt by the unconscious victim once more. The clothes, he noticed, were of quality; the hands, soft and well kept. A gentleman. Gom felt his temple, taking again the measure of his blood. Then he looked to Stormfleet standing over him. "He'll be fine."

"Good. Now come, or we'll be shut out," the cito urged, but Gom had not finished. He went back to where the thief lay, arms spread, mouth open. Having caught the first smoke burst full on, the man should, according to Folgan, stay that way for three full days. However, Gom bound the ankles with the thief's own belt for good measure, then tied the hands behind with the man's own neckerchief, knotting the ends firmly. Now Gom explored pockets, found a leather pouch fat with gold coins, and set it aside.

Lastly, Gom searched the man for any sign of skull, whistled with relief. No tattoo, no ring, medallion, or bracelet. No sign of Katak at all. Just a common thief, thank the skies. He dragged the robber up the alley and laid him at his victim's feet. As he straightened up, the gentleman began to stir. Gom thrust the purse into his hands, and retreated, Stormfleet trotting after.

"Come back, sir! Sir, I say!" came the cry.

Gom leapt astride the cito and sped away. As they reached the drawbridge, bells chimed midnight. Even so, since they were in sight of the gate guards, Stormfleet had to check his gallop and stagger up the ramp with slow, arthritic gait. By the time they reached the sentry box, the last echoes had died away.

"Umph," the sergeant said. "You live close to the edge, lad. Oh, well, off you go, and pray your stars your master won't mind."

"That was fun, though I'm not sure if it was wise," Stormfleet said, as Gom led him into the stables.

"I know." Gom retrieved his pack. "But we couldn't let that robber go, could we? Anyway, no harm's done, so good night."

Gom lay, looking down the rows of silent cots, going over the evening's escapes. It made him feel good to think of the gentleman waking up and finding his stolen pouch of gold returned, and the thief lying bound by his feet. What had that man thought to see Gom running off, a horse at his heels? Gom smiled. How would he explain it? His smile faded. And how would he explain the thief's not waking up for three whole days? *What if it came to Folgan's attention?* Gom turned over. Pen'langoth was a big city. Why should anyone connect the incident with him? He turned back again.

Saving the man had been folly. And going to The Jolly Fisherman had been no less. Seeing his old friends only made him miss them more, and he had surely upset Essie.

Fool!

Then there was Brody.

Married. And her man there with his arms about her, and her laughing back at him. She'd no doubt forgotten Gom. And why not, he thought, staring up into the dark. Why not, when he'd taken off without a farewell into the blue and wouldn't be back for years, if ever. And besides, he thought somberly, with all the weight he had on his shoulders, what room had he for such as Brody Leggat?

. . . *you, instead of preening yourself and strutting for the hens, you shut yourself away . . . with a bag of old, dried bones. Why?*

. . . *I have important work to do.*

Gom sighed heavily. Destiny, was why. *Destiny.* It sounded so grand, and mysterious, and important, and, indeed, it was. But—oh, if only it didn't feel so lonely.

He was just drifting off, when someone poked him in the ribs. "Are you Folgan's apprentice?"

Gom came bolt upright on his cot. "I am."

The servant jerked his thumb. "He's hollerin' for you, and by the looks on his face, I'd say you'd best get goin', quick!"

Chapter Eight

GOM EYED the breathless servant apprehensively. Why? Why did Folgan want to see him, now, in the middle of the night? Gom had obeyed him, gotten back in time, just. He fell out of bed, pulled on his clothes again, then hurried along to Folgan's chambers.

The wizard was sitting by the fire, eyes half closed, puffing his cherrywood pipe. "Ah, boy. Come." Folgan pointed to a stool by the hearth. Gom went, sat, and waited.

Presently, the wizard looked up. "There's been some excitement over in the city."

Gom's mouth went dry. "Oh?"

"Lord Lugen, Vice-Chamberlain and Lord Leochtor's second cousin, has had an adventure."

"Oh?"

"Yes." Folgan examined the bowl of his pipe, knocked out the dottle into the hearth, and set the empty pipe aside. "Down Goldsmith's Lane, just off the main square. It appears," he went on, clasping his hands in his lap, "that a pack of thieves set upon him, left him for dead, but then a stranger popped up out of the blue, caught one of the thieves, and left him at Lugen's feet. As Lugen awoke, the stranger ran off, followed, he said, by a horse. You came home just now, I hear."

Gom nodded. A *pack* of thieves?

"Well? Speak, boy! Did you hear anything? See anything?"

"Well, I—" Gom faltered, tried again. "I was hurrying; it was late."

The wizard looked at Gom's face hard and long. "Hmmm. The thing is, they can't wake the thief. He seems to be under some sort of magic influence. Agarax, I'd say." Folgan's brows came down. "Now who on Ulm would know about that? Or dare to use it?"

"Only a wizard, sir?"

"Or his apprentice."

Gom swallowed. The little wooden box in his rear pocket seemed to grow in size. He leaned back, letting his jacket hang loose. "Did he say what the stranger looked like?"

"Oh, yes. My lord reported that he was high as a house, a giant of a man, and that his horse went like the wind." The wizard laughed. "Lugen's a big man. Proud. He'd hardly be inclined to tell a tale that might diminish him. What do you think, boy?"

Folgan knew, he knew! "Well, I—" Gom began.

There came a tap at the door.

"Tcha! Answer it," Folgan snapped.

Standing on the mat was a short, round man in a purple robe and nightcap.

"Blifil!" Folgan stood up. "What is it? Come in, come in."

Blifil? Gom watched him cross the floor. Blifil Bludge—Hilleray's master. Gom closed the door and stood, while Bludge took the empty chair Folgan had pulled up to the fire.

"It's—well, I can't sleep," Bludge said. "So I thought if you were still awake, you could maybe offer some advice."

Gom shrank into the wall. Wizard talk! With any luck, they'd let him stay and hear it!

Folgan sat down, leaned back in his armchair, and refilled his pipe with fresh tobacco. "Why, certainly, dear fellow. Say what it is."

"A client has asked me to move his house across a field without taking it apart. The house is large and creaky; the field, uphill."

"Hmmm." Folgan lit his pipe, the taper flaring, lighting the folds of his face. "What have you done so far?"

"Well, the house is built of mologrite."

Gom came to attention.

"You've tried smeddum, of course," Folgan said.

"Of course. We cut the foundations, set bars of smeddum on the roof, to draw the load upward some. Then I set twelve two-ton bars in front—eight teams of oxen for each bar—to draw the whole thing forward. And twelve at the back, reverse polarity, to push it."

"And?"

"The house won't budge."

"Mmmmm. The structure is large, you say."

Bludge nodded vigorously.

Gom eyed Bludge in disbelief. No wonder the man ranked low in the Hierarchy. Ractite, man, ractite, he urged silently. And waited for Folgan to explain.

Folgan jabbed his pipestem in the air. "The house is large, and the field slopes. I'd say . . ." He looked up. "Use more smeddum."

More smeddum? Gom frowned. That was not the answer, so why had the old man given it? Maybe—maybe Folgan didn't really want to help Bludge. No. Members of the Hierarchy always helped one another. He eyed Folgan more closely. The old man looked tired. It was very late and there had been much excitement. Evidently his master was not thinking clearly.

"I suggest," Folgan went on, "that you find the critical mass of smeddum required. Then that you smelt it, refine it to get the greatest strength working for you." He looked across to the door, as though to make sure that Gom was taking it all in.

Blifil Bludge's beard wagged up and down. "That is so! Dear fellow, I thank you! Why did I not think of it!"

But— Gom could scarce contain himself. These two were reckoning themselves into a mountain of the stuff. What about the ractite? One pinch, and the house would fly into place!

Bludge stood up to go. "I'll send directly," he said. "They'll have things ready for the moment I get back."

Gom could bear it no longer. He went to Folgan's side and whispered in the wizard's ear. "Ractite."

Folgan's head snapped up. "Eh? What's that, boy?"

"I said 'ractite,' sir," said Gom, and wished he hadn't.

"What about it?"

Gom cleared his throat, looking from one wizard to the other. "If you add a trace to the smeddum, sir, you can get by on less."

"By on—" Bludge stared down his nose. "Get-by-on-less?" He turned to Folgan. "This your apprentice? Good ones are hard to find. Well, I'll be going. Thank you, my dear Folgan, for all your advice. Good night."

The moment the door closed, Folgan leapt up. "How dare you!"

"But—I was trying to help, sir," Gom said. "To remind you."

"*Remind?*" The wizard paced to the fire and back again, a bad sign. "Remind me of what, boy?"

"If Maister Bludge adds even a trace of ractite to the smeddum he'll surely have more than enough for the job."

Folgan frowned. "Ractite? *In smeddum?* Have you lost your wits?"

Why . . . Gom stood astonished. Folgan did not even know!

"When we set out, what did I tell you, boy?"

"But I—"

"I told you to see and not be seen, to hear and not be heard. Remember?"

"Yes, sir, but I only—"

"You have committed a very serious breach of form. You are guilty of conduct unbefitting a first-year apprentice, not to mention gross ingratitude! Is this the thanks I get for most graciously allowing you to stay to hear the consultation? To bed! I've half a mind to send you packing!"

Gom went out, his face set. Not fair, not fair, when he'd only tried to help. But he couldn't speak up, lest Folgan dismiss him.

When Gom went to the stables the next morning, Stormfleet had already related the night's adventures. Gom told his side, what happened after.

"Folgan suspects it was us," he said.

"But he can't say so," Keke chipped in. "That would flatly contradict Lugen's tale."

"Lucky for us." Stormfleet's tail switched. "Well, off you go to breakfast. I wonder what the story is down there!"

The servants' mess hall buzzed with rumor. "Everybody's talking," a footman said. "Upstairs and all. They say—" The man lowered his voice, looking around. "They say as it was magery, although not one of them spellcasters upstairs was out last night."

"What did Lugen say his rescuer looked like?" A small woman farther down the table spoke up: Reggia, a chambermaid.

"My lord said as how it were a giant of a man, head and shoulders over him. My lord called out, meaning to reward him, but the stranger just ran off, his horse following." He leaned over the table, looking around the spellbound faces. "They still can't wake the robber."

Reggia nodded vigorously. "It's magery, all right. I heard the ladies talking before breakfast. 'The Sandman,' they've called him." She took a bite of bun. "Me, I hope he's still about. That's the kind of magic we could do with right now, the sort them scrinchy old men should be working to rid us of these awful upstart ruffians."

Gom kept his head down. *Sandman . . . sleep-bringer.* He touched his back pocket, fingered the hard edges of the little box under the cloth. He felt proud and afraid, both at once. *Sandman.* Folly, rushing in to help like that without thinking. Now look what trouble he had brought upon his head! Folgan was certainly not done with him!

"I wonder who it could have been," said Afen thoughtfully. "Perhaps one of them was out, after all."

"And not taking credit for it? Well, it wasn't Mathery, for sure," Zobe said. "He'd have shouted it from the citadel tower!"

"So would Potra," Dingle declared. "She's so ambitious."

"Well, it was certainly not my master," Hilleray shrugged, bringing on a roar of laughter.

"Of course," said Cory, a cook's boy, eyeing the apprentices sourly, "it don't have to be anybody in the citadel at all."

"Don't be daft," sneered Afen. "Our masters are the only ones in all Ulm who know magic—"

"Unless—it was one of us," Zobe said.

A quiet came over that part of the table. Gom, looking up from under his brows, saw that they were all staring in one direction: toward Mat.

Mat looked sly. "Well, chaps," he said, with a sideways smile. "Whoever won't let on. I mean, one isn't supposed to practice one's magic, is one, until one is qualified." He leaned back nonchalantly, eyeing the ceiling.

"It's him, I'd bet on it," Afen muttered. "He's the only one of us we know who could."

"But," Zobe said, "we weren't allowed out last night. Only him." She glanced Gom's way.

Dingle laughed out loud. "Well, it wasn't him, for sure." He held his hand so-so above the floor. "High as a house?"

"And a horse that went like the wind," Afen said, and there was general laughter from those who'd seen Gom walk Stormfleet into the stable. Afen turned to Mat. "You're the tallest. You fit the closest. How did you sneak out and get back in without anyone seeing?"

"Yes, how did you do it, Mat?" said Zobe. "Come on, we won't tell."

Mat, still leaning back, only put a finger to his lips.

Gom eyed him angrily. The nerve! He was encouraging the lie without uttering a single word! The imposter! The cheat, to get the credit for someone else's risk!

Down the table, the women were crowding around Reggia, their empty teacups all pushed up together.

"What's up, then?" Afen leaned over.

Cory looked up scornfully. "Wouldn't you want to know! You all think yourselves so clever," he cried. "Well, you're not the only ones to have magic, so there!"

The apprentices looked at one another. "Oh?" said Mat. "How is that?"

"Reggia here can read your tea leaves," Cory said. "And tell you things that's going to happen. And she's never wrong."

Reggia looked up, dismissing Cory with a smile and a wave. "Now, Cory," she said. "It's only a bit fun, you know."

There came a chorus of protests:

"Don't you listen to her."

"She told me that my latest would be a boy."

"And about my dad getting thrown from his horse."

"And where to find me a bonny lass last year," a groom said. "We got married two months since."

"And me—she told me I'd wed a tall dark stranger," said a lady's maid. "And now I'm walking out with Hewel, our head steward."

". . . never bin wrong yet," said Cory, "so you lot can keep your magic. It's Reggia for us."

Mat stood, stretched, then ambling down the table to where she sat, set his empty cup in front of her, winking at the rest. "Read me," he said.

Reggia looked up. "What do you want to know, lad?"

Mat turned back to Gom and the rest with a nod and a wink. "Tell me about this nice young lady I'm to meet."

Reggia took his cup and studied the dregs. "In three summers' time. She's short, about midway up your chest. Brown hair, brown eyes, bit on the full side for you, but you'll never love another better, lad."

As Mat, smiling, sauntered back to his place, Afen slid his cup down the table. "Me," he said. "Now me."

"Don't, Reggia." Cory looked indignant. "Them uppity fools are only making fun of you."

But Reggia leaned over the cup with a good-natured smile. "I see a tall, dark maid," she said. "I can't say exactly when, only that it's not this year or next. I see you wedding her. A little house, roses around the door—"

"*Wedding her!*" Afen grinned around the table. "That's hardly likely," Afen said. "A wizard may love, but he doesn't marry."

Reggia looked back at him, her mouth saying nothing, her eyes saying all.

The table went quiet.

Afen jumped up, stony-faced, setting off a regular bustle of activity. Folk moved off, and within minutes, the table was almost deserted. Only Gom lingered, and Reggia, sipping her tea.

A wizard may love, but he doesn't marry. Harga had married, and had ten children. But then she, being outside the Hierarchy, was not bound by its customs. *A wizard may love* . . . He thought of Brody's face, the look in her eyes as she had sat on her husband's knee. What of Gom? An idea formed in his mind, a thought that made his blood pump faster. What if Reggia really could speak the future? Thought became desire.

He set his empty cup before her.

"What would you want to learn, lad?" she said, looking around dreamily.

"What—what you told the others," Gom said, feeling sheepish now.

She bent her head over the cup, staring down at the half-dried dregs. And there she stayed, for the longest time.

Gom cleared his throat. "Well?"

"It's only a silly game, you know."

Gom jumped up angrily. "You told the others, so now tell me: what do you see?"

Reggia turned the cup upside down. "I would tell only the good, lad. It's always been my way. But you force me to speak—" She looked him in the eye. "The truth of what I see is this: for as long as you live, and you may live long, you'll never love a mortal maid of Ulm."

Chapter Nine

THAT NIGHT, Gom crowded with the other apprentices and many of the citadel folk in the servants' gallery, a high balcony situated at the back of the Great Banquet Hall, close under the dome, overlooking the prenuptial feasting. Such a hubbub and a clatter there was up there, rising from the floor way below. Gom moved forward with his fellows and leaned over the railing. The banquet tables formed long lines down the hall, with one High Table running crosswise at their head. He scanned the assembly, as around him, his fellows did the same, pointing out where their masters were seated.

"No trouble picking yours out, dear." Reggia appeared beside him, pointing. "See, at the High Table, only six seats from Leochtor himself."

Gom saw. Folgan, in ceremonial gray robe with purple hood at his back, and looking rarely affable, was talking to a bejeweled woman next to him.

"Balivere, Queen of Quend." Reggia was following his gaze. "Isn't she handsome? That's her husband, Goulan the Prince Consort, beside her. Next to them's King Furly and Queen Rialan of Ringing Valley. All the nobs of Ulm seem to be here: kings, queens; lords, ladies. Anybody who's anybody."

"Excepting Galt of Sundor," a scullery boy piped up behind her.

Reggia looked scornfully over her shoulder. *"Not* excepting. He's but a scurvy, cutthroat brigand no self-respecting body would let across the doorstep! Though," she went on, relenting, "I daresay he wouldn't have minded an invitation, with all this wealth on display. See, Gom—there's my Lord Leochtor, right in the middle, doesn't he look fine?"

Gom's eyes continued along the table, so much to see, and all at once! The Lake Lord on a high-backed throne: Leochtor, overlord of all the Lakelands, listening with long grave face to Urolf, on his right. Urolf, Lord of the immortal Yul Kinta—and happy bridegroom, although one would never guess it, thought Gom, gazing down on that haughty and disdainful face. But Leochtor seemed well enough. A modest man, and fair, according to Carrick. At Leochtor's left hand sat a stately, dark-skinned woman. Her black hair, piled on top of her head, was crowned with a golden diadem.

"That's the Lady Nasidda," Reggia whispered. "Our Lady of the Lakes."

Gom nodded. Leochtor's wife. He looked along the row, seeking out her sister, Urolf's bride, and, finding her, exclaimed. Reggia laughed.

"No, you're not seeing double. It is Leana, Nasidda's twin."

Gom looked from Leana to Nasidda and back again. Truly, he'd not tell them apart, save that Nasidda was in gold, while her twin sister Leana, being the bride, wore silver and white. "They are both equally beautiful," Gom murmured, wondering how Leochtor had managed earlier to distinguish between them and marry Nasidda. Next to Leana sat another mage, white-haired as Folgan was grizzled, dressed in the gray of the Hierarchy but in a golden hood. Mecrim Thurgeril, the Grand Archimage himself! To the wizard's other side sat the Lady Vala, then Feyrwarl—and, Gom ducked back unconsciously, Thrulvar. At one end of the table, Gom noted with interest, was the man he'd rescued the night before: Lord Lugen, Leochtor's second cousin, impressive in blue-and-gold Vice-Chamberlain's robes. He looked quite recovered, Gom saw; eating, and talking at the double.

Just below the High Table sat the other wizards—no sign of Tolasin, but then he'd not be likely to attend such a public and stately occasion. In among the wizards were more dignitaries, both humans and Yul Kinta folk, all in bright silks and flashing stones—so many of them, Gom noticed uneasily.

In the minstrels' gallery directly beneath him, six bards plied harp, and lute, and tambor, the sounds wafting over the heads of the glittering assembly. Just then, Lord Lugen stood, and, taking up a gold-tipped ceremonial mace, he rapped three times for silence.

"My Lords, Ladies, High Mages, and other honored guests," he began.

The scullery boy groaned. "Oh, no! They're going to make spee—" He broke off under the head valet's stare.

But the boy was right. For upward of two hours, folk stood, one after another, first expressing their good wishes for the happiness of the bridal pair, then extolling the virtues of each and their respective families: of the rare alliance that was to be forged on the morrow between mortal and immortal, human and Yul Kinta; and proclaiming the great future that lay ahead for both races. After the first hour, Gom began to think wistfully of his friends down in the stables, chatting together, freely taking their ease. He was just wondering when it would ever end, when Lord Lugen stood, rapped his mace as before, and called out Mecrim Thurgeril.

Gom leaned down, his interest rekindled.

The Grand Archimage rose, and went to stand before the bridal pair, and addressed the assembly. "My Lords, Ladies, and other honored guests . . ." The old man's voice was quite loud and strong. "Never before has Ulm seen such a union as this. To mark it, the Hierarchy has been pleased to assist in an exchange of gifts between Pen'langoth and Aelyth-Kintalyn."

He beckoned a page bearing a large velvet cushion. As the boy moved forward, light caught it, sending out bright flashes of rainbow brilliance. Gom's eyes narrowed. More gemstones! As if there were not enough of them to worry about already!

"These three gems are invested with spells worked with the combined power of the Hierarchy. On behalf of my Lord Leochtor, I do present this first one to my Lady Leana." The old man reached out, lifted up a bright gold pin that flashed yellow in the light. "Til-Ambyr, heart of the sun; to bring the bride good health, a long life, and a fruitful union."

A murmur ran around the assembly, quickly stifled. Lady Leana stood, took the pin, and fixed it on her bodice. Then she turned to her brother-in-law. "I thank you, my Lord Leochtor," she said in a firm, clear voice. "And you, Maister Thurgeril. And all your Council."

When she was seated, the old man took up a second stone, set in a thick gold ring. "For my Lord Urolf: Peryth-nyn, blue as deep Langoth, to bind the link between tree and water."

In full sight of the assembly, Lord Urolf accepted the ring, slipped it onto the middle finger of his left hand, then held it up for all to see. "I thank my new brother, and all the people of Pen'langoth. May our kinship flourish," he declared loudly, but to Gom's mind the Yul Kinta looked as haughty and disdainful as ever.

Now the Grand Archimage took up the third and last stone, an emerald, which he dangled on its thick gold chain, sending out rays of bright green fire: Urolf's gift. "For my Lord Leochtor: Herelys, which shall hereinafter be known as the official Seal of Pen'langoth. May its power keep all the Lake peoples forever in peace, harmony, and prosperity!"

Leochtor took the chain and, handing it to Lady Nasidda, let her place it about his neck. Then everyone sat down again amid tumultuous applause, not least of which came from the servants' gallery. But Gom stayed quiet and still, looking down. Three stones, each one of tremendous power and importance. If any one of them should ever fall into Katak's hands! He sighed, and straightened up, but still the applause went on.

"On account of the speeches at last being over," the scullery boy remarked, and as he said it, one of the musicians struck an extra-loud chord, and began to sing of the coming union. After the first couple of lines, the folk around Gom started to hum and tap their feet with the rhythm of the lay.

Come, let us all rejoice,
And celebration make;
Now sing we with one voice
As Wood doth join with Lake!

Upon this truth, all must agree:
That Wood doth better flourish,
With deeper root and taller tree—
When water doth it nourish!

So let us all rejoice, etc.

Full blest are they within Love's thrall,
Bound by its subtle power:
And lucky, they who heard its call
From Forest and from Tower!

So let us all rejoice, etc.

May fortune smile upon this pair
As here they do combine;
And may their issue prove full fair:
The noblest from each line!

Now let us all rejoice,
And celebration make;
Now sing with one glad voice
As Wood doth join with Lake!

Full blest are they within Love's thrall . . . Gom turned away.

"Cheer up, lad. You're much too young to be so down. It were only fun this morning, and not a bit true, whatever they say," Reggia said.

Gom nodded unhappily. Were his feelings so obvious? He wiped his face on his sleeve. The air was hot and close up here, and the noise from the guests was rising in waves to echo around and around the hollow dome. Abruptly, he pushed through the throng and ran off down the stairs.

"I'm glad I was not there," Stormfleet said. "All that heat and noise. It makes me thirsty even to hear of it."

"Why did it go on so long?" Keke said.

"Speeches," Gom said. "One after another. Then the exchange of gifts."

"More gifts?" Keke cried. "You'd think they'd had enough!"

"These were special. Leochtor and Urolf swapped stones to seal the kinship of their peoples. First, Leochtor gave the bride and groom each a stone, which the High Council invested with spells this morning."

"Oh," cried Keke. "I should have liked to see those bags of old bones wagging their beards and waving their arms about. You saw the investment?"

Gom shook his head. "Apprentices were not allowed."

"Tell us more about the stones," Hevron said.

"Urolf got a blue one to bind the two peoples. Lady Leana got a yellow one to bring long life and a fruitful union."

"Fruitful union!" Stormfleet snorted. "There's been more talk about the mixing of the blood. So many folk are scandalized."

"I agree with them. It isn't natural," Keke chipped in. "Kind should keep to kind. Urolf is immortal, while Leana has but a normal, human lifespan. They say no eggs will come of the match. What do you think, Gom?"

"I think," Gom said carefully, "that if they truly love each other, then they deserve to be happy. And these stones surely will ensure it, Mecrim Thurgeril promised."

"And Leochtor's stone?" Hevron asked.

"An emerald pendant invested with spells to ensure peace and harmony among his peoples."

"Humph," the roan said. "I'd say they had that already."

"True," Gom conceded. "But the emerald will prove more than that. While the other two stones are personal gifts, this is to be the State symbol, the official Seal of all the Lakelands from the Lord of the Yul Kinta, no less. The lake folk will take great pride in it."

"Maybe, but to us it just means more worry," Stormfleet snorted. "It is not good."

"Not good," Gom echoed. "Especially right now. There's too much power gathered in one place: these three gifts, the wizards' runes—not to mention all those uninvested gems the guests were wearing. I hate to think who might be waiting on the shore to slip past the sentries into Scandibar." He looked up. "I'll sleep down here tonight. No one will give it any mind."

"Wise," Hevron said. "Our stall window commands the gate; and the aisle window, the inner arch. You could get by one hundred sentries, but you'd not get past us unseen. We'll all share watch, Gom. I'll be first, then Stormfleet, then you."

"And I'll watch through daylight," Keke said. "Tell me," she went on pointedly changing the subject, "what they wore at the feast, the cocks, and the hens. Your friends are doing well for themselves. They've been hanging around here with a hen on each arm. And you? What have you found?"

The night passed quietly. On the hour, every hour, a pair of sentries walked the courtyard, swinging their pikes, peering into doorways, pausing for a word with the stable watch. But when Stormfleet nudged Gom awake at three in the morning, the watch was slumped on his stool, snoring loudly.

That morning, the kitchens were bustling with preparations for the wedding. But just after elevenses, Feyrwarl whisked Gom from the servants' hall up a dusty passage to meet Vala. She waited in a small cubbyhole at a round table, lit with a single lamp. She was just as Gom remembered her, solemn, dark-eyed and mysterious. As he entered, a smile briefly lit her face. "Master Gom!" She stood up, reached across the table, and took his hands. "You've grown! And your shoulders have broadened out!"

He had? They had? Gom straightened up. It was nice of her to say so, even though he couldn't see it. He bowed low. "Lady, I owe you much."

"Not so," she said gravely. "Let us say it was for Harga. She is our true friend, even though there are some who forget it. Please." She waved Gom to a chair.

They all three sat around the table and talked of Harga, Vala telling of journeys they shared. After a while, Feyrwarl stood. "I'll be back," he smiled, and went out.

"So. You are working to become a wizard." Vala eyed Gom steadily across the table. "You are troubled," she said at last. "Truly, there is much heaviness on your shoulders, and it is not born of your studies, I think."

Gom said nothing. She had seen Harga in Gom's vision, had seen the tears on Harga's face. Had heard his mother's cry. *Oh, if you could only see the devastation . . .* From one of the Seven Realms Harga had spoken, but Vala could not know that, and he could not tell her, for he had promised.

Vala leaned forward. "Master Gom, I do not seek to pry. But know this: I am your friend, as I am Harga's. If ever you are in trouble, and your mother is not near, then call on me. Just send your little harrier to Aelyth-Kintalyn. I will hear—and I will answer you."

"Thank you," Gom said. Now there was a friend, he thought, his spirits rising.

"I had not looked to meet you here," she said, and there was her quick smile again. "So I have no great gift to give you."

Gom looked at her in surprise. "None was expected," he said. "I must say that I am right glad to see you."

Still smiling, Vala reached under the table, brought out a handful of shimmering gray-green stuff. She shook it out and laid it on the tabletop. "Never know," she said, "but that this might come in useful—wear it with discretion."

Gom took up the stuff, feeling its lightness, its softness, enjoying the play of lamplight on its folds. A Yul Kinta mantle. Impervious to wet, and wind, and cold, and its wearer could pass unnoticed through wild and dangerous places. He knew, for he had worn one. "Thank you, lady," he said. It folded up so small, it fitted easily into his jacket pocket. "I regret I can give you nothing in return."

"Not necessary," Vala said. "But wait, I have not yet done." She leaned down, brought up something he recognized at once, and set it on the table between them. It was a little copper bowl, that same bowl she had used at Urolf's command to get news of the cito. Now she took up a ewer and filled the bowl with water. "We have not long," she said. "But I would give you something, a vision, perhaps, to cheer you. What would you know?"

Gom stared at the bowl. What would he not know! Where was Harga? How was she? And the starstone meant for him—was it on the way? The mailed warrior, who was he? Why had he appeared when Gom called Harga? And . . . how come that one knew so much? And then there was Katak. Was he still secure beneath Great Krugk, and like to stay so?

Gom bit his lip. All these questions he wanted answered, yet he may not ask one, lest their secret be revealed. So . . . What else could he ask, so that he not wholly waste this precious offer?

"There is one thing," he said, and felt the heat rising in his face. "A woman told me yesterday that I'd never love a mortal maid of Ulm."

Vala nodded. "And you believe her?"

"I—I'm afraid."

"Don't be." Vala turned down the lamp. "Your hands, Gom. Courage."

He let her take them, and cup them, and lower them into the bowl. They filled with water. The water began to swirl, then to glow with a golden radiance. Then it disappeared, and in the hollow of his palms a shadow began form, a soft dark mass. Slowly, it solidified, took shape and Gom was gazing down at an armored figure, visored head, green plume waving above.

"Stop!"

The image vanished, and, released, Gom snatched his hands from the bowl and covered his face. Reggia had been right! No maid for him, no nuptial feast, no homely hearth and child. Long as he lived—as clearly it was meant to be—his only love would ever be a battlefield and war!

Chapter Ten

VALA TOOK him in her arms. "I should not have let you go on," she said sorrowfully. "No good comes for those who fear." She held him out at arm's length. "But it might not signify as ill as you think, Master Gom. The bowl works in subtle ways."

Subtle. Gom pulled away. What was subtle about a mailed warrior? Soon as he could, Gom escaped to the stables.

His friends greeted him excitedly. "Mat's been hanging about all afternoon," Hevron said.

"Over by the main gate," Keke said. "Until about an hour ago, when the guards began to notice him."

"Then he came in here to an empty stall, two doors down."

"Stood looking out the window," Keke said, from her current favorite rafter. "Watching the gate, just as though he were waiting for somebody."

"Then what happened?" Gom said.

"A groom called him out. He looked for you, too. You're all supposed to be getting ready for the wedding ceremony."

Wedding ceremony! Gom began to run.

"Not too long since," Hevron whinnied after him. "Anyway, you're only going up into that high gallery, so why do you have to bother?"

Ask Folgan, Gom thought, hurrying back to the dormitory. Every wizard was jealous for his reputation. Every apprentice had been ordered to look his best, even up in the spectator's gallery.

The dormitory was deserted. Gom changed hurriedly, ran up the narrow winding stair, past the minstrel's gallery, already ringing with melody, and up to where the servants crowded, looking out.

A splendid sight met his eyes. The tables had been cleared, and a glittering assembly sat in rows facing down the center of the room. Twin processions were winding up the aisle: Urolf and his train approaching along the left-hand side, Leana and her attendants along the right, toward a dais where the Lord and Lady of the Lakelands waited, Mecrim Thurgeril between them.

Gom nudged Afen's elbow. "What's up now?"

"Leochtor will wed them," Afen said. "And my master will bless them."

"Then Lady Nasidda will call for the festivities to begin," Zobe said.

Gom looked around for Mat. There he was, drooped over the railing, languid, elegant. Gom studied his former friend uneasily. What had Mat been doing, out there? That one was weak, and slightly . . . bent. As if sensing Gom's scrutiny, Mat glanced up. "Such a bore this is," he yawned. "Disrupting our work."

Dingle smothered a laugh, turning heads nearby. "Work! I should say—if by 'work' you mean certain females who even now give you the eye!"

The others snickered.

"Where will you meet this time, eh?" Hilleray held his nose. "The smell of stable is not very romantic, I warn you."

Gom looked from one to the other. Was that what it had all been about down by the stables? Mat had been watching the gate, the horses claimed. But they could be mistaken. Agh, they were seeing plots everywhere! The stables overlooked both gate and inner courtyard. Meeting girls sounded far more likely than waiting for a skull-thief in broad daylight—and under the gate guards' watchful eyes. Gom turned back to the glittering procession.

"I don't like it." Gom set his pack and staff down, and went to the stall window. "The citadel—the whole of Pen'langoth has gone mad. Three in the morning and everyone still wide awake, drinking and fooling around. The lords and ladies in the hall, the servants below stairs, even the guards on the gate—I swear, without their pikes, they'd fall flat on their faces!"

"Not mad," Hevron said. "This is the wedding of a lifetime—nay, many lifetimes. And no one knows the real risk but us."

"True. Except that the Hierarchy knows enough to be on their toes. Yet even they seem to be as addled as the others. Oh, that Tolasin were here!"

"Well, he's not," Keke said drowsily. "So what will you do?"

"I'm not sure. But say there's even just one man out there, waiting his chance to nip through. If a man could slip a wizard's bonds, he's certainly a match for tipsy guards. Once over the drawbridge and through the gate—" Gom turned from the window. "If only I could warn folk in some way."

"Well, you can't, but you can keep watch. It's your turn," Keke said. "As for me, I'm going back to sleep."

Gom went to sit by the door. The stable watch was carousing also, and wouldn't be back. He stared out across the empty yard. There were shadows in the spaces between lamps. If one moved, he'd see it fine. . . .

A warning whicker brought him upright. The stable lantern flickered in the drafts, and boards creaked in the quiet.

The whicker came again. "There's a man, going by the far wall. See?"

Gom peered around the door, saw nothing.

"There, by the inner arch."

Still he could not see. But once the man went through that arch, Gom would more than likely lose him. He dashed across the courtyard, reaching for his dream-sand. He was just passing under the shadow of the arch when he heard the soft hiss of breath. The intruder stood right beside him!

The man seized Gom and put a hand to his throat.

Gom struggled, but the man only tightened his grip. Gom's breath began to labor, and lights popped back of his eyes. He must do something, he told himself. Quick, while he still could. He ceased to struggle, went limp. "Stop, let go," he wheezed, "if you value your *s-s-s-skull!*"

At the last word, the man released Gom. "Who are you?" He peered down at Gom suspiciously. "Where's the tall feller with the sandy 'air?"

"Delayed," Gom said, rubbing his throat tenderly. . . . *tall fellow with the sandy hair* . . . He was shocked, even though he'd somehow known all along. "So I came instead."

The man laughed. "Hah! A squinty little squirt like you?"

"We come in all shapes and sizes," Gom said shortly.

The man grabbed him by the collar, and drew a knife. "Show me proof—afore I slit your gizzard!"

"Nay, you show me—by our master's command."

The man frowned, unsure again. But he didn't let go of Gom's collar. "Look inside my shirt," he growled.

Gom pulled the man's shirt open, exposing broad, hairy chest—tattooed with a death's-head. Gom swallowed. This must be the man who'd broken into Riffik's house and escaped again—and now Gom knew how he had done it!

"Your turn," the man said, giving Gom a shake. "Make it quick."

Reaching into his pouch, Gom slid his middle finger through the silver skull-ring, and pinched it to fit. Then he stuck out his hand. "Satisfied?"

"'Ere, lemme lookit that." The man reached out.

And have him see how much too big it was? Gom snatched his hand back, and glanced around. "You're wasting time. Do you want to be caught?"

The thief scowled. "Where's Spindleshanks? Has things gone wrong?"

"Of course not!" snapped Gom. "You've not had a chance to mess up yet, as you did at Riffik's."

"Why, you—"

"Oh, come on." Looking bored, Gom pulled the man toward the stable.

"'Ere." The man drew back. "I'm goin' in, not out."

Gom sneered. "The way's not clear. Mat'll come when it's safe."

"Mat?" The man's eyes narrowed. "Is that Spindleshanks?" He glanced to the inner archway. "Our master must be 'ard up to let you lot wear the skull! Move, I'll foller." The skull-thief started back across the yard behind Gom.

Now Gom felt under his jacket for his back pocket, took a pinch of agarax. By the stable door was a water trough. Twelve paces away. Gom counted them off. Reaching the trough, he took a deep breath, held it, and dropped the sand into the water. Then he ran in and slammed the stable door. From the other side came a hiss, a cry, broken off, then a heavy thud that rattled the whole stable wall. Still Gom held his breath, but little smoke came through. Only the smell, the harmless after-fumes.

He waited, listening for sounds of the man stirring, of running feet.

Nothing.

Nearby horses peered over their wickets. "Whatever's going on?"

Gom opened the door a slit, and the man fell through to lie on the floor, out cold, praise the skies.

"Hay-yey! What's that!"

"Looks as though the cat's had it!"

"Rat bait, more like!"

Gom dragged the man down the aisle, and dumped him inside his friends' stall. "Ugh," Stormfleet sniffed. "He smells bad!"

"What shall you do with him?" Hevron said, edging back.

"What shall I do with Mat, is more the question," Gom said grimly. "You were right, after all. Mat may have let this man into Riffik's house. Certainly helped him escape. He claims Mat wears the skull."

"I never did like the looks of that one," Stormfleet said. "From the moment I set eyes on him in Pen'langoth market."

"Talking of whom," Hevron whuffled warning, "look outside."

Gom peeped around the window frame. Mat, stalking the shadows past the stable, going for the gate. Gom sniffed the air. Spent fumes lingered still. Did Mat know of agarax? Its telltale odor?

Gom thought fast. He must get Mat into this stall. How? Taking a deep breath, he called out, in as nearly the man's voice as he could get. "Hey up! In here, Spindleshanks."

Mat looked toward the stable door. "Grandy?"

"Shut up, 'less you want a slit gizzard," Gom said. "Come in 'ere, quick, and shut the door."

"But—"

"Quick, I said!"

Gom heard the stable door open, then the sound of scuffing straw.

"Grandy?"

"'Ere, in 'ere." A cough tickled Gom's throat from the effort to sound hoarse. But his ruse had worked. Mat was coming.

"Where? What are you doing—"

As Mat's head drew level with the open wicket, Gom reached out, and jerked Mat's sleeve, hard. Mat fell inside, tripping over Grandy.

"Let go!" he cried. "What are you doing? What is this?"

"That you know right well, Mat," Gom said.

Mat straightened slowly, a wary eye on the horses.

"What will you do, my dear fellow?" He slid out a foot, prodded Grandy delicately.

"Don't bother," Gom said. "He won't be waking for a day or two."

Mat sniffed the air. "Dream-sand. So it was you! I thought so. What will you do with Grandy, dear chap? You wouldn't care to tell?"

Gom looked at Mat in disbelief. "He'll not leave Scandibar, I promise you. Not like Riffik's house—oh, yes. I guessed that. How did you do it? You wouldn't care to tell, dear fellow?" he mimicked. "No, I thought not," he went on, as Mat stayed silent. "As for you . . ." He fell quiet now himself. What should he do? What *could* he do?

"I thought you were my friend," Mat said hopefully, then he stopped, his eyes gleaming. "Why, you can't let them know you caught Grandy, any more than you dare tell about helping Lord Lugen." He broke into a smile. "So you can't tell on me, either! Hah!" He turned to leave, backed up again as Stormfleet reared, and Hevron blocked the door. "Get them off! Back, back, I say!" Mat pressed himself into the wall.

"Grandy said you wear the skull."

"I don't know what you mean."

"Yes, you do. Have you any idea what you're into, Mat?" If he didn't, Gom certainly couldn't explain.

Mat spread his hands nervously. "Look, dear boy. Remember how I tried to help you last year? Gave you a good job, I did, when you were penniless."

"I got you one, too, with Folgan—only you went one better, remember that? Now you have a master, and you're well on the way to becoming a wizard. You want to throw that away?"

"Help me move Grandy to a safe place, and he'll see you right. He'll see both of us right. He can get us wealth you'd never dream of!"

"You don't need wealth right now! Have you any idea how lucky you are to have Riffik for master? You risk your life, your neck for this—this scum—"

"You are a fool, dear boy. Think back to this afternoon. The jewels, the riches. What have those folk done to earn them? Nothing. They inherited them. That's not fair. I told you about my folks, didn't I? The sort of life I had. Well, I'm clever as any of those bigwigs, just as deserving. Come on, use your wit: help Grandy and me. No one need know."

Gom held out his hand. "Your emblem of the skull: give it here."

"No. It's mine, and none of your business! I—"

Stormfleet kicked the wall beside him.

"—have it right here." Mat slipped his hand inside his shirt and pulled out a silver medallion on a leather thong.

Gom stood still, hand out, waiting.

Sighing loudly, Mat slipped the medallion from around his neck and threw it at Gom's feet.

Gom let it lie.

"Now let me go," Mat said, his voice flat. "You've spoiled the caper, had your way." He laughed then. "But you can't tell on me, you can't say how you did that, or you're out." He pointed down at Grandy.

"Mat," Gom said, "promise me you'll keep clear of that sign. You must, or you will fall into peril worse than you could dream of."

"Promise!" Stormfleet neighed for good measure.

"Promise, promise, dear boy!" Mat cried. He sprang

for the wicket, leapt through, and ran up the aisle. "Promise!" he called again, "promise, promise, promise!" The echo of his mocking laughter faded away.

"Promise, promise," Hevron snorted. "What were you doing to let him go? You think for one minute that he'll keep his word?"

Gom turned on him angrily. "What would you have had me do, then?"

"Fix him as you fixed that one," Hevron said. "Scotch the snake in the egg."

"You heard what Mat said," Gom said sharply. "Folgan has not yet done with me over Lugen, I told you that."

Hevron shook his mane. "Hmm. That is a thought. But on balance—"

"Gom did right," Stormfleet said. "The skull-thief's caught, Mat has lost his medallion, and Gom still has Folgan. What will you do with Grandy, Gom?"

Gom scratched his head. He didn't know. But he couldn't just leave the man there, for no one would know to put him away, except—He looked up. "Riffik. Riffik would know him by the skull on his chest."

"But how will you get Riffik down here?" Stormfleet said. "If he's still in the Great Hall, celebrating."

"Let me think." Gom dragged Grandy out and dropped him by the stable door. Now what? He couldn't go to tell he'd found a stranger in the citadel, because how could he know the man was one, being a stranger himself? No, the citadel people would have to discover that. He ran back down to the stall.

"I have it," he said. "I'll tell the head steward I've found a man taken ill inside the stables. The Scandibar folk will come, see he doesn't belong, and then they'll report to the gate guards. The gate guards will tell the higher ups and sooner or later it'll get to the wizards. Then Riffik is bound to come in and see the skull. How's that?"

"That should do nicely," Hevron said. "Hurry."

"No need," Gom said. "Grandy won't wake up for three days."

Nevertheless, Gom hurried out across the courtyard, but he was no sooner through the arch, when he pulled up. Mat's medallion! It mustn't fall into anyone's hands, for it was likely tainted. But how to get rid of it?

On a sudden idea, he ran back, took up the silver talisman, and, climbing a high turret overlooking the lake, he hurled it out.

Gom waited, heard the splash as it hit the water. Now it was gone, into the deep currents down to Scandibar's very foundations. Satisfied, Gom briskly brushed his hands together and set off to find the head steward.

Chapter Eleven

B Y DAWN the next day, the wedding festivities were suddenly over. The wedding party had been whisked away, gone. Gom and the other apprentices were rousted out and on the road home with their masters without so much as a farewell, even to one another.

Two hours after sunup, Gom was riding from the lake valley after Folgan as though their lives depended on it.

For one hour after his message reached the wizards, Gom had stood before them answering questions.

"How did you find the man?" Mecrim Thurgeril had asked him.

"I'd gone to see the horses, sir. When I left, I opened the outer door and the man fell inside."

"Did you notice anything unusual about him?" Potra asked.

Gom had thought hard before answering that one, decided not to mention the tattoo. "He wouldn't wake up, ma'am."

"There are quite a few lying around similarly afflicted," Riffik said. "Why should the sight of one more have bothered you?"

"He—didn't smell the way he should, sir," Gom said. "I thought he might be ill, that's why I summoned help."

"But not of us. I say he doesn't know, Folgan," Thurgeril murmured. "He summoned the head steward quite properly in the circumstances. It was the head steward who came to us. So I say let the boy go." The Archimage had turned then to Gom. "It was good that you reported the man's condition. You may have saved us much harm this night. Would that all other apprentices were sharp as you."

Folgan was clearly not of the same opinion, but in the face of Thurgeril's judgment, he said nothing. Doubtless waiting until they got home, Gom thought, apprehensively. What then? Had the risk been worth it?

Whether or no, he'd had no choice. Grandy lay dreaming his head off in the Scandibar dungeons, and the talisman was safely buried, deep in the cold lake waters. Pray the skies they both stay put, he thought, climbing the first rise into the foothills.

They rode hard, and long. And in three days they were in sight of Folgan's mountain.

The first morning back home, Folgan sent Gom out with a long list of roots and stones to collect that kept him busy all day. All four of them went: Gom, Stormfleet, Hevron, and Keke, and, indeed, without his friends to help, Gom might have been out all night as well.

But a little after sunset, Gom climbed the steep slope, two full bags across Hevron's back. He fed the horses, then hauled the bags upstairs.

Folgan was waiting in the kitchen. He pointed to Gom's door.

"Pack your things. Now."

Gom stood stunned. "What—"

"Now!"

Gom made for his room, then stopped. "If you'd tell me—"

Folgan stood, crossed to the outer door. "Be gone within the hour."

He went out.

Gom stared after him. A row, he'd expected. After all, there was the matter of the ractite, and Folgan still had not really questioned him about the dream-sand. Gom looked toward his door. Folgan had threatened to dismiss him often enough, but this time . . . The man was serious. Why? Gom lit a candle, took it through into his room—and stopped still. His books, which he had kept under his bed, lay haphazardly about the room. Two were open on his coverlet.

Gom stepped forward, and scanned a page.

. . . and I'll bet that's how magic was made in the beginning; through things bumping together by chance. And I'll bet it happens in my mother's workshop all the time. That's why she's the greatest wizard in all Ulm, and Folgan is not . . .

His private journal: Folgan had pulled it out and read it from cover to cover. Gom slowly put it down and took up the second. A workbook, left open at the page recounting his ractite discovery. He looked around at the rest of his chronicles. All read, all lying open. Folgan had seen everything: thoughts, feelings, opinions . . . on everything since Gom's arrival there.

He sat down and covered his face. Folgan had made up his mind in Pen'langoth. Had meant to do this. That's why he'd sent Gom out all day. Of all the tricks! Why, that was worthy of—his mouth tightened. Mat.

Gom jumped up. He wouldn't stay another moment in that place, wouldn't do another thing for such a man! He sat down again. How would he become a wizard now?

There were no second chances. Blindly, he began to stuff his belongings into his pack. What of his books?

He ran into the kitchen and snatched up the bags in which he'd collected Folgan's roots and stones, and dumped their contents out onto the floor. He refilled them swiftly with his chronicles, then, slinging pack and staff, he scooped up the heavy bags in his arms and went to the kitchen door. Gom took one last look around that room, then he staggered downstairs to the stables.

"Now what?" Stormfleet said. "Not another errand at this hour?"

As Gom told what had happened, the cito pawed the ground, waking Keke. "Let's go!" he neighed. "I know the paths. I can travel in the dark."

Gom fastened Stormfleet's saddle, hung the bags at either side. Then he turned to Hevron. "You're quiet, friend. Have you nothing to say?"

"What Folgan did was bad." He stuck his nose into a pile of straw. "I am sorry, I shall miss you."

"What!" Keke cried. "You'd stay behind? Have you no pride?"

Hevron kept his head down. "He's my master," he said.

Gom patted the roan's back. "Good-bye. You've been a good friend. If we meet again, I'll be right glad." He strapped on gauntlet and pad. "Come on, Keke, Stormfleet."

Keke flew to Gom's shoulder, and together, the three of them started down the mountain, Gom on foot and going slowly, for, despite assurances, Stormfleet's feet were inclined to stumble. The farther down they went, the lower Gom's spirits sank.

Stormfleet paused, nuzzling Gom's cheek. "Cheer up,"

he said. "We'll think of something. We always have."
Gom stroked the cito's muzzle absently. True. But oh,
to have lost so much in the space of one hour: master,
home, and friend.

"I pity Hevron," Gom said softly. "He'll be so lonely
now. That old man doesn't deserve such a loyal companion."

"That he doesn't," a voice snorted in the darkness above
them, "so make way."

"Hevron!"

"I've been expecting you," Keke said drowsily. "Now
be quiet. It's the middle of the night!"

"But Folgan will be angry," Gom said.

"So what?" Hevron said. "That's nothing new!" He
tossed his head. "All this time I've envied Stormfleet,
the way you took him from the High Vargue. Well, now
you've rescued me as well!"

Chapter Twelve

THEY TRAVELED steadily down, through marsh and twisting valleys, going due west, by the safest paths Hevron knew, until at last the air began to lighten. Beside Gom, Stormfleet and Hevron plodded slowly on, ghostly shapes in the graying mist.

Gom was exhausted. All through the night, his thoughts had gone around and around, revolving on the axis of his hurt and shock. "So fast," he muttered. "It was all so fast." He could still see the old man's set face, his chronicles scattered about his room.

"My master's a cruel, vindictive man," Hevron said. "Poking in another's papers I don't know about, but to turn a fellow out and leave him homeless with fall well under away!"

Homeless? Gom took out Harga's ring. "See this?"

"Oh," Hevron said. "Another ring."

"Ah, but it's more than that. It's also a key—to Harga's house." He stowed the ring back in his pouch. "My house, too. We'll go there, live in peace and safety—while I work to become a wizard!"

Stormfleet tossed his head. "I'd like to see that place again."

"Where is this house?" Hevron asked.

"In the Dunderfosse. It's west, beyond the Wilds. We can't miss it."

"The Wilds." Hevron looked doubtful. "Not many dare cross that waste."

"I know. But we have to chance it. We shall go swiftly, and Keke will keep a lookout." Gom knew the risk; Harga had warned him to keep his wits about him when crossing that barren, stony wilderness dividing west from east almost from Great Krugk right down to Sundor's fens.

They pressed on, until they reached the Wilds. From there, the horses rode swiftly through the day, stopping only when absolutely necessary, while Keke kept incessant watch. At night, they sought what shelter they could, and kept out of sight. It took three days to cross that inhospitable place where springs were few and bitter-tasting. Toward the end of the third day, they sighted a distant mountain range.

"The Dunderfosse should be the other side," Gom said, shading his eyes against the evening sun. He was right, Keke reported early the next morning. Over the other side of the peaks, a dark forest stretched away north, and south, and west, as far as the eye could see. They went forward, over peaks, through deep and secret valleys cut by waterfalls, until, at last, one midmorning, they found themselves gazing down on endless waving green, the dark, rich green of midsummer, although trees elsewhere had long succumbed to autumn's blight. Gom let out a deep sigh. To be in that ancient, magical place again! His worries vanished, his heart lightened, and peace settled over him like a mantle.

Impatient to reach the forest, Gom led the way down, out of the crisp, high mountain air into the moist mists of the forest lowland. Down, down, and around slopes they descended, until a wall of green soared above them, a curtain of impenetrable vine.

"Well," Hevron said, stopping. "Now what?"

Gom took out his ring and placed it on his fourth finger.

Your key to the Dunderfosse . . . If you would come home, come to the edge of the forest, turn the ring three times following the path of the sun, and the ways will open to you. . . .

Gom stepped forward. "Harga's son greets you on this fine autumn day. I would go to my mother's house, if you'd lead me, and my three good friends." Slowly, carefully, he turned the ring three times sunwise.

For a while, nothing seemed to happen, then, with a soft rustle, the vine curtain parted slightly, revealing a dark and narrow path beyond.

"Ke-ke-ke-ke," Keke chattered softly.

Gom bowed. "I thank you," he said. "It is good to come again!"

A wind lifted the high and hoary branches, rustling myriad leaves. Gom stepped forward onto the path, motioned Stormfleet and Hevron to follow. Keke rode Gom's shoulder, keeping still, and, for once, silent. As before, the way opened in front, and closed behind. The light was dim under the high branches; the air, cool. And yet Gom's energy soared, until he was whistling under his breath, then presently, he broke out into song.

> Lucky the few who tread these ways,
> And dwell within these bounds;
> Where cool bough shades the sun's bright rays
> And rushing stream resounds.

Thus with glad song to Harga's lake
We take the forest's course;
On Harga's isle new lives to make,
For boy, and hawk, and horse!

" 'Boy, and hawk, and horse.' That was a good song,"
Stormfleet said. "Sing it again."

"Gladly," Gom answered. "If you will sing it with me."

"I?" Stormfleet tossed his head. "I cannot make your
human sounds!"

"So make your own," Gom said. "Come on, all of you.
The song is a round; all four of us can sing in turn. I'll
go first, then you, Stormfleet, when I give you the signal,
then Hevron, then Keke."

And so Gom began the song again, at the end of each
alternate line nodding in the next singer, and soon the
forest rang with the strangest assortment of neighing and
whinnying and snorting, and strident bird call, all kept
together with Gom's own human voice.

"I liked that," Keke said. "Let's sing it again."

And so they did, over and over, until their voices gave
out. Gom looked up into the trees, feeling happier than
he had in ages. "Skies," he said aloud. "It is so *good* to
be coming home!"

That night, as the horses grazed, and Keke dozed on
an oak-tree branch, Gom sat back and looked around,
thinking of that other night under the dreaming trees,
when he'd sung Stig's songs; of the strange creatures who
had crept out to hear him: Faramors, Harga had called
them; ancient beings who walked Ulm long before humans, or even Yul Kinta. If he sang now, would they
come again? Gom began an old song that Stig had taught

him long ago, about Lollybob, the foolish apprentice. After that, he sang a lullaby, and was into a third, the new round he'd made that morning, when Hevron raised his head.

"Hold."

The Faramors were standing behind the broad tree trunks, their shining eyes fixed on him. Oh. Gom breathed out. He'd forgotten just how big they were: taller, broader than full-grown bear, crowned with stag-like antlers. Gom remembered how afraid he'd been on first seeing them, sensing latent power. "It's all right, Hevron. They've come to hear the songs."

"They're harmless," Stormfleet said, barely looking up. "Don't worry."

Gom resumed his singing, and at once the massive forms began to sway among the trees. Gom sang, and sang, and when he was done, he started over, and all the while the Faramors swayed in dreamy silence. Then, as before, the moment he was through, they vanished, soundlessly as they had come.

Every night thereafter of the nine-day journey across that forest to Harga's domain, Gom sang, and the Faramors came, seeming never to tire of Gom's singing. Gom was only too glad to oblige. When Stig had been alive, his father had made music every single day, being the fine singer and songmaker that he was. So Gom sang, and as he sang, he recalled Harga's surprise that the Faramors had gathered to hear him, even waited for encore.

Twice over, you say? They'll be in your debt forever. . . .

Midmorning on the ninth day, the ground began to rise.

"Gom," Stormfleet said excitedly. "I remember this climb."

"Yes," said Gom, filling his lungs with the pungency of pine. "We're almost there."

"We are?" The harrier shot up through the sloping pine trunks and disappeared. Gom led the way, as Harga had that morning long ago, just after their meeting. As they climbed, the ground became rocky and uneven under matted needles, but this time Stormfleet did not stumble.

Keke came back. "I see no lake," she complained. "Nor any house."

Stormfleet snickered, and Gom laughed aloud. "No more should you," he said. "But you will, only be patient. Here," he called, as Keke rose to fly off in a huff. "Ride my shoulder, and you shall see!"

The little bird came to settle on the leather pad, and began to preen her ruffled feathers. Another hour's walking, and, cresting the last rise, they stood looking down on a round, green, grassy basin.

. . . But when you reach this spot, this is what you'll see . . .

"I still don't see any island," Keke cried.

"Nor any house," Hevron said.

Gom nodded. "Good."

Turn the ring thrice sunwise and the lake will reappear. . . . Come home, Gom, when you need, only mind when you leave to "lock up" by turning your ring countersunwise. . . . Know this is your home—workshop, and all in it. Study my books, my chronicles with care, but be sure before you would use any magic that you know how to work it well first—and keep things orderly against my return. . . .

Raising his hand, Gom turned the ring.

Hevron shied, Keke flew up in alarm, even Stormfleet

stepped back as grassy sward vanished, replaced by a shining expanse of lake. And there, in the middle, Harga's island, a yellow sandstone plug of cliff.

Gom ran down to the shore. "Come on," he cried. "We're here!"

By the time the horses had caught up, Gom had retrieved Harga's raft from its mooring, and was waiting to help them aboard. Now Keke raced ahead, across to the island and back, crying jubilantly at all she saw. Gom remembered the bank swallows, and called her to him.

"Keke, small creatures live here: this is their home. While I respect your needs, you must respect them. Touch not one feather or hair of any who live on or near this island, you hear?"

Keke chattered agreement, and set off again, circling the island in big, sweeping curves. By the time they rounded the cliff to the shore, there was not another creature in sight. Never mind, Gom thought. Get in and settled, then he'd reassure everybody how well Keke would behave.

They beached the raft, secured it, and pushed through the holly screen. It was much overgrown, and in need of attention, as was the garden beyond, for everything had gone to seed. But there was still plenty to eat, he saw, as they picked their way among the vegetable and flower beds.

Stormfleet whinnied with pleasure. The grass by the orchard was in great need of cropping. "Do what you have to, Gom," he called. "I'll show Hevron around." The cito led Hevron off toward the fruit trees.

Gom peeped in the little dairy. No sign of Jilly, the nanny goat. Oh, well, perhaps she was off grazing somewhere. He walked the pebble path to a spot midway along the cliff base, and pressed a crack waist-high in the stone.

He sighed in satisfaction as the narrow slab swung inward, revealing the front hall behind. His excitement mounting, Gom ran across the hall, and up the stair to the second level. All was as it had been: dusty, perhaps, but as bright as ever, the blue-washed walls reflecting the sunlight beaming in through round holes in the hollow cliff. He went into the kitchen.

The hearth was laid with a fire waiting to be lit, a pile of logs at the side. Cups and plates shone on the dresser shelf, and Harga's glass jars were filled with beans and dried peas and herbs of all kinds. He went out, along the passage to his room.

Gom stood in the doorway, remembering that far time when he and Harga had stood looking in at the carved bed, the wooden Hoot Owl presiding over the canopy: his bed, that he'd not yet had a chance to sleep in! He closed his eyes. The outer world seemed far away; the teeming lake valley, the city, the citadel. Folgan, and his unkindness. Gom set his staff against the wall, dropped his pack, and threw himself face down across the bed.

Home!

Chapter Thirteen

GOM LAY spread-eagled on the coverlet, looking at the play of light on the ceiling. He caught Hoot Owl's eye. Get up, keep moving, it seemed to say. You have much to do before dark.

He ran to the end of the passage and up a little stair to the third level. Harga's workroom—his workroom, too, now, to work in, to learn in, without that old curmudgeon peering over his shoulder, watching his every move, waiting to pounce at his slightest mistake! Gom walked down the curving chamber, in and out around the jumbled benches, pushing cobwebs aside. To his right, the large globe stood against the wall. He gave it a push, sent it spinning. Beside it, lay piles of Harga's books, blanketed in dust. He picked one up, blew the dust off the cover, opened it—and closed it again in a fit of sneezing. This whole place needed cleaning. Three, four days, it would take, at least, to bring it to a decent state.

Down the far end of the workroom stood the stove, a portly ghost.

He and Harga had sat before that stove the night they'd traveled alamar to the crystal stair. Images rushed in, of Harga lying in her chair, eyes closed, locked in mental combat with Jastra. Jastra, who had taken Harga to serve the people of the stars. Jastra, who had looked Gom up and down and found him . . . unready. Jastra, who, according to the mailed warrior, had set aside for him a starstone to use against the Spohr. Gom shuddered, for with old memories had come old fears.

He walked slowly on. The little table still stood before the stove, the two chairs they'd sat in. And . . . Gom reached to touch the glass globe at its center. No wires, no black box to house it. And yet that sphere had summoned them alamar to the stair; in its lighted depths Gom had seen Tolasin's workshop; by its means Harga had left her old master a message to meet Gom in Pen'langoth.

Harga's globe, attuned to her hand.

Gom cupped his own palm over it.

At his touch, the globe began to flicker, then to glow with a steady light. Leaning over, Gom gazed into its depths, and exclaimed. Harga!

He lowered himself into his chair, his eyes fixed on the image of his mother: perfect, tiny; caught and held within the curve of the sphere—seated in her old chair, her hands clasped on the table before her.

"Gom, son. I'll not waste words. Obviously, what I thought might happen, has. Tolasin could not take you, you've gone with Folgan, and now there's come a parting of the ways. I cannot say I'm sorry. I was expecting it. But I'm hoping—in fact, I'm counting on it—that you now can read, and say your tables. And perhaps you know a little magic too—not much. Simple, basic stuff: an ointment, a cure. A liniment. But no transformations, yet. Nor any knowledge of investment: to store magic you'll need a high degree of mind control, and Folgan will be slow to teach you that.

"So: here you are, with the workshop all to yourself. If you've just arrived, you're feeling pretty good about things. I hope Stormfleet is downstairs, helping himself to a backlog of grass. Oh, don't worry about Jilly. I let her off to find herself a husband. She'll come back sometime, maybe, then you'll have milk again. I'm sure you'll manage, otherwise.

"But sometime you'll start to think of work again. My dear son: I have spent this, my last afternoon, compiling a sort of word map to lead you through the maze that you must tread alone. Look under the globe."

Gom looked, and saw now that the globe stood on a small book, bound in dark brown leather, with dull gold letters along the spine. Gom tipped his head, reading sideways: *Gom's Waybook.*

"Open it when I have done, and you'll see that I have listed things you need to learn, and the order I would teach them. Beside each entry I have noted in which volume you'll find the work, and the page. Also where necessary rock and root are stored. You'll also see that I have drafted out a weekly and a daily scheme." She smiled. "I imagine that at the moment, the last thing you want is to be told what to do by anyone. So maybe for a few days you might just do little more than enjoy the garden—if the season's right. And then browse, maybe start to choose your own work, in your own time and order. That would be fine, too, for I trust you'll heed my wishes, and not undertake anything over your head, and that you'll restore things to their proper order when you're done. But the book is here if you want it, for when you want it. That's how you'd have worked with me, my son."

Harga lowered her head, hiding her face. When she looked up again, her eyes shone with tears. "As I speak these words, you walk the forest still, wondering if you'll meet your master. Whether you'll run into Yul Kinta. But as you hear me speak them now, years will have gone by for you—though maybe only days for me up there, the way time bends among the worlds—a way I still can't understand." She wiped her eyes. "I hope that we shall meet again. I pray for your safety, and your success. Never forget how vital it is that you get your wizard's scroll. Remember what I said before: when you hold the Covenance's scroll of necromancy, then you'll climb the crystal stair, not alamar, but for real. Then you'll learn at last the trust that Jastra would vest in you. If things permit, I shall speak with you alamar. But if not, know this: you are everything I hoped for in a son—nay, more. Whatever becomes of us, Gom, remember that I love you very, very much, and that I'm proud of you.

"One more thing: after I have done, and the globe fades, know that it will be attuned to Tolasin's house. From my books you'll learn in time how you might use the globe to reach him. Don't be afraid to call on him. He knows what provision I have made, and will answer you. So don't feel entirely alone, my dear. Good luck, work hard, and, who knows, if that luck prevail we may meet again at last!"

Her image faded, and Gom was staring at a dull glass globe.

He reached forward, rubbed it shiny, and cupped his hand again, hoping to bring the image back. But nothing happened, of course. Hadn't she said the globe was now attuned to Tolasin's house? For a while, Gom sat, thinking over his mother's words. *When you hold the Covenance's scroll of necromancy, then you'll climb the crystal stair . . . for real. Then you'll learn at last the trust that Jastra would vest in you. . . .* Thanks to the Spinrathen warrior, he knew what that was. *Jastra has a starstone, a crystal seed plucked from the very heart of the Tamarith-awr-Bayon. He keeps this starstone for you, against the hour when you must take it up against the Spohr. In the First Realm he has it, and I know where.* Come to think, the warrior had said nothing about asking Jastra first. Who was this warrior, and how did he know where the stone was stored? And who gave him authority to decide that Gom must have the stone over Jastra's head?

He set the globe aside, took up the book beneath it, and dusted it off.

Every page was covered in fine, neat writing: Harga's instructions, just as she'd said. He turned the pages, skimming the lines. Tables of Basic Elements, the titles began. Lists of Compounds. Tabulated Organic Complexes . . . These, he knew, but soon he was lost in words he'd never seen before. He skipped to the end of the book and found a note. "Mark where you are in your studies, then go back a way, and begin from there. Don't skip, unless you'd do things the hard way. As for the mind exercises—if you find them too easy, as I expect you found Folgan's, then you must devise your own!"

Mind exercises. Gom was tempted there and then to sit down and read. But . . . he stood up—reluctantly, waybook in hand. He ought to go and see his friends. Tend to their needs. And his own! Feeling hungry now, he hurried downstairs. He'd make a fire, bake some oatcakes, and prepare a broth. Then, as he ate, he'd look through his waybook and decide where to make his start.

That night, Gom took his waybook to read in bed. But before he began, he took pen and ink and parchment, resumed his habit of keeping daily journal. *At last,* he wrote. *I lie in my own bed, in my own home for the first time since I left Windy Mountain. Truly, it feels good, although the place is in a sorry state! Now as I cleaned and swept for that mean old man, so I shall work to make this place as Harga would have it, and I vow not to try any magic until I have done.*

True to his word, for five days Gom washed, and cleaned, and swept; he weeded, he gathered autumn crops from the garden for his winter store. Oats there were in plenty, he found, in a lean-to behind the dairy, still fresh and sweet in airtight bins, protected from mouse and weevil. Back of the orchard, he found a small barn, where Harga had obviously once kept a horse. It was badly in need of repair, but the work would be easy, Gom decided, and there was more than enough old timber lying around for the job. By winter, his friends would have a warm and comfortable shelter, lighter and more cosy than Folgan's chill stone stall!

The fifth evening, Gom stood in a clean and dustless workroom, by Harga's books, his own ranged alongside. Tomorrow, he'd begin. And where? He scanned the pages, found what he sought. Harga had known, as the other wizards had not, and that was where he would begin: where ractite met with smeddum seemed a fitting place to start.

By sunrise the next day, Gom had finished his daily chores and was free to climb the workroom stair.

"You must admit," Hevron said, "you learned something at Folgan's—if only how to get up early and put your chores behind you."

All morning, Gom worked from Harga's notes on ractite-smeddum interaction, learning much from her detailed account. She had even compiled tables on quantities critical for certain results, all verified with practice. He mixed, and melted; fused and annealed the various strengths of alloy, testing, noting, until elevenses time. Then, in the afternoon, looking in his waybook, he saw that she had planned to have him practice his first mental exercise. He found the volume concerned, took it to the stove, and began to read. Part chronicle, part diary, the book was very old, and Harga's hand, immature. Why, she must have compiled it during her apprenticeship!

. . . *the Hierarchy teaches this way. But while their scheme is all very well for those who have no gift in that direction, I find it a waste of time. Already I have quicker and easier ways to "bring on the hum." (My name for what Tolasin calls "reaching the focal point necessary for working magic.") I simply sit, in the dark, if possible, and close my eyes. Then I relax and let my mind go, allowing it to seek a way out, as water seeks to flow from its container. I sit, and sit, until the hum sounds. Then, suddenly, my mind draws to the focal point, as a lance poised for the throw. . . .*

Water? Lance? Gom read eagerly. She put it very well.

In time, maybe in two years or so, in the heat of the moment, I shall have the power to find the focal point instantly, wherever I am, yet I shall still repeat this exercise to keep my mind attuned, just as an athlete trains to race; the hunter, to hunt. And the warrior, to do battle . . .

Gom set the book aside. *Bring on the hum.* A far cry from Folgan's cumbersome ring of stones. He had already managed to do it once in his own clumsy way the night he'd reached the Spinrathen warrior.

Bring on the hum . . .

He was suddenly back on Windy Mountain, watching by the creek, hand beneath the water, waiting for a fish. Not to drag it, suffocating into the air, but just to cup it in his hand, for one moment to touch it, to bid it good day. Then to let it go, watch it circle in front of him then streak away, a flash of silver in the sunlight.

Times like those, when he was quiet, oblivious of his surroundings, his mind bent on fish, he'd fancied he'd heard the rune humming. But the sound had always been inside his head. He, too, had unwittingly done as Harga, bringing his mind into focus without all that other rigmarole.

He skimmed through, until he reached a note near the end of the book. This he read slowly, and with care.

I have counted three main uses for the hum, but I think that Tolasin—and the others—know only of the first. The other two I'll keep to myself. They are not taught, I suspect, but are gifts—rare gifts, for I have heard no hint of them anywhere this past seven years. The primary use, which the Hierarchy teaches, is to make, store, and retrieve spells.

But I can also bring on visions. And I can also seem to travel, to see and hear things far away, through the hum—and my crystal sphere. I'm sure that it is possible to use the mind alone, stars know that I have tried. But after all these years it is still beyond me. I suspect that even greater gifts are

*needed, and if ever one is born with such, then that one will
have power exceeding any other born of Ulm.*

Gom set down the book, went over to the others piled
up, and scanned their spines. At last he took up the
chronicle from which Harga had read to him at their
meeting, turned the pages until he found the place.

*. . . I only can defend Ulm from destruction. And yet this
charge is too great for me alone. But to whom can I turn? Only
Tolasin, and he is old . . . I myself could have a child, a
special child . . . to share this task. . . .*

Gom read on a while, then closed the book and stood,
rubbing his face. Poor Harga, bearing all that weight
alone. She had surely been glad when he was born. "My
little tool to save the world," she'd called him.

Sighing, he went back to the table. He was getting
ahead of himself. Before he would run, he must walk.
This afternoon, he would begin the first simple exercise,
just as his mother prescribed. He set his feet squarely on
the floor before him, clasped his hands on the table as
he'd seen Harga do, then, letting out a deep breath, he
went still.

Minutes passed. Gom's head lolled forward, but he
was only dimly aware, and he could not have raised it
had he wished. He felt a slight shift. The hum was
beginning, back of his head. It spread forward, through
his skull, swamping his thought. His head began to spin,
faster, faster, then suddenly the spinning stopped and he
shrank to a single, clear point.

His mind was focused. Now what? He'd been so set
on bringing on the hum Harga's way he'd not thought
what to do with it. Enough, he told himself. Learning
how had been the exercise. What to do with it came

next—and that, in stages. Now he must let go, bring his mind back to normal.

He hung on. Seemed such a waste. Perhaps he could just drift, as he'd done in Folgan's house. Enjoy the clouds and rainbows. But—what if he thought instead of Katak? And skull-thieves? What if—

As the air went dark, Gom knew that he was somehow in that same waking nightmare he had dreaded so long. Powerless to stop it, Gom drifted down into deep and deadly cold. He tried to rise, but he could not, for he was somehow part of where he was. His fear grew stronger. Katak was near. And ever moving. Oozing like slow rock slime, degree by slow degree, through cold and dark. Gom's mind recoiled. Katak moving?

Terrific forces seized and pulled him away at speed until his head began to spin, and the world about him vanished.

Gom came to lying across the table, face down. Late afternoon sun poked in through the tiny round windows, dotting the chamber behind him. Gom lifted his face from the tabletop, still locked into his vision.

Katak—moving through deep rock mass?

Meaning broke in upon him. Gom stood, and, scraping back his chair, he made for the stairs. So long ago his vision had tried to warn him: the sealstone was still lit, and the kundalara watched by Katak's flooded cave—but the Spohr was no longer there!

Chapter Fourteen

"**K**ATAK LOOSE?" Stormfleet rolled his eyes. Hevron came racing up. "Where is he, then?"

"I don't know." Gom stood between them, at a loss. "Only that he's going down deep, *under*." He described his vision.

"It could have been a nightmare," Hevron suggested. "You've had them before."

"No." Gom shook his head. "This was no nightmare." He told them about his new mind exercise.

"But how can he have gotten out?" Hevron said.

"Who? Who's out?" Keke flew in, alighted on an apple branch.

Gom explained. "Wherever he is, he's slithering, very slowly down; thin, like a sheet, sliding through rock, it felt like."

"But the sealstone is still lit!" Keke cried. "And Ganash flooded—"

"This is what I think: there is a crack, a hairline crack, in the cave floor. He found it, slipped into it, and now he's sliding down through the bedrock, feeling his way until he comes out under the Sound. Oh, to think I didn't see it before!" In his agitation, Gom walked off into the orchard and back. "Who knows when he might come out into the open currents?"

Stormfleet tossed his mane. "What can we do?"

"I don't know."

Keke spoke up. "Ganash might have an idea where Katak would come out."

"Aye." Gom nodded. "He knows the waters well."

Keke flapped her wings eagerly. "So when do I leave?"

The hawk took off shortly after sunrise.

"Don't look so anxious," Stormfleet said. "She'll be fine."

"It's the quickest way," Hevron said. "And you can go on working."

"Gom," Stormfleet said, "couldn't you call on Harga through this new mind exercise?"

"I could try."

The cito butted Gom's shoulder. "Sit with us. We'll keep quiet."

"No. I'd better go inside." Gom climbed to the workroom, sat down. But each time he relaxed, and let his mind flow, he found himself drifting off to sleep. Why? He'd done it once, why not a second time? He tried again. The next thing he knew, he was lying face down across the table. He came up, frowning. His mind was like a balky horse, when it had been so good before. Why? He found his place in Harga's book, and read on. *Simple as the practice is, it is not easy, even for one gifted. After the first session, I was so exhausted that I was done for a whole week. I had to temper my impatience, and learn to follow the natural rhythm of things; to build my strength gradually, and not force the pace. For the longest time, I sat every other day, and if on those occasions my mind rebelled, then I let it be and turned to other things.*

Gom closed the book in disgust. Every other day! He took up his waybook, opened it, then closed it again distractedly. The crystal globe—perhaps he could learn to use that.

He found the place, and read through slowly. To summon Tolasin in the globe, he had to picture him. Gom closed his eyes, recalling the night in Hannan Whitlock's shed. It had been dark, and the wizard had worn a cloak. But he remembered Tolasin being tall, very thin—gaunt, with white hair, and piercing eyes, like a cat's. Good enough?

Gom cupped his hands about the globe, and stared into it intently, imagining Tolasin within, the workshop behind as he'd last seen it when Harga had called on her old master in this very globe. Tolasin had not been there, but Gom had seen the empty chamber clearly: many shelves, he recalled them well, and boxes, and bottles, and books, all jumbled together.

Nothing happened. Gom sat back in exasperation. Hadn't Harga said it would be thus—for at least a week? He straightened up, tried again, willing that old man's image to appear inside the glass. The globe flickered, then began to pulse with light. Gom watched with growing excitement. In each flash, he saw the old man clearly, bending over a bench: long gray robe caught with a blue sash; silver beard and craggy face in the glare of a small white flame on which a crucible steamed and bubbled. The old man looked up sideways, a crease of annoyance between his brows.

"Yes?"

"I—" Gom fell silent. What to say? He hadn't thought.

"You're Harga's son—young Gom. You've grown, I'll say. Steady, *steady!* You keep coming and going. Hold *on,* that's it," the old man nodded approval as Gom tightened his focus. The globe stopped pulsing, the image inside shone bright and fixed.

Gom breathed out carefully. It felt good, to be holding the picture like that. Sort of *right.* Like when he'd brought on the hum, and with not nearly the effort. The old man was watching him.

"What is it? I'm right in the middle."

"Sorry. I was—testing," Gom said. Well, that was true, mostly.

"Humph, you pick the most awkward of times. Folgan didn't work out?"

"No, sir."

"Pity. And pity I can't take you. However, if you've a problem, don't hesitate to call. Hunh?"

Gom nodded, wondering how to break the link.

"Oh—before you go—" The old man leaned forward, his face distorting in the bulge of the glass. "Harga's still away, yes, she must be, or you wouldn't be bothering me like this." The wizard turned away, muttering to himself. Then he turned back. "You two talk, from time to time?"

"Er—yes." Gom hoped so.

Tolasin foraged in his gown pocket. "Remember this?" He pulled out a little box and held it up. A snuffbox, the snuffbox Tolasin had taken from the thief in the Wilds!

"I do, sir."

"Tell Harga there's been another thief—tattooed like the one they caught at the wedding." He cocked an eye at Gom. "You wouldn't know anything about that, I suppose? Put to sleep with agarax, they say."

Gom held his tongue.

"Well," Tolasin said, "this latest one was caught inside Scandibar also. They think he was after my Lord Leochtor's new stone. When they went to question him, they found him—" The wizard turned away again, this time tutting in irritation. "Bother, it's passed the fusing point. Look, just tell Harga this last one fetched up dead, like the one at the wedding."

Dead? Grandy—dead? Gom felt his color drain. "But that one didn't—"

"That one, as you call him, was found in his cell, cold. Not a mark on him. Couldn't have been the dream-sand, of course. Strange, eh?"

Gom stared back at him, speechless.

"Ah, well. Tell Harga the Hierarchy are in a lather. They hate unsolved mysteries, you see. Take them quite personally. I hope it will all blow over soon. Umph? Oh well, I'm sure Harga knows what she's doing. Now: if you need me, call," Tolasin said, and the globe went dull, leaving Gom with but his own reflection in the glass.

Another thief! And the Hierarchy in a lather. Gom frowned. It seemed that when caught, the men simply died—or were killed. . . . *in his cell, cold* . . . Could Katak do that? Gom shuddered, folded his arms, hugging himself tight.

Storms came during the night, blowing away the last warmth of autumn. The air grew sharp and frost wilted the tall grasses. Gom finished repairing the stable roof, gathered in what hay there was, watching constantly for the harrier. But it was not for two weeks more that she came barreling in.

Ganash sent his love. The cave was still sealed, the kundalara said. Even so, he'd gone to scour the Deep for sign of the Spohr. "But if Katak seeps through bedrock as you fear," Keke said wearily, "Ganash says we have trouble indeed, for water flows beneath everything, under the roots of the world. Once out in the Deep, Katak could go for long, and come up anywhere."

Gom listened, his spirits sinking. "What to do now?"

"Just go on," Hevron said quietly. "Work, and watch, and wait."

Blizzards came early: vicious gales that threatened the barn roof and felled two old apple trees. The snows came, smothering the island, burying the frozen lake. Gom labored from dawn to dusk up in the workroom, following his mother's schedule. By midwinter, he was halfway through the waybook. And he was sitting every day, bringing his mind to focus point without any trouble.

From here, Harga wrote, *from this one place, the mind is ready for all the many things Tolasin would have me train for separately. I find it so simple by this method that I can do so many things in half the time it takes my master, yet I will not let him know, for I honor him, and would not diminish him. But I list here magic one can do from this point, including investment and divestment, and even transformations!*

Transformations! Gom ran his finger down the page, until he found the place. He began to read, his brow creasing with concentration. Too advanced for him as yet.

But the word had started up the thought in his mind. Harga had transformed Stormfleet into his present sorry state to protect him from greedy men, and angry Yul Kinta. Harga had warned them at the time that the spell had been hasty and crude, and would be most difficult, perhaps impossible, to reverse. But the sight of the word started up the hope in Gom that his friend might soon be restored to his true, magnificent form.

All through that bitter winter, Gom pushed his mind to the limit. On the first day of the thaw, when the horses ventured out across the soggy ground to walk the shore, Gom went running out, waving his crystal on the end of its chain. "See, see!" he cried.

They raced to meet him. "What is it?"

"I have invested it!"

Stormfleet sniffed the crystal. "How, invested?"

Gom explained impatiently. "I made a spell in the crucible upstairs, then I put the magic from the spell into the crystal! It's there, in the stone!"

Hevron bared his teeth. "What magic?"

"I made a simple invisibility spell," Gom said. "Now it's in here. I can use it any time I like."

"How can you tell it worked?" Hevron said.

"I . . ." Gom scratched his head. How to describe it? "When you drank from the lake just now, you took up the water with your tongue, and sent it down to your belly, right? Well, when I made the spell in the crucible, I sort of drank up its power with my mind, then emptied it into the stone. I felt it go, so smoothly." Gom smiled. "It was easy."

"Then test it, see if the spell is really there, as you think."

"Pull it out again?" Gom frowned. "That's divestment."

"Divestment," Keke cried. "I know divestment: Ganash divested the skull-ring!"

"Yes, he did. But divestment can mean many things. Say you have a runestone: you store your spells in it, like food in a larder. And you can pull them out as you need, and put each to use. Or you pull a little bit of a spell at a time, or you can pull the whole thing at a weak level, leaving—"

"Hold!" Hevron lowered his head. "You make my brain whirl!"

"Go on," Stormfleet said. "I'm listening."

"You can also pool your individual spells, fusing them into one massive thrust of power—if your mind is strong enough to redirect it. Or again, you can pull the power and destroy it, if you need."

"As Ganash destroyed the skull-ring's power," Keke said. "Sounds like hard work to me."

"And difficult," said Stormfleet.

Gom agreed. "Putting in one simple spell and pulling it out again is the beginning. So far, I've practiced this one investment. Now to see if I was successful." He swung his crystal under the sunlight. The spell was quite small. Indeed, its magic would hold for no more than a minute, but it was a start. "Be still and quiet," he said, looking straight at Keke. He'd never tried to bring on the hum outside the workroom. He closed his eyes, his mind to the friends standing around him. He shut out their images, their curious stares. Wind gusted by, lifting his jacket, blowing his hair about his face. He ignored Wind, and the sounds of lapping water, and the rattle of dry holly leaves. He withdrew, and there! He found the focal point! Now he bent his mind to the crystal in his hand, saw with his inner eye the myriad secret patterns of its structure. Like a honeycomb it was, full of empty cells waiting to be filled. He saw deep in its inmost recesses, Harga's spell, sealed safely within its cavity, shining like a tiny sun. And there, near the crystal's tip, quite close to the surface, the pinpoint light of the spell he'd just deposited. He sent out a tendril of thought, gently dislodged the small nugget of simple power, drew it to the surface of the stone. Then he pulled it out, stretched it, and, throwing it high, he let it fall around him like a mantle. He barely heard the startled snorts close by, Keke's cry, the start of a wing. For a long moment he stood, locked in concentration, then he felt a shimmer pass through him.

The power was used up.

He shifted, opened his eyes, feeling giddy suddenly, and weary, although it was barely past breakfast time.

His three friends were staring, unmoving, like statues in the sand.

Gom pushed his hair back and rubbed his brow. "Well?"

"You—you vanished!" Keke cried.

"There one minute, gone the next!" Hevron blew out his lips with force.

Stormfleet, breaking the stillness, pranced about. "What did you expect? Isn't that what he was supposed to do?" He pulled up in front of Gom, and bowed his head to the ground. "Well done! You are a wizard born!"

Gom raised the crystal and eyed the gold flake at its

center. "Thank you," he said. He drew cold air into his lungs, felt his strength returning.

"You'd never done that before you say?" Hevron was clearly impressed. "You've come far in a short time!"

Stormfleet snickered. "He's no one to hold him back now, no master to dole out his learning in miserly pinches."

"Folgan had his reasons, and not all bad," Hevron said. "But, truly, Gom, as you're a wizard born, you'll know all you need to know years before the rest."

Gom shrugged. "The basics, maybe, thanks to Harga. I'm more than halfway through the waybook." He dropped his crystal back under his shirt.

"But how shall you become a true wizard," Hevron said, "unless you stand accepted before the Hierarchy to receive your scroll and staff?"

"I don't know." Even if Harga had stayed on Ulm, she'd have had to send him come Covenance time to take his examinations with the other apprentices.

Stormfleet tossed his head. "He's wild, like Keke and me. He'll never take to bit and bridle. Rune and staff he has already. As Harga herself works outside their law, so shall Gom. No?"

Gom slipped an arm around each horse's neck. "If that's the only way. I shall make magic and store it in my crystal against the day that I might meet the Spohr. And if I should win and Ulm is saved—who's to complain?"

"Those old men," Hevron snorted. "You'll never learn!"

That evening, as was become his habit before going to bed, Gom took a lamp upstairs, and browsed through Harga's chronicles. For many evenings he had pored over

Harga's account of Ulm, now he was reading about the Realms: of their establishment; the Spinrathen sky-ships, their fall into disuse when the stargates were built. To his delight, he found a chart of the Seven Realms, neatly inscribed across the page.

Here I draw a chart of the Realms, Harga wrote, *listing their names and their rulers as Jastra told them to me, lest I forget:*

The first Realm is Bayon, and the Lord Jastra rules it.

The second is Mythruin, and the Lady Serula governs it.

The third is Fain-yl-Bour, and Lord Logund rules it.

The fourth is Lantyn, and the Lady Grymedra ruled it.

The fifth is Maluc, the Lord Karlvod rules it.

The sixth is Sparad ythalar, and Lord Thrun ruled it.

The seventh is Uftos, and mayhap the Lady Huthryn still rules it.

{Ulm lying between the first and second Realms, thus I mark it on this sky chart, just as Jastra described it:

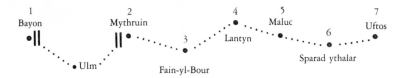

Gom studied the chart, remembering the peppercorns Harga had used to make this very map on her kitchen table. He ran his eye down the list of rulers, seeing all the names for the first time, noting the ominous change of tense in two cases.

. . . Lady Grymedra ruled it . . .

. . . Lord Thrun ruled it . . .

The Realms on either side of Karlvod. Their gates had

fallen under Karlvod's subtle workings. But what had happened to their rulers? Gom read on. . . . *At the fall of the fourth gate between Maluc and Lantyn, the High Houses began to fight among themselves. The Lady Grymedra, head of the ruling House, then died by her brother's hand in this way: The rumor was put about at Karlvod's subtle instigation that Grymedra, not content with her own estate and ascendancy above all others in the Fourth Realm, coveted her brother's fortune and estate, which was not inconsiderable. Incensed, her brother stormed her halls, put her to the sword, and razed the palace to its foundations. Of the widow's son and daughter, they say Anja fell also to her uncle's blade, while the young lord Kurnyn passed secretly through to the Third Realm by the help of retainers. Since then, he has been often seen joining battle under his mother's blazon of the horned hind rampant, his helmet crested with the mourning green. Some contend it is his ghost who fights, while his ashes lie with Anja's and Grymedra's. Certainly, none has seen my lord Kurnyn ride to the field, and none has seen him go. Neither is there soul who's heard him speak, or has seen his face—not even Lord Jastra, though they've fought together, side by side, upon the battlefield. . . .*

Gom looked up in excitement. *Blazon of the horned hind rampant? Mourning green?* He leaned back. The warrior's voice had sounded deep, like a man's, a seasoned veteran's. But . . . He looked down at the lighted page. In every other way the description fit. *Kurnyn.* The boy had lost his father, just like Gom. His mother, too—but not the same way, pray the skies! "Kurnyn." He said the name aloud. Then he set his feet, and clasped his hands, of a sudden, ardent mind to call this Kurnyn out.

Chapter Fifteen

OM SETTLED himself down, prepared to let his mind go. He had practiced hard. Had a good measure of control. Now was the time to set his thought again on the stars. He focused his mind, then let it out, yet keeping hold, as though it were a hound on the leash. *Kurnyn? Kurnyn!* He waited, picturing the Spinrathen warrior, alert for sign of response.

Nothing.

Gom sent out farther, his power stretching and growing thin. Suddenly, there was noise all about him: of clashing steel, the clamor of men's shouts. Out of the general din came a loud cry, the whinny of a startled horse, a moan of pain. Then the darkness lightened, and Gom caught a glimpse of sky; low, and dark with swollen cloud. He was standing on a plain. About him, men fought hand to hand, some on horseback, most on foot. Gom recognized the armor, and the great helmets, and the strange swords with metal shafts and blades of blue fire that flashed in the dull light. Even as he watched, one man raised his right hand and with his light-blade felled his opponent.

Gom caught sight of the pale green plume not ten paces away. The warrior stood, back turned, in the act of bringing down his sword.

Kurnyn!

The warrior completed the stroke, cutting down his opponent. Then the figure whirled about. *What! Again —you!*

Gom's heart leapt. The voice was higher, younger! *Kurnyn, I would speak with you!*

I am not Kurnyn. Get away! Leave! You distract me! the answer came. The voiced thought was a man's again. Deep. Gruff. And angry.

I had to come! Gom cried defiantly. *For your sake as well as my own. Katak is loose! I need the starstone urgently!*

At the mention of the stone, the warrior glanced around. *I can't help you right now!* He ducked as a light-blade cut toward him. *What do you expect me to do in one day! Can't you see I'm still—* He ducked again. *Get away, leave me—* The figure wavered, broke, reformed as Gom grimly held on.

Wait—who are you, if not Kurnyn?

The figure whirled about again, the sights and sounds of the battlefield momentarily receding. *How do you know of him?*

From my mother's records. Who are you? Where is Kurnyn?

The warrior glanced around again. *Kurnyn is dead; I am kin. Now let me free, if you'd see me more!*

Gom released his concentration, and all went dark. For a while, there was silence, then he heard the crack of wood and the shift of burning coal in the stove. Not Kurnyn, though at first, Gom would have said so, hearing as he'd thought a younger voice. . . . Kurnyn was dead, the warrior said. Pity. Gom had felt such a strong kinship with the young lord. Had felt that there might be a friend. But not in that grizzled, seasoned fighter—*kin.* Another uncle, perhaps, out to avenge his sister, and his sister's children. And if in doing so, he fostered the legend of Kurnyn's avenging ghost—so much the better for morale.

Strange, though, for all the soldier's gruff manner, Gom could have sworn the man had been startled, almost afraid, at his appearance. How had he in turn looked to the warrior? Like a ghost, as the warrior had to him at their first meeting? The man's anger had had a touch of fear.

What do you expect me to do in one day!

Harga had warned Gom, but still it came as a shock to know that although months had passed for him, the warrior was still fighting the same battle on the same field!

So now what should he do? The warrior had said that Harga was too far to hear him. Even so, Gom tried to reach her the next day, but without success. Every day from then on, he tried, as part of his mind practices, but still there was no response. The days passed, and weeks, and months; spring turned to summer, summer to fall.

One whole year on Harga's island, Gom thought one late autumn morning, as he gathered in stores for the root cellar and cut hay for his friends. He had over the months been gathering stores of quite another kind, investing his crystal with magic: healing spells, invisibility enough to last one day; light for dark places, and from his work on polarity the power to repel and to attract more than metals.

The seasons passed and nothing happened; Gom's sense of urgency and danger eased. He progressed steadily through his waybook, until at last he reached the tables of Transformations. He began with a simple spell, changed an apple into a pear. He chose a green apple, a windfall from the orchard, not telling Stormfleet what he was about. He placed the apple on the bench before him, then set himself to bring on the hum. Now he could see the apple's inner shape, the intricate pattern of lines and spaces that made it what it was. Gingerly, he began to prise the lines apart, widening the spaces. With his outer sight, he saw that the apple was apparently dissolving into mist, minute droplets hanging loosely together. Now came the critical point, when Gom must steer those droplets into their new configuration. He imaged the pear, on the bench before him, the droplets recohering, coalescing into the different shape. The mist began to shimmer and sparkle with restless light, and on the bench a pear began to form. Sweat started on Gom's brow. The pear shape wavered, the shimmering ceased, and there! On the bench before him was a real, solid pear.

He picked it up, weighed it in his hand, sniffed it. He took a bite. It was a pear, all right. Jubilant, he rushed down to tell Stormfleet, but out in the garden he changed his mind. That had been the simplest of spells. Changing the horse would be quite a different matter. He must do a lot more work before giving his friend cause to hope.

The next day, Gom changed another apple into a pear, but this time he left it intact, for now he must go one stage further and change it back.

Again, he broke the solid form down into particles, saw them hover, misty, formless. He began the spell again, and the apple started to form. At that moment, he lost concentration. The half-formed apple twisted into a blotchy mass. No! Gom pulled his mind together, but it was too late. He stared in dismay at the mess on the bench before him. It was only an apple, he told himself. There was no real harm. He covered his eyes. What if that had been Stormfleet?

He worked on, the weeks and months a blur. From simple transformations, he moved on to more difficult ones, then to practice investing them. At last, he was ready to reveal his new skills to his friends outside. But he did not. He did not want Stormfleet to know until he was sure.

Was that really the reason? he asked himself one night, as he was writing his journal. Or was he afraid?

Afraid or no, Gom carried on, aware of the growing power he wielded. But for all his care, a second disaster occurred. One midautumn afternoon, he was halfway through changing a cup into a dish, for simple practice. He'd been investing a polarity spell all morning, and he was tired. He should have finished for the day, but he was so eager to practice transformations that he worked on. He had broken down the cup and was just reforming it when Harga's globe flickered, then blazed brilliantly, flashing light through the whole room.

Tolasin!

"Ah, Gom. Your mother there?"

Distracted, Gom's tired mind stumbled, and he found himself saying words from quite another spell.

The mist flashed—and vanished!

Quickly, Gom said the transformation again, but the mist did not reappear. He tried again, and again. No use, and he should know it. For the words he'd accidentally said were that morning's spell to reverse polarity!

Instead of drawing the cup particles together, he'd made them fly apart—for good! There was no way in the world to bring that object back, for its very essence was scattered to the winds.

"Gom?" The wizard called again. "Your mother there?"

"N-no, sir."

"I must reach her. Where is she?"

"I cannot say."

The wizard hemmed and hawed. "She heard of the trouble?"

"Trouble?"

"Obviously not," the wizard said, as to himself. He leaned forward. "Where have you been the past few months, young man? Oh, don't bother to explain. There's a mess brewing in the Lakelands. King Galt's gotten big for his britches again. Happens every now and then. But this time . . . Four raids this past summer into outlying settlements, though he denies responsibility. That caused some grumblings, two of us were commissioned to go and make representation.

"But now he's gone and seized the Lake Lord's emerald Seal." He frowned. "Wherever your mother is—you can tell her this?"

"I-I'll try, sir," Gom said. Herelys, the official Seal of Pen'langoth, which the whole Hierarchy had invested with powerful magic almost two years before. The thought made him uneasy.

"Some in the Hierarchy are of a mind that magic stands behind the Marsh King. A mage who thinks to work outside the law, someone who perhaps works under this crest." Tolasin held up the little silver snuffbox. "You look shocked, my boy. Well, you may look more shocked than that before we're done. Already there is dissent within the Hierarchy, accusations are flying about like dust in a gale, and fingers are pointing this way and that."

"You're not saying—they can't think that Harga—"

Tolasin put a finger to his lips. "Not only Harga. Old feuds are reviving, grudges, suspicions. Oh, I'm not saying Harga's name hasn't come up, but so have others—and not without reason, my boy. For while I am certain Harga's name is clear, the fact remains that whoever gives Galt courage to defy us has magery of a very high degree, and so that whoever must be one of us, umph?"

Gom stared mutely into the globe.

"Several of the Order went to Sundor, demanding the Seal's return: Galt laughed in their faces. *And nothing they tried against him worked!* Send Harga, I said. They refused, of course!" He shook his head. "Now the armies gather in Scandibar. Any day now, they march west. Gom: Harga must go at once to Sundor, find the Seal, bring it out. If she doesn't, the blood of the Lakes will stain that stinking fen but there'll be no victory."

Chapter Sixteen

"**Y**OU SHOULD have told him," Hevron said. "Surely the combined power of all the wizards in the Hierarchy could put a stop to Katak's will—if it really is Katak's will."

"*If?* Can't you see? All the signs are there: men at one another's throats, the Lakelanders on the brink of war, even the Hierarchy rife with feud and suspicion. Wherever Katak is, he sows his seed, even as his brothers sow the seed of anarchy across the Realms at Karlvod's bidding."

"Then all the more reason to go to the Council and tell them. They have a right to know, to deal with Katak of one mind."

"Hevron, again I say: I may not speak of this to any human soul on Ulm!"

"But why, *why?*" Hevron demanded. "It's all very well for this Jastra fellow to give orders, it's not his world at stake."

"But it is!" Gom cried. "If Ulm fall, his world is forever cut off!"

"Therein lies some difference," Hevron said. "If I could tell those wizards, then surely I would!"

"First you'd get past me!" Stormfleet reared, sending Hevron back. "Think what a sniff of Katak's power might do to them in time. Saving Tolasin, there's not one who wouldn't bend a little, or a lot, in the end."

"Frrrrumph," Hevron said. "I don't know. Take Folgan. He is proud, but corruptible? I don't think that he would—" The roan fell silent.

"This is all very well," Keke said, "but it doesn't tell us what to do."

"There is only one thing to do," Gom said soberly. "I must go to Sundor and find the Lake Lord's Seal."

"You?" Hevron bared his teeth. "You're not the wizard yet!"

"So? Folgan has done no good there, nor even Mecrim Thurgeril himself. I must go, I know the stakes, and besides," he added, as though to himself, "this is as it was meant to be." He looked up. "I shall leave for Sundor this day."

"Count me out!" Keke cried.

"Call on Harga, Gom. Be wise. Think," Hevron urged.

Gom faced Hevron squarely. "I've called on my mother every day for months, but she does not respond. And even if we spoke this minute, she could not be back in time to stop this massacre."

"I wish that I could bear you on a cito's back," Stormfleet said. "You'd be there in no time!"

Gom patted his friend's neck. "Maybe you could, if you'd risk it."

"What? You have the transformation spell? Already?"

Gom took out his crystal, dangled it on its chain. "I invested it this very morning."

"You did? Then change me, now!"

"Wait," Hevron said. "Could this spell go wrong?"

"Don't listen," Stormfleet snorted. "Get on with it."

"Just a minute, Gom!" Keke cried. "Let's talk sense! You'll never get to Sundor quietly, parading on a cito."

"She's right," Hevron said.

Gom looked from one to the other, then to his friend. "The power is here, I can use it any time."

"Brrrr, I suppose. Go pack."

"And put on gauntlet and pad, Gom," Keke said.

"Oh? You said you'd not go near that place."

"That I shan't! But I shall scout your way out to the marsh border. After that, well, perhaps I'll get a cousin to lead you in."

Gom packed a few necessities: water bottle, rations, Vala's cloak, Carrick's map. Then, the house safely locked away behind them, they moved swiftly through the Dunderfosse, Gom having told the forest of his urgency, and where he would come out. As before, they emerged by the little river that led south, and moved fast along its eastern bank, over ground that Gom and Stormfleet had trodden on their journey to Pen'langoth to find a wizard master. Now Gom wore Vala's cloak, keeping a wary eye out for Yul Kinta, Keke scouting constantly ahead.

As they went, trees along the riverbank flamed yellow and orange and red, and thickets of bramble and hobblebush began to shrivel. "This was where Urolf took me prisoner," Gom said as they passed through the remembered place. "Aelyth-Kintalyn is just to the west, not far from here."

On the eighth day they left the river, struck out southeast through hill and woodland toward Sundor's barrier hills without trouble, reaching them in only nineteen days. It was twilight when the low, crescent hill-range came in sight, dark smudges on the horizon. Beyond them lay Sundor's deadly waste. "Ke-ke-ke-ke!" Keke shrank into Gom's shoulder. "That is where we part, I think."

"That is where we all shall part. The marsh is deadly uncertain, even for human feet. A horse would not get far. And Sundborg is at the marsh's very center. I shall go in alone."

Stormfleet lowered his head and pawed the ground. "You think to leave me behind now? Think again!"

"One wrong step and we'd both be sucked down."

"Not if a cousin showed you where to tread," Keke said. "We'll stop this side of the hills, and I'll go find us a guide tomorrow."

"What guide?" Hevron said, as they moved on toward the distant range. "How would any creature of the air know where a horse should put his feet?"

"Why, any bird that would survive in that place will know where men go," Keke retorted.

"Brrrr." Hevron sniffed the wind. "You really think we should stop here tonight? There may be sentries in these hills. Come to think, there'll be watchers across the fen. How will you get by them to the king's fortress?"

"I don't know." Gom unslung pack and staff and set them down. Vala's cloak worked well in woodland, but over open fen? He had the invisibility spell stored in his crystal, of course, but he'd rather save that power to use inside Sundborg. "You know, you're right about one thing," he said. "I'd be a fool to travel through the dark. I'll move on in the morning, with Keke's help—Keke's kin's help," he amended hastily as Keke started up. He took out his map, spread it, and examined the great wide marsh with the single peak right in the center. There was no other way to reach that mountain than across the marsh. And that marsh was bottomless, he'd been told. A thick skin of mud and grit floating on an inland sea. If he were to tumble into that bog, he'd be sucked down through the mud into cold black water that ran beneath down to the roots of the world. Gom shivered, his eyes on the map. Somehow, he must cross that open waste, find a path to tread.

Sunset deepened into dusk; dusk darkened into night.

Gom wrapped himself in his cloak, and lay down, looking up at the stars. He was just dropping off when he became aware of someone standing over him. He turned his head, tried to sit up, found he could not move any further. The figure crouched, bent-backed, looking on him intently. Gom moved his eyes, caught a glimpse of Stormfleet and Hevron close by, still, silent sentinels.

"They do not see me, traveler." The voice was old and plaintive.

"Who are you?"

"Sit, sit," the old man said. "Be comfortable."

Gom, feeling his body release, sat up slowly. "Are you of the fen?" He moved his hand to his belt, to the clasp of his knife. To his surprise, the figure began to rock to and fro, as though in pain.

"Of the fen? Oh, I like that, I do. I do. Oh, oh. Am I of the fen!" To Gom's astonishment, the man began to cry. "Lost," he mumbled. "Lost . . . all lost."

Gom touched the man lightly on the arm. "What have you lost? Perhaps I can help you find it."

The man looked up slowly, his face pale in the starlight, the tears shining on his cheeks. "Yes, you will at that." He began rocking again, muttering to himself all the while.

Gom eyed the man uncertainly. Was he ill? Unhinged? Did he wander in his mind? "What is your name, old fellow?"

The man looked up. "My name?" He laughed; a sharp, disconcerting sound. "It is not yours. 'Destroyer' is your name, yet it is not accursed. The curse is yonder." The man waved his arm toward the fen.

"You are wrong," Gom said. "My name is not Destroyer. You mistake me for someone else. Listen, do you know Sundborg?"

"Aye, better than most," the man said.

"Then do you know a quiet way in?"

The man pointed down. "Under—but that way is closed." He shut his eyes, and began to sing.

In days of old this barren waste was bountiful and fair;
The marsh was filled with shoals of fish and birds
flocked through the air.
Marshaven was this country called when Good King
Gorfid reigned;
And at its center rose the peak with lofty hall
maintained.
Its Gate was ever open to traveler in need;
In peace and honor dwelt its folk, in noble word and
deed.

Until one day a savage horde came in with purpose
harsh;
They stormed the peak and took the folk and drowned
them in the marsh.
Their leader made himself a king, and Sundborg,
named that peak,
And on the land, with cruel hand, did great
destruction wreak.
Now in this desolation few creatures still persist,

And few things live amid those pools, beneath that
dismal mist.

And so today the haven seems a dying waste, forlorn;
A withered place, quite without hope that virtue be
reborn.
Yet Gorfid, with his final breath, when pushed into
the fen,
Foretold the peak's destruction; claimed that it would
rise again.
And now at last that hour doth come, the evil king
must drown;
The hand no bigger than a child's must bring the
mountain down!

Lo! The Sleeper doth awake, to bring thee on thy way,
That curse may now its vengeance take and evil
monarch pay:
Gorfid's Chimney is the crux over which you'll kneel;
Trace the Waters to the Bung, foul Sundborg's taint to
heal!

The old man's voice trailed away, leaving silence between them. Then, in one quick, smooth movement, he
stood up, tall and straight, the tatters of his garments
flapping against his emaciated body. "Now it begins, and
will not end until Sundborg lies under the marsh." The
man turned away, tears shining on his hollow cheeks.

"Please," Gom said. "If you'd only tell me—"

The figure vanished into the night.

Gom leapt up, ran after him. But of the stranger there
was no sign. Shrugging, he turned back. Old beggar?
Feebleminded vagrant? No. That had been no ordinary
man. All the time the stranger had crouched there, Gom
had sat, lacking the will—the power—to move. Those

cryptical things of which he'd spoken, the mysterious prophecy.

And that song: a strange ballad it had been, an ancient lay, a simple saga of tragic proportions. Gom sat down suddenly. King this, mountain that, the words had gone. Until the end, when he'd been looking straight at Gom.

Gorfid's Chimney is the crux over which YOU'LL kneel!

Gom drew up his knees, hugged them tightly. And all that about a hand no bigger than a child's bringing the mountain down! Gom brought up a hand, inspected it, hastily replaced it around his knees. This had been no chance encounter. "Just as if the old man had been waiting for me—but how could that be?" he muttered uneasily. The horses stirred, and shifted their feet.

"What, Gom?" Stormfleet said drowsily. "Still awake?"

Gom said nothing. Tomorrow, perhaps, under the light of day, when his mind was clear, he'd try to tell what had just happened. He lay down again, composed himself to sleep.

Keke's cries awoke him. He sat up, blinking, as she wheeled against a blood-shot sky. The sun was just about to rise.

"Cowards!" She came crossly to his shoulder. "Every last one of them! It looks as though I'll have to go in there after all."

Gom reached up and stroked her head, smoothing down her feathers. "You don't have to go anywhere. You can wait here with Stormfleet and Hevron."

"I'm not waiting here," Stormfleet snorted.

"Nor I," Hevron said.

"And if you think I'll stay here by myself, prey to any

who'd feast on one small marsh harrier," Keke cried, "then you are much mistaken!"

Gom shrugged helplessly. "All right. We'll go together through these hills, and then we'll see."

"That we shall," Keke said. "The other side is the marsh, just my sort of place if it weren't for those evil folk."

"What's it like?" Hevron said.

"Low ridges, scarcely bigger than the furrows in a field. A flooded field, for most of it is under water."

"Any shelter?"

"A few runty bushes on the ridges, not enough to hide you far. And it's very misty out over the fen. You'd likely get lost, for it all looks the same. I couldn't see the mountain. I didn't see much of anything else, either, until I was right on top of it."

"But could I move in from ridge to ridge?" Gom said. Hevron snuffled nervously. "I said *I*," Gom went on. "It sounds much too dangerous for four legs to walk."

"Or for two," Keke retorted. "Those ridges curl and curve about like a maze. It could take you hours to walk them, and you'd be terribly exposed. Anyone could come out of the mist—and every step you take might prove your last. There are safe paths, for I spotted a few men here and there, but I can't pick those paths out, Gom."

"Then how shall I reach the mountain?"

"Only by the official approach," Keke said. "The Causeway to the east. Even that is sunken in places. But it's the only possible way."

Causeway. Gom knuckled his face thoughtfully. A road into Sundborg. Safe—but exposed. How would he travel it? He picked up his things, ready to move on. There was only one way to find out.

                                    *   *   *

It was midafternoon when they crested the hills and
looked down on muddy waste receding into marsh gas.
Keke had described it well: scrubby ridges writhing like
fat maggots over a wide expanse of reed and water. Somewhere in there, invisible through the gray, rose Sundborg,
King Galt's mountain fortress. Gom sighed. Keke was
right. He couldn't guess which direction to take.

"Ke-ke-ke-ke!" Keke sounded warning as a large dark
shadow circled overhead. A huge carrion bird, sweeping
in to see. Gom looked up warily, thinking of the skull-
bird, but Keke only gave it a shrill good day.

"Well?" Hevron said.

Stormfleet sniffed the air. "It smells bad. What do you
think?"

"Come on," said Gom. "Let's find that Causeway."

They turned eastward, keeping to the marsh's hill
boundary, reaching the Causeway in late twilight. Even
as Gom surveyed that uncertain cobbled path, a noisy
band of horsemen galloped by toward the distant fortress,
vanishing into the mist.

"How far?" Gom asked the harrier.

"Hours, for one on foot," she said. "It winds, and it
dips. You'd have to go slow if you'd not wander off into
the marsh."

Stormfleet pricked his ears. "Many slow hooves, coming this way."

"And wheels," Hevron said. "Big ones."

Keke flew up into the air. "A caravan!" she shrieked.
"Mules, and wagons, a whole line of them!"

Out of the hills they came, about fifty supply wagons,
led or driven by a band of tired-looking men. One by

one, the carts rumbled past, their wheels bumping off grass and onto cobbles.

"Hrrrum," Hevron snuffled softly. "Looks as though King Galt is preparing for a siege."

Gom took off his cloak, and stuffed it in his pocket. "Keke—watch for me tomorrow. And you two—will you wait here?"

"What will you do?" Stormfleet said.

"If all goes well," Gom slung his staff and moved after the last wagon, "I'll be going into Sundborg in broad daylight—at the back end of a bag of salt!"

Stormfleet reared his head. "Remember what happened the last time you took a ride in someone else's food cart?"

"Why, yes." Gom looked back, grinning. "I bumped into a horse!"

Chapter Seventeen

GOM SAT braced for sign of trouble. He felt for the crystal under his shirt, wishing it were the starstone. This evil king seemed to possess so much power, even against Ulm's highest wizards. Such a critical time for Ulm, standing in twofold peril! A powerful stone at risk, and, for the first time in living memory, strife was stirring folk to war. War was one of Katak's aims on Ulm, short of finding the stargate. If this battle were not stopped, it would be a great victory for the Spohr. With the Lakelands in disarray, Galt could at his leisure plunder the cities; murdering, destroying, seizing countless wealth at his master's bidding. Gom fingered his stone. This was all he had: a few simple spells stored up, and a mind as yet unschooled.

The slow miles passed, and Gom grew drowsy, lulled by the swaying of the wagon. Just before dawn, a shout aroused him, and a loud clanging, then the clatter of many feet over the cobbles brought him fully awake. Gom reached for his crystal, to pull his spell of invisibility. No time! The sounds of shifting bales and boxes came from all around him. He raised the flap and peeped out. They were in a sort of forecourt, a widening of the Causeway at Sundborg's gate. Above, in the darkness, a row of sharp spikes pointed down: a raised portcullis. Men swarmed about, heaving, pulling out bales and barrels, rolling them up a ramp under the mountain arch.

"Hey, you! Come here!"

Gom ducked back inside the wagon, his heart thudding. Stormfleet had warned him. He unslung his staff and held it tightly, poised for challenge.

"Hey—come on out, you lazy good for nothing. Hold this lantern, unless you want a whipping!"

Gom slung his staff, and slid down over the tail of the wagon. A thin, stooped man in a spattered butcher's smock shoved a lantern into his hand. "You cooks' scum, you're all alike: idle, free-loading sons of no-good—" The man's curses were cut off as a soldier shoved them both aside to make way for a cart stacked with barrels. Gom dodged back, swinging his lantern, into the general turmoil. He blended well with the crowd of tattered ragamuffins, kitchen boys with lanterns. Going with the flow, Gom walked slowly, holding the lantern high, under the portcullis, past guards with deadly pikes, lighting the way as men rolled barrels of salted fish up the ramp, through an outer hall smelling of mold and mildew, and down into a vast smoke-filled cavern so high he couldn't see the roof.

King Galt's kitchen.

Gom ditched his lantern, and, unslinging his staff, took refuge behind a pile of crates. There he stayed, crouching, until the bustle subsided and the unloading was over, safely inside Galt's stronghold—by his wits alone with his magic store intact!

Gom could not stay there long. From their temporary spot at the foot of the steps, the goods were now being shifted into nearby pantries. In a matter of minutes, men would come for the crates and he would be exposed.

Quick, he must bring on the hum, make himself unseen. He retreated to the back of the pile, took out his crystal. The sounds of the kitchen retreated, then surged anew, breaking his concentration. Bringing on the hum was all very well on Harga's island, but here, in this unfamiliar place—Gom tried again. Sounds of shifting feet drew nearer. Only moments left. Relax, he told himself. Relax, let your mind go. . . .

It was not easy, when common sense told him to do the opposite, to stay alert, poised to run. Gom gazed at the crystal, watched it shift and change, watched the secret cavities open to his inner vision, tiny spaces filled with sparks and specks of different colored light. Swiftly he sought, and found, the one he needed, pulled it out, stretched it, and let it fall.

Burly hands lifted the last crates, and there Gom crouched, in full sight. He waited, not daring to breathe.

"Come on, Han. Last one, heave ho."

"Heave ho yourself. My back's fit to breaking!"

Grunting, one of the men hefted the crate and carried it away.

Gom let out his breath. The spell had worked—but for how long he could not tell. Dodging busy kitchen hands and cooks' boys, he crept to the stairs and was just starting up when a loud bell clanged. Gom shrank against the stair wall as men stampeded past, streaming up to the floor above. Gom followed them up the steps and crossed to the far side of the dim front hall. The portcullis was down now, Gom saw, as he walked with the men into a big, round hall lit by smoky torches. To its rear was a dais. On the dais was a throne: empty.

Gom dodged back just inside the door, feeling exposed.

It was difficult to remember that he was invisible. Every moment, as he caught a man's eye, he expected the man to cry out and seize him.

A sudden silence fell. The crowd parted, leaving a pathway to the dais.

King Galt had arrived.

The king paused in the archway, barely an arm's length from Gom, a middling man: middling high, middling wide, middling face—save for the expression. Catching it full on as the king's gaze swept the crowded chamber, Gom prayed he might never stand in plain sight of that corrupt and wasted face.

Flanked by guards, others bringing up the rear, Galt stalked down the hall and mounted the dais. There, he sat upon the throne—a wooden, high-backed seat crowned with gold finials comprising the heads of fabulous beasts; strange monsters, whose contorted bodies, carved out of the chair's wooden pillars, groaned under the king's weight.

Galt looked out over the gathering. "This very day," he said, his voice ringing harshly through the hall, "do the fat fowl waddle to the slaughter. Not an hour ago, the Lake armies finished crossing the Wilds. By dawn tomorrow, they'll reach our border; come for what they claim is theirs." He raised his hand and from it dangled bright green fire.

Gom stepped from the wall. There it was, the thing that he had come for: Herelys, the Lake Lord's emerald Seal.

A great shout split the air, overlaid by another, and another. The king raised his hand for silence. "They shall not have it, and we have nothing to fear, for the power in this stone is mine, and therefore must we prevail! So we shall let the plump tame fowl walk the Causeway, even to our door. Then you and I shall pluck their fancy plumes! So now go eat and drink, and tomorrow shall I call you to untold plunder!"

The king stood, walked out amid more tumultuous cheering.

Gom waited while the royal retinue passed, then he followed, going up three levels more to a hallway lit by slits of daylight in sloping mountain wall that must be near the top of the peak, as Gom would guess.

The king strode down the hallway between ranks of guards, and through into a high chamber alone, shutting the door behind him. Gom followed, squeezing through just in time. The chamber was sumptuous, hung with embroidered panels and overstuffed with finely carved furniture—all booty, doubtless. Galt crossed through into a smaller, inner room, no less sumptuous, this time leaving the door ajar. By the time Gom caught up, the king was standing before an open vault set waist-high in the wall—a large, square hole crammed with gemstones. Even as Gom watched, the king took Leochtor's emerald Seal from around his neck, and laid it with the rest of his hoard. Then he shut the vault door, locked it with a great key, and hung the key at his belt.

Gathering his courage, Gom bent close to inspect the key's clasp—and found it embossed with a skull! He stepped back with a hiss of indrawn breath, froze at the king's sharp glance.

"Master?" Galt's soft call was almost fearful.

Gom held still. If the king reached out, they'd touch.

"Master, is that you?" Galt cocked his head to one side, as though listening. Then he cleared his throat loudly, smoothed down his tunic. "The stone is here, Master, all ready for you." Galt waited, then, after a moment, when nothing happened, he relaxed, and walked away down the room, muttering.

Master . . . waiting . . . Katak—expected here! Gom's worst fears were realized!

Gom moved to the wall vault, tried the door. Solid iron. He felt for his crystal. He had the power to open it. But . . . was this the time, with Galt right there? Dare he wait? He must, if he wanted to get away alive.

A tap came at the door.

The king turned. "Open!"

Three men stood there. "Majesty."

"Come in! Come in! The scouts are back?"

One man bowed. "Sire."

"Good. And our captives: how do they?"

The man bowed. "Sire, one has taken to bed. They say he may die."

Galt laughed. "Die? Surely they mistake, Wural."

Wural bowed his head. "Majesty, the captives demand to speak with you."

"Tomorrow. Oh, yes, then shall we speak indeed!" The king rubbed his hands together. "Now where are the scouts' reports?"

The three men bowed Galt through into the other chamber, partly closing the door behind them.

Captives? One dying? Poor, miserable wretch! Gom crept to the door, peeped through. The four were seated around a table, deep in talk. The Seal must wait. He crept across the room, and out.

The four levels above ground, Gom found, descended in order of magnificence. At the top were the king's chambers, next came two floors of staterooms, even whole apartments for folk of rank. Then came the ground floor with the general assembly halls and front gate.

No captives.

Gom moved down.

The first level below ground, as Gom had already discovered, was the kitchen level. Behind the kitchen, many rooms stretched back into the mountain: servants' quarters, larders, stock rooms. Still no captives.

Gom, ravenous, helped himself to bread and cheese and moved on.

Below the kitchen were cellars, cavern after cavern stacked with barrels of ale, and wine, and cider, some caskets big as a shed. He helped himself to a cup of cider, downed it in one draft, and moved on. Off the main cavern were more steps going down, badly lit. Gom trod carefully, testing loose slabs, the air getting colder, and smelling of mold. Moisture gleamed on the walls, and half the torches, long spent, rotted in their sconces. Gom paused near the foot of the stair. Ill-lit tunnels, branching like fingers, ran off into shadow. He reached for the bottom step, slipped on slime, and scraped the toe of his boot.

Some way down the third tunnel from the left, a shadow moved, separating from the deeper shadow beyond. "Who goes there?"

A guard. Gom held his breath. The man strode to the foot of the stair, and stood beside Gom, listening. Then, with a muttered oath, he started up the steps, head cocked, pike raised.

How long until he was back? Gom surveyed the tunnels in front of him. Five, and only one guarded. He moved forward slowly, cautiously, in the direction from which the guard had come.

To either hand lay deep alcoves, their openings barred. Cells, all empty, except—Gom slowed—for the one he'd just reached. He peered through the bars, counted half a dozen figures in there, one of them lying down.

The dying captive. Gom stood, at a loss. He'd come to help, but how to get inside the cell unobserved?

A slight tremor ran through him, a sort of shimmer. The spell—it was spent! He was standing now in plain sight! He ran, pulling Vala's cloak from his pocket, throwing it on. If he could but reach the foot of the stair unobserved, he could maybe hide in one of the other tunnels. A good idea, but as he reached the meeting of the ways, the guard, on his way down again, rounded the bend in the stair.

Gom swerved sharply right and took off, cloak flapping, down the endmost passage, away from shouts and the sound of running feet. That cloak had not been a good idea after all, for it got between his knees, hindering him. He ran on through the dark, drawing ahead. He was getting away! He was just congratulating himself, when he fetched up smack against a blank wall. He felt around but found no opening, not even a crack. The sound of heavy boots grew louder, and torchlight shone as his pursuer rounded the last bend.

Grasping his staff in both hands, he turned and stood at bay.

Chapter Eighteen

HE LASHED out, but the guard, stepping aside, put the pike to Gom's throat. "Young varmint—haven't you lot been told to keep upstairs, eh? Get a pike in your gizzard, won't have time to wish you'd minded orders."

Gom lowered his staff. Why, the man thought him a kitchen boy, bent on mischief. The guard marched him to the foot of the stair, pointed his pike upward. "You tell your friends I'll skewer the next one as sneaks down here—all ready for the spit, got it? Now . . . off!"

Gom started up the stair.

"Wait a minnit." The guard grabbed Gom's shoulder, pulled him back. "What's that you're wearing? Here, let's have a look." The man hauled Gom over to the nearest torch, and turned him about. "That's one of them shimmery cloaks, like what—" The guard glanced back to the occupied cell. "Where did you get that thing, you thieving little—? Hey"—the man peered into Gom's face—"you wouldn't be one of 'em, would you? Come on, let's see."

The guard began to drag Gom back down to the cells, but Gom, pulling free, made once more for the stair—only to find it blocked by a monstrous man in a long robe, a swatch of keys clinking at his belt. The man caught Gom's arm, held on until the guard reached them.

"Well, well, what have we 'ere? Another customer?" The jailor thrust his face into Gom's. "Where shall I put 'im?"

"Anywhere you like, Scudgeon. Me, I better go and tell his nibs."

"You'll tell 'im nothin' now, if you value your life. He's parleying." Scudgeon rubbed his scalp. "Now let's see . . ." He looked along the rows of dark cells.

"Put him with them others," the guard suggested. "Where he belongs."

Scudgeon nodded, his jowls wobbling. "Hey, then, come on, lad. Join the merry throng." He led the way back up the tunnel, stopping before the occupied cell.

At their approach, one of the captives came forward.

"Back, back, or you'll get nowhere." Scudgeon waving a hand, stuck a heavy key into the cell door, turned it, and pushed. The door swung out.

"But have you—"

The guard thrust Gom inside, and stood, pike cocked, while Scudgeon relocked the door, shaking his head in dismissal. "The king 'as got your message, now it's up to 'im."

The guard and Scudgeon walked away.

Gom stood, his back against the cell bars, peering through the gloom. There had been something about that voice . . .

The captives eyed him, silently. Then the spokesman stepped forward. "Gom Gobblechuck," he said. "If you don't turn up in the oddest places!"

"Feyrwarl?"

"What are you doing here?"

"I might ask the same of you, Gom." The Yul Kinta

· 190 ·

gestured behind him. "A party of us were on our way to Pen'langoth with a pledge of Urolf's support against Sundor. They took us by surprise."

Yul Kinta, taken by surprise? Collecting himself, Gom peered around him. "One of you is hurt."

Feyrwarl turned to the figure lying by the back wall. "Thrulvar. He's lost blood. Vala has sustained him for days. She can do no more."

"The Lady Vala—here?"

Vala came forward, took Gom's hand. "Oh, my dear." She lifted the hem of his cloak. "Much good my gift has done you. About as much good as Urolf's gift has done my Lord Leochtor. Ironic, is it not, that the very stone intended to ensure peace now rallies the Lakes to war? These are dark days."

"And getting darker," Gom said grimly. He took off the cloak and stuffed it back in his pocket. "Leochtor's army arrives tomorrow—and the way I hear it, the lakemen do not stand a chance!" He moved to Thrulvar's cot and knelt beside him. The Yul Kinta was covered in blood, still seeping in places, the seepage plugged, ineffectively, with torn up cloaks. Gom felt Thrulvar's brow. Cold as death. He bent down, listened to the chest, measuring the heartbeat. The Yul Kinta was almost spent.

Gom thought back through the healing spells stored in his crystal. One to staunch blood, and another to restore it. Would they be strong enough? He pulled the staunching spell, sent power plug by plug to seal the seeping wounds. There were eight gashes in all. With his inner sight he saw them plainly, like rivers on a map, and one stab wound that the Yul Kinta had not discovered. For this ninth wound, a deep and ugly puncture that was badly festering, Gom sought, and found, a green-blue light, pointed it like a needle and thrust it down into the wound, drawing out the poison, which welled out, staining Thrulvar's tunic. Gom probed again, until the wound was clean. He closed it, and soothed the heat. Only then did he bring out the clear red light and direct it to Thrulvar's throat to rouse his pulse and restore his blood flow. It was over.

Gom came up, exhausted.

Feyrwarl helped him to a second cot, where he sat, bent over. Making those spells was tiring enough, and the practice of divesting them. But it was nothing compared with discharging them for real!

Feyrwarl held out a flask. "Here, taste the waters of Aelyth-Kintalyn."

Gom took a swallow, felt it go down. Spring water, cold, bubbly, pricking his mouth, his throat. His spirit rising, he sat up.

"I thank you, Gom," Feyrwarl said. "Thrulvar would, if he could."

"I'm sure," Gom said dryly, and they exchanged looks, recalling how unkindly Thrulvar had treated him.

Vala came to sit beside Gom. "Whatever was between you and our people is over," she said. "If ever Urolf learns what you did today, you'll have his undying friendship."

Gom cocked his head. "And a cito?"

She smiled. "He'd make you gift of it himself. Of all his male blood kin, Urolf loves only Feyrwarl better."

"Ummm," Gom said, feeling stronger by the minute. "Maybe I'll put that to the test one day."

Vala laughed softly. "I wouldn't be surprised. But

what are you doing here, Master Gom? Where's Maister Folgan?"

"We . . . parted company. I've been learning magic at my mother's house."

"Ah." Vala met his eyes. She knew, her look said: Harga was still away; he worked alone. She went on in a low voice. "You have come far in such a short time. No one in the Hierarchy could have done better."

"Thank you. They were simple spells."

"I'm sure. But you plied them as a full-fledged mage."

He looked at her sharply: no, she was not mocking him. "I'm slow, I have to stop and think each time," he murmured.

"Gom, I've watched mages of twenty years or more who lack your skill." She smiled. "Your mother will be proud." Her eyes clouded. "She would not let this happen, if she were by. What would she say to know that you are here, I wonder?"

Gom held his tongue.

"Your pardon, Gom. I must treat you as the mage you are."

"Not for two and some years more," he said.

"And yet you keep a wizard's rune. May I?"

Gom followed her gaze, realized he still held his crystal. Slowly, he uncurled his hand.

Vala took it, turned it over, then gravely handed it back. "A fine stone," she said. "I have never seen the like."

"Harga gave it to me," he said proudly, slipping it back under his shirt. "The flake I found myself."

"Ah, yes, the gold. But the crystal, it is rare. Tell me, you still haven't said how you came to be here."

A dozen tales came to mind; glib, easy. But looking into Vala's face, Gom could tell only the truth. "I heard about the Seal. I'd give anything to get it back and stop this war." How grandiose he sounded.

Vala did not smile. "You're clever, and brave too," she said. "A true son of your mother. She'd never stand to see the carnage that will surely be tomorrow."

"No," Gom whispered fiercely. "There won't be war, there has to be a way to stop it. Surely you—"

Vala shook her head. "I have tried to bend Galt's will, but something prevents me."

Gom nodded grimly. Katak was near, he felt it as one feels the air charge before a thunderstorm. "What do you know of this place? Is there a curse upon it?"

"Oh, yes." Vala shot him a look. "And if I had the power, I'd pull that curse this very day."

"So there is truth behind the old man's words."

"Old man? What old man?"

"I met him in the hills."

"You did?" Vala's eyes gleamed. "What did he look like?"

"Tall, thin. Straight. At first, I thought him feeble-minded, but then I got to thinking he knew me, that he'd, well, he'd been waiting for me." Gom shifted uncomfortably. "He sang a song, 'Gorfid's Lay,' he called it. About how one day the mountain will be destroyed and—" He stopped short. Destroyer, the old man had called him. "He said it has begun!"

"How, Gom?" Vala took his hands. "Tell me exactly what he said, from the beginning, leaving nothing out."

Gom told her everything, including the words of the

Lay, word for word. "What is this Bung, and how will its removal bring the mountain down?"

Vala sighed. "As the Lay said, this mountain was called Marshaven, and it really was a refuge for travelers, and home to many wild creatures, large and small. Gorfid's folk were *Kila:* human, for the most part, with what you might call a goodly pinch of saltwater." She smiled. "You may know that under this mountain and the marsh that surrounds it lies an inland sea, joined to the oceans by currents so deep man has never fathomed them."

Gom nodded. He knew, but he listened, mindful of Katak's slow seepage.

"In fact, there is so much water beneath the mountain you might wonder how the peak holds up at all. Well, underneath it is a hollow pillar, going straight down. Here, let me show you." Taking up a chip of stone from the floor, Vala scratched a map on the wall behind them.

SUNDBORG

drawn from Vala's diagram

"Gorfid's Chimney, they called it," Vala went on. "The base of the mountain perches on this column, like a seedpod on a hollow stalk, see?" She pointed. "Inside the pod is air; outside, below the level of the marsh, is the inland sea, pressing against the pod, seeking to break in."

"How is the water kept out? Oh!" Now Gom saw the significance of the Bung. "Gorfid drained the lower levels of the mountain, and somehow sealed the waters out."

Vala nodded. "When Gorfid settled this place, the lower levels of the mountain, as you've guessed, were flooded. He spent ages stopping up leaks in the mountain's walls, and draining it, until these three levels below the Great Gate were added to his domain."

"And somewhere down there," Gom murmured, pointing at the tangle of tunnels below the dungeon level, "is the one keystone that could break open the mountain and let the waters back in—the Bung." He frowned. "You spoke of three levels below ground. But this lowest one makes four."

"True. They call it Under. In the beginning, it was left open, but after all the levels were excavated and the mountain shell was made secure, Gorfid saw that it was too unhealthy for use—and dangerous, with children about. So he had it sealed."

"The Lay mentions water running inside the mountain. How, if Gorfid stopped all the leaks?"

"Gorfid left just one small jetstream in to wash away the mountain's waste. Anyway, all went well for many years until the day Galt's ancestor rode up. He sacked the place, massacred the Kila, and threw their bodies into the fen, making way for his own brood. The first to die was Gorfid himself, forced to walk into the fen before his people. Since then, as you know, marsh and mountain have been nothing but a source of evil, the stronghold of the robber kings. And so it looked to stay so, except for one thing: Gorfid laid a curse upon Galt's line. So great would the weight of evil become, so Gorfid said, that the mountain would sink beneath the mire. And now I hear the song, I see how this would be. Say the words again, Gom, slowly."

Gom did so, and this time he saw more clearly than ever the sense of the words. "So if the Bung were found and removed, the mountain wall would cave in and the sea would flood the mountain with force enough to snap it from its stem. Then the combined weight of stone and water would be too much for the marsh to sustain."

And now at last that hour doth come, the evil king must drown;
The hand no bigger than a child's must bring the mountain down!

"If only someone could get down there and pull the plug before the battle—there might not be one after all." Gom raised his hand, held it palm-up between them.

Their gaze met, and Gom saw the hope in Vala's eyes. Then, sighing, she looked down, and reaching for his hand, closed her own over it. "Gom, the risk is so great. I could not let you!"

He shrugged. "Sounds simple enough."

"Simple—and impossible."

"Yet I would try," he said.

Chapter Nineteen

"**G**ET YOU out of here, Gom? If that were possible, we'd all be off!"

"Feyrwarl, he's serious." Vala turned to Gom. "We cannot hope to get away, not with Thrulvar, not through that Gate. But we can help create a diversion to let you out of this cell. Have you anything in mind?"

"Agarax." Gom pulled out his little box, opened it. "Dream-sand."

Feyrwarl frowned. "What of us? How would we avoid its fumes?"

Sighing, Gom put the box away and took out his crystal. "I have a spell to break the lock. The only problem is—"

"—the guard outside. He'll be onto you before you take one step."

"Then I'll have to use something else." Gom held up his stone. "Light, that's it."

"To do what, Gom? What would you do if you got out of here?"

"Find Gorfid's Bung and let the waters in."

Feyrwarl looked to Vala, then back to Gom. "They'll surely catch you!"

"Not a second time."

"But how would you even find Under? This place is a maze of tunnels."

Gom nodded. "And this one slopes down."

"To another dead end, likely."

"Not this one."

"How do you know?"

"The way you know the forest."

Feyrwarl nodded. "Do you really think you'll find the Bung?"

"I've an idea how."

"How?"

Gom smiled. "By putting one foot in front of the other," he said. But he was thinking of the Lay.

Gorfid's Chimney is the crux over which you'll kneel;
Trace the Waters to the Bung, foul Sundborg's taint to heal!

If Vala spoke true, only one stream flowed beneath that mountain, and that must empty out down Gorfid's Chimney. So find the Chimney, and he'd find the stream. Then he had only to trace the watercourse back to where it flowed through the mountain wall and there would be the Bung. According to the Lay.

"It is a dangerous place," Feyrwarl was saying. "Men shunned it even in Gorfid's time."

"Good," Gom smiled. "Then I won't have any guards on my heels."

"If you do find Gorfid's Bung and pull it—who can guess the force of that flood? How will you escape it?"

"How will any of us?" Vala said quietly.

Feyrwarl folded his arms. "I go with you, Gom."

"Thanks," Gom said, shaking his head, "but you might prove more—"

"—hindrance than help." Feyrwarl sighed. "Oh, well. I don't like it, but I'll allow that things don't look promising for any of us as they are." He went to the bars, peered toward the stair, and came back. "Soon they'll bring what they're pleased to call food. There'll be that jailor fellow, two guards, and a couple of kitchen hands with trays. What would you have us do?"

An hour later, there was a clank of keys and a clatter of dishes.

"Now," Feyrwarl whispered.

Gom unslung his staff, grasped it in his left hand, took the crystal in his right. Vala went to sit by Thrulvar, while the other four Yul Kinta moved to form a solid line inside the cell gate with Gom behind them, concealed.

Scudgeon appeared, key in hand, the rest following: two guards, two menials with heavy trays, just as Feyrwarl had said. As the man stuck the key into the lock, Gom readied himself, weighing the crystal, picturing the light stored in there, waiting to flash forth. Steady . . . steady . . . Gom braced himself.

"Hey—give way!" One of the guards was jabbing his pike through the cell bars. "Or them trays goes back upstairs!"

Gom's hand tightened on the stone. He could feel Vala's gaze on him, the power of her goodwill. Hefting his staff, he caught the wooden sparrow's eye. Strength surged through him, and a sort of fearful excitement. He of the sparrow and the bear: how could he fail!

The Yul Kinta retreated a pace or two, and the gate groaned outward until a wedge of space appeared; open, inviting. "Now!" Gom raised his hand.

The Yul Kinta charged through, ramming the cell door back against the wall, knocking the kitchen hands off-balance. The men staggered, the trays crashed to the floor. The guards cried out and raised their pikes to strike, and in that moment, Gom pulled a charge of light.

A flash exploded in that narrow space. And in that brilliant instant, Gom, inspired, willed the spreading light into a tight ball and sent it flying toward the stairs.

Stunned, their captors turned to watch. Then someone shouted, and suddenly, all was confusion, Yul Kinta and Sundor men one struggling mass. Alarms sounded, and feet pounded down the dungeon stairs.

Gom fled, away from the light and the noise, the clatter of his boots unheard in the commotion. He turned the corner: no more torches here. He rounded a second bend, then a third. The noise behind him was a distant echo. If any would follow him, it would not be for a while. He stopped, leaned against the wall, his breath coming loud in the dark, damp, quiet. The Yul Kinta would not get far, probably not even to the foot of the dungeon stair. But they had gotten him free. Gom hoped that Galt would not punish them for their abortive escape. . . . Such courage they'd shown on his behalf! If he did start that flood—he must be sure to free them on his way back.

Having gotten his breath, Gom came off the wall, and cocked his head, listening. No more headlong flight: now he must move slowly, cautiously, using all his senses. He started off again, trailing his fingers along the wall. Which way? Which way for the hole that would lead him Under?

Sessery? His old friend from Windy Mountain who had taught him most of what he knew about going underground.

"Good-bye, Sessery, I shan't forget you," he'd said,

taking his farewell of home. *I know you won't,* had come her mocking reply. *Wherever you go there'll be a relative of mine and that will be me. . . .*

And thus had Sessery—or her cousin—come to him under the Far Fjords. Would she answer him here? He called again.

Sessery?

Light fingers of air tickled his cheek. *MMmmmmm . . . ? Who is this that knows my name, and dares to trespass about my upper halls?*

Gom Gobblechuck of Windy Mountain greets you, and begs leave to visit your domain.

Ho, you do? She whisked away down the passage, away from him, then came back. *For why?*

Gom hesitated. To flood the mountain and destroy your spaces, was the truth, but say that and Sessery surely would abandon him, leave him to find the way alone.

She laughed. *You think I do not know? I have been expecting you, you little quick thing. Or something like you. The Old One is back, and you're the one to find that stopper, aren't you? Well, I shan't help you: he'll have to guide you himself.* She coiled into a small whirlwind, then shot off.

Sessery! Sessery . . . please?

Silence. Somewhere in the dark, condensation plop-plopped into a pool.

Gom waited, but she did not return. With a sigh, he moved on.

For some hours, Gom traveled the tunnels, until he realized that he was going steadily down—just as though someone were pulling him.

. . . he'll have to guide you himself . . .

Gorfid, certainly. That was who had sung to him out

there. And now the old king—or his shade—was drawing him steadily in the right direction. Gom picked up his pace a little, not too much, for one did not rush headlong into unknown dark and stay alive. Every now and then he stopped to test for sound, until, presently, the echoes changed: a gap in the tunnel, ahead, to his left. He edged forward, his fingers tracing the wall until cold hit his face; icy, wet. The doorway to Under. It had been sealed, Vala said. Now it was unlocked, and waiting. Gom paused. Above lay the world of light and air. Up there, Stormfleet and Hevron and Keke awaited his call. Beyond them, near the edge of the marsh, the Lakeland armies massed for battle.

Below lay . . . Gom took a breath of clammy air. He had a sudden urge to turn and run, back into the light of day.

Agh, there was no turning back now. He slung his staff, squared his shoulders and stepped through the gap. There, he took his bearings. More tunnel, going down. Same stone, same rough walls, and yet . . . The upside world felt farther away with every step he took. Gom moved on, inching along wet rock face. Moisture dripped and trickled under his fingers, up his sleeve, to his elbow. The tunnel opened out into a cave. Where now? Gom wondered, but he already knew, for someone was guiding him still, pulling him, almost.

"Gorfid?" he whispered. There was no answer.

He crossed the cave to the other side, where the tunnel continued narrower and lower. Gom walked almost bent double now, his head barely scraping the tunnel roof, then, abruptly, so abruptly that had Gom not been used to going under mountain he might have fallen headlong, the floor ended on a stair. His heart pounding, Gom paused, trying to recall Vala's hasty drawing. He tested the first step with the toe of his boot. Solid—barely. He felt to either side, encountered empty air.

"Gorfid?"

Again, no reply, but he felt the pull inside him getting stronger.

Gom started down.

The steps, treacherously uneven, sometimes scarcely wider than his heel, wound around and down without wall, or guide, or rail of any kind. Like the crystal stair, Gom thought. Or the Onder's bridge. Only in reverse.

Down he went, crabwise now; one step, two, three . . . one hundred, two, three, a thousand . . .

The stairway ended as abruptly as it had begun. Had Gom not been feeling his way with such care, he'd have gone tumbling out into space—a space filled with spray, and a hissing and a roaring.

He ran his tongue over his lips.

Salt.

Gom backed up a step, lowered himself gingerly and knelt, clinging to the edge of the stair. "Gorfid? What now?"

The old voice came faintly over the tumult:

"Gorfid's Chimney is the crux over which you kneel:

Trace the waters to the Bung, foul Sundborg's taint to heal!"

Gorfid's Chimney. All at once Gom had the feeling of height rather than depth, as though he stood atop a high turret. He stood, pulled a light, set it on the tip of the crystal, then held it high. He found himself just inside a high, hollow column, a natural stone chimney, like a giant well. Above and behind him, the spiral stair twisted up into darkness. On his left, waters tumbled out of sight to join the inland sea far below. This must be the stream he was to follow back up to its source, Gom realized. Do that, and he'd find the Bung. He turned to retrace his steps up the stair, but as he did so, a coldness wafted across his face, keener than the air, and the icy salt spray. With that coldness, a feeling stole over him: a want, a need, a *compulsion* to go not up, but down.

As in a dream he turned back, and raised a foot to step out into space.

Gorfid's voice shouted in his ear. "No! You have come as far as you should! This is the Crux! Do you not hear the waters that you must follow back upward? Listen: shut your mind to the Other! It is evil that draws you to the depths! Back! Go back!"

Other? Evil? To the depths? Gom shook his head, confused. "Who, who draws me down?"

An image came into his mind, faint and far, but growing sharper and clearer with every breath. Katak! Gom teetered on the edge, lost his balance, and fell out, over the abyss.

Chapter Twenty

GOM CLUTCHED at the last step and hung on, while the waters twisted and thundered down. . . .

Let go, a voice within him urged. Gom's head spun, his heart leapt with fear. His fingers lessened their hold. Then over the cold insistence came Gorfid's voice: "Back, back, or all is lost and evil reigns forever!"

Sweat pricked Gom's brow. He tightened his grip, and flailed his legs wildly. Then with great effort, he pulled himself up, scraping his body over the stone sill. There he sat, on that bottom step, while strength returned, enough to get him back up that deadly spiral. The power of Katak! Had it not been for Gorfid, had Katak been that much nearer . . .

He thought of Ganash, wondered if the kundalara was down there in the sea beneath the fen, roiling around in the cold currents, striving to block Katak's path. Time, Gom thought. If Ganash could only win him time.

Trace the Waters to the Bung . . .

Gom climbed to the top of the stair, listening to the distant sound of water. He must find it again, higher up. For hours he walked the tunnels, striking out, doubling back, while the sound of rushing waters drew closer. Up above, it surely must be night. The eve of battle.

Gom came to a stop. How long since he had eaten?

He felt in his pockets, found a remnant of cheese. It was stale now, and sweaty. Better than nothing. He bit into it, made a face. He thought of the Lakelanders camped on the edge of the fen. They'd have fires, likely, to warm their hands and cook a hearty supper. Would Carrick be there? The tinker was brave, and liked Leochtor well. Gom's mouth tightened. If it came to battle, then Carrick's good and honest blood would spill! Gom swallowed the last of the cheese and moved on, his mouth tasting bitter.

For hours more, he traveled the twisting tunnels, tracking the sound of the current until, at last, the rush of running water broke clear upon him: the stream was flowing by his feet. Gom followed the stream until the tunnel ended and he could stand straight. Beside him, water fell from way up. Gom pulled a light to the tip of his crystal and looked around. Directly ahead rose a massive wall, great stones laid in rows, smaller ones wedged neatly in between. Behind that wall surged the waters below the marsh, seeking entrance.

Gom gazed up in awe. How many hands over how many ages had it taken to accomplish such a feat? He went to the rock face, and, raising his crystal, peered into the heights. Fifty feet up, as far as Gom could see. And about ten feet from side to side. Somewhere in that wall, according to Gorfid's song, was the Bung: the one small stone which, when dislodged, would bring the whole mass caving in, then an avalanche of water to sink the mountain. Gom edged back. Beside those massive stones, he felt small and fragile.

Gom moved back some more. So many large rocks, so

many little stones wedged in between. How would he ever find the one? He raised the light.

"Gorfid?"

Something caught his eye: to the left, some thirty feet above him. He blinked, looked again, standing on tiptoe, his arm upstretched. A patch of shadow shaped like a man darkened the wall. As Gom watched, it grew tall, emaciated: Gorfid. Without a word, the king beckoned Gom to climb. Gom let his crystal go and started up the rock face. The climb was treacherous; the boulders, splashed by the torrent overhead, were slippery in places. Gom made his way carefully toward the spot where Gorfid hovered.

Almost there.

Gom glanced up. The king was leaning down, watching intently, his aged face ghastly above the crystal's glow, and the dark eyes a-glitter.

As Gom drew level with Gorfid, the king pointed to a narrow wedge of rock between two boulders. The Bung, at last. The moment Gom saw it, the old man disappeared.

Left alone, Gom surveyed the wedge. From close up, it was not as small as it had seemed. It would take both hands to pull it. Gom studied it soberly. It looked set in its bed. Too set to move? If not, as soon as Gom budged it, he'd surely be overwhelmed by tons of rock and rushing water!

Shutting off these fears, Gom pulled the light from his crystal and sent it spinning overhead. Then, slipping his stone inside his shirt, he put both hands to the Bung, and tugged. Nothing happened. He tried again.

The Bung was set in tight.

Gom rested, braced against the wall. His hands were not strong enough; the rock was tearing his fingers. Clinging to the rock face with one hand, he unslung his staff with the other and poked around. There, a space at the top of the Bung, just large enough to give him leverage. Gom rammed in the staff as far as it would go, and pushed upward. The Bung shifted—not much, but perhaps enough. Gom slung his staff again, and, seizing the Bung with both hands once more, he pulled.

Chapter Twenty-one

"**G**O, DESTROYER," the king cried in Gom's ear. "Quick, for the death of the mountain is begun!" In the light still spinning overhead, the old face looked anguished, and yet touched with a fierce joy. "You have taken, yet you have given, for the waters will cleanse the taint, destroy the ill. The peak shall rise again one day, and this land will once more be fair!" The king began to fade. "Hurry, I will . . . guide . . . you. . . ."

A waterspout hit Gom in the face, making him gasp. He slung his staff, then scrambled down the rock face, scraping himself on jutting wedges. The jet, arcing, falling, beat upon his head and shoulders, tore him from the rock and threw him to the floor. Gom struggled up, regained his balance, and fled, the water beating at his back. No listening now to echoes, or waiting for the feel of Sessery's light breath. The air was filled with the sound of crumbling rock as the inland sea pushed against the weakened dam wall.

Gom fled up through tunnel and stream, Gorfid's unseen presence, like an instinct, guiding him. He had not gone far when there came a loud boom, and the floor trembled. The dam, given way already? If so, the pent-up flood was even now hurling those giant boulders like flecks of foam. And that flood was about to overwhelm the little streamed, and roar on, to drown the deep spaces. Soon, the weight and force of the flood would tip the whole mountain. And then? Gom went faster. The mountain would break off from its hollow stem, and slide into the Deep.

Another shock shook the tunnel underfoot, and another hollow boom reverberated up through the tunnel behind him. Gom broke into a run, picturing the cleft that would lead him through into the dungeon level. Surely he was almost there? He took a quick breath and called aloud. "Oooooh-oh!" Yes, the echoes said, the cleft was but a dozen steps ahead!

Gom passed through into distinctly warmer air, then fled on through lightless galleries, up and up. The first flickering torch seemed bright as daylight after the long hours of total dark.

Turning the last corner, Gom looked along the dungeon passage to the stair. Empty. He ran forward, passing dungeons on either hand, toward the Yul Kinta cell. He found it empty, the door, wide open. Gom paused an instant, anxiously. Where had Galt taken them? The floor rumbled beneath him, speeding him on, up steps now reeking of wine and ale. The cellar floors were awash with it, spilled from great casks that, fallen from their cradles, lay smashed about the floor.

As Gom reached the kitchen stair, he heard the clamor of many voices. He ran up the steps, into noise and confusion; folk ran about excitedly, talking of earthquakes, unaware as yet what was really happening. Did they not know of the curse?

Gom paused. He'd come to get Leochtor's Seal and stop a massacre: but things had taken quite a different turn.

Katak was coming.

Gom recalled another time, another place. Ganash trapped beneath the Isle of Lorne, and Katak, using Zamul the conjuror, scavenging the kundalara's gemstone hoard.

He saw the evil king, standing before an open wall vault crammed with booty: a fortune in stones. That treasure would still be up there, in that vault, awaiting the king's return. If Katak should get hold of it all— the Seal and all the other stones, too—Gom started up.

The front hall was thronged with people, milling aimlessly about, arguing as to what to do. Gom pushed through toward the upper stair. If he would retrieve the treasure, he must go now. He was halfway to the stair when a really bad tremor shook the mountain. People screamed and ran, some to climb the king's stair. A shout from above, and a solid phalanx of pikes appeared, forcing the people back down. Gom halted in dismay. Galt had left his chamber guard behind: so many of them, crowding that spiral stair, that they stood shoulder to shoulder, disappearing up around the first bend. How on Ulm was he to get past them!

Gom pushed to the front of the crowd. The tip of a spear prodded his chest, prompting him back. He looked upward, over the sea of gleaming helmets going up around the stair. Even with the invisibility spell, he'd never squeeze through that solid mass! Another jolt, and the floor tilted slightly, setting off another wave of panic. What to do? He tried to think. Soon, no human would be able to get inside this place, not even Galt. And without human help, Katak could not retrieve those stones. So if Gom watched that Galt did not go back inside, then the treasure would be safely buried! And the emerald Seal? Another jolt tipped the floor and Gom was swept back with the crowd, out under the raised portcullis.

Gom moved down the ramp, and onto the Causeway, emerging under a low gray sky. Behind him rose Sundborg's low, bare peak; ahead stretched the fen. He gazed out over the Causeway to the dim horizon. Way out there, on the edge of the Marsh, the Lakelanders were already fighting to storm the mountain and take back the Lake Lord's stone. No sign of battle. Gom was not surprised. The only way in was by the Causeway. With no more room on it for more than four men to fight abreast, Galt's men could hold the lakemen back for a long time. Folk streamed past, fleeing out on foot. Forerunners of doom, Gom thought grimly, willing them to hurry. Their news would surely halt the war.

He was just about to follow, when a shrill cry sounded above.

"Keke!"

She circled overhead. "Stormfleet and Hevron are coming, see!"

On a ridge to his left, the bushes parted and his two friends emerged. Someone shouted. "Hey! Horses! Come on!" Two burly men ran past.

Gom sprinted, overtook them, and leapt astride Stormfleet's back just as the men came up. "Ride—ride!" The two horses struck out at a gallop, Keke wheeling urgently overhead.

Gom, settled into Stormfleet's stride, looked back, saw tiny figures way in the distance, well and truly left behind.

Stormfleet glanced around. "Glad to see us?"

"Hah! Very! When did you come? And how?"

"After you left us," Hevron called across, "things got . . . crowded."

"Crowded!" Keke cried. "Thousands rolled up. Lakemen. Yul Kinta. The place was packed with tents and fires and wagons. Soon as it got dark, we decided to move. And this was the only way we could go."

Not true—at least, for Keke. She could have flown away. But the little harrier had chosen to follow the horses in. It must have taken great courage on her part. "You mean, you walked the fen?"

"No." Hevron moved closer. "We trod the Causeway, dodging off whenever we heard folk coming. There was traffic all night, fen spies, taking the measure of Leochtor's camp. When we got to the mountain, we walked all over the mountain, then around the mountain, and around the mountain."

"And around again." Stormfleet snickered. "Until it began to shake. Then we got off, fast, and let Keke watch for you."

"I've had hardly a wink of sleep this past night and day!" Keke complained loudly. "Ever since sunup they've had me flying back and forth keeping an eye here and there."

"The battle's started?" Gom glanced up, the wind whipping his face.

"They've been at it since midmorning. Lakemen and Yul Kinta trying to advance along the Causeway, but it's impossible. Galt made quite a splash riding out from Sundor, feathers and flags and trumpets. He's just sitting back watching, and hurling insults—and threats. He's got a cage out there, with half a dozen folk inside—Yul Kinta. If Leochtor doesn't surrender by noon, the cage goes into the fen.

"Things are very tense. The Lakelanders won't back down. They were still fighting last I saw—if you can call it that. Galt's soldiers lure the lakemen off the Causeway and out into the marsh, then back off, leaving them to drown. The way it's going, there'll be no Lakeland army left come sundown!"

Gom listened grimly. The waste! "How much farther?"

Keke soared up, came back again. "Over the next rise!"

Even before that, Gom heard shouting and neighing, and the harsh clash of metal. Clearing the rise, they pulled up.

"The battleline," Keke cried. "See, ahead!"

Gom saw only bands of men all over; thick on the Causeway, spread over the ridges to either side. Then he saw the thickest of the throng, men pressed together hand to hand, purple colors of Sundor this side, blue and silver and green and primrose on the other—colors of the Lakelands and Aelyth-Kintalyn. Gom scanned the scene for sign of Leochtor and Urolf—and Galt. On a low, bushy ridge behind the Sundor battleline stood the cage Keke had described.

Gom dismounted. "Wait here." He left his friends standing, dodged from ridge to ridge, ducking, weaving, until he reached the cage. There, he edged forward, crouched behind a rear wheel.

"Feyrwarl!" he called, loudly as he dared. Peering up over the floor of the cage, he met Feyrwarl's startled gaze.

"Gom!" Feyrwarl looked back over his shoulder. "Vala—it's Gom!"

"I did it," Gom said. "The mountain is sinking."

"By all that's wonderful!" Feyrwarl broke into a smile. "Although you wouldn't guess it, from here."

"It'll take a while," Gom said, then bowed his head respectfully as Vala came into view.

"For the mountain to sink?" she said. "Or the news to come?"

"Maybe both, my lady," Gom said. "Folk are bringing the news, on foot. The word is spreading. With luck, the war could be over within the hour."

"Too late to save us, I'm afraid." Vala grasped the bars of the cage.

"Perhaps not." Gom crept forward, and, kneeling up, he inspected the padlock on the cage door. He felt for the crystal inside his shirt. "If I unlock the cage, can you get away?"

"Aye," Vala said. "If Feyrwarl would carry Thrulvar, we shall walk from this place, even through Sundor's battleline, and no fen man shall mark our passing."

"Then make ready." Gom shut his mind to the tumult around him, found the polarity spell stored within the crystal's spaces. He needed two points. He pulled one, directed it into the padlock. He pulled the second, then set it in the catch. "Step back, my lady."

Vala obeyed.

Gom charged the two points then reversed polarity on the catch. It snapped out of its hole and the padlock dangled from its loop. Gom snatched it off, and, after a quick glance around, slid the cage door aside.

One by one, the Yul Kinta stepped down, Feyrwarl last, bearing Thrulvar.

Vala looked back. "You're coming?"

Gom nodded. "I'll follow in a while." He could not leave that place until he was sure the treasure was out of Galt's reach.

Vala bowed her head gravely, and moved on. To Gom's astonishment, the Yul Kinta left the ridge and walked through the thick of Sundor's forces toward the body of Leochtor's army—and no one saw their passing, except him.

Gom sighed, watching after them. Well, they were saved, at least. He turned to go back to his friends. They must find a vantage spot from which to keep watch for Galt, in case the king tried to make a dash for the treasure.

"Hey—where's the prisoners?"

Three soldiers, guards, heading his way. Gom ducked. Heavy boots thudded onto the ridge and surrounded the cage.

"The lock's broke!"

"Broke? 'Ere, lemme see!" There came a loud oath, a chink of metal. "Spokin spikes! He'll kill us for this— go on! Git! It's nearly noon!"

"They've not gone nowhere, I've bin watchin all the time. There's only one place they can be!"

Three heads, helmeted, slid into view under the cage, three mouths hung open. "What's he doin here?"

Gom gripped his staff, but there was no room to strike. Hands dragged him out and stood him up beside the empty cage. Soldiers, in chain mail and purple colors, surrounded him, pikes cocked.

"Who're you?"

"Where did you come from?"

"Where's them Yool Kinty gone?" A pike tip prodded Gom's shirt, making a tear. "If you're the one what disappeared 'em, kiss your gizzard good-bye!"

Gom knocked away the pike. "You, too, when Galt hears what's happened!"

"Why, you—" cried one.

"He's right," another said. He put a hand on Gom's shoulder. "Listen, pipsqueak, tell us where they're gone, and we'll let you off."

Gom pointed, right through the middle of the fighting.

The soldier, enraged, leaned down, nose to nose. "You—you scummy varmint—making jest with us! We'll kill you right now!" The man drew back his pike to spear him through.

In the next moment, the soldier cried out and fell into the mud, pulling Gom with him. Gom looked up, and found the last person he expected to meet in that place and at that moment standing over him, light-sword shining in the gray murk. The Spinrathen warrior!

Gom opened his mouth to speak.

Save it! the warrior growled. Gom's captor lay still, staring blindly at the sky. The sword flashed again, in a curious circular motion over Gom's head, and the other two went down, like grass before a scythe. The warrior helped Gom up.

He stood gratefully, feeling the strength of the man's arm. No alamar warrior this time. This one was real. "How," Gom began.

Oh, shall we sit in the mud and have a reckoning? The warrior's plumes bobbed in the wind. *Look behind you!*

Through a gap in the fighting, Gom caught sight of Galt on a high gray, sword raised, looking angrily at the empty cage, a soldier before him, explaining, pointing. A word from Galt, and several others started Gom's way.

Gom thought fast. They could stand and fight, back

to back, sword and staff. He raised his head and shouted. "Stormfleet! Hevron! This way!" He turned to the warrior. "Follow me!"

He ran down from the ridge, leapt onto the neighboring one. The warrior followed, then checked. *I will not flee a fight!*

"Who said anything about fleeing!" Gom retorted. "You'll do better on a horse."

Horse? The warrior turned about to face the oncoming detail. *What horse?*

"That one!" Gom cried. "Hevron, here!"

His two friends were picking their steps delicately toward them.

"Hevron, let this man up!" Gom commanded.

Hevron trotted obediently up to the Spinrathe and stood. The man swung into the saddle, his mail clanking. And yet, Gom noticed, scrambling onto Stormfleet's back, Hevron didn't seem to mind the weight. *Go.* The warrior raised his weapon high. *I shall deal with this scum. Find a safe place, and I shall follow.*

"But—" Gom hesitated. He was no soldier, but it didn't seem right to quit. A loud whoop cut over the general noise of the battle as the riders leapt onto the ridge.

Go, I say!

Gom went, Stormfleet teetering over the ridges, slipping, sliding, until they had left the whoops behind, and the clash of blades, until he found a safe place, out of the fighting. He looked back: the warrior and his attackers were lost to view. He'd been right to leave, he told himself. He'd only have been in the way. He slung his staff, wiped his face on his sleeve, felt his breathing slow.

Keke swept down, settled on a low bough. "You should

see Hevron! He's fighting like a stallion! They're holding the Sundor rats at bay! And that stranger's sword—it sings!"

Stormfleet reared, throwing Gom forward, threatening to unseat him. "A stallion!" The cito neighed fiercely. "And here I stand, a cowardly hack, meat for the lamest blade! Gom Gobblechuck, give me back myself! I would stand with Hevron—and in mine own proper form!"

"Now? But there is neither time nor place!"

"This is the time, the very place! Here! And now!"

"But there is peril in it." Gom leaned his head on the cito's neck. "Stormfleet—I can't—I daren't!"

Stormfleet shook him off. "You who have just brought down a mountain—you can and must do this for me."

"But I—" Gom peered through the bushes. No sign of the warrior, no one seemed to be looking their way. It would not take long . . .

Dismounting, and slinging his staff, Gom slipped the crystal from under his shirt. "If you're sure," he said.

Chapter Twenty-two

GOM REMOVED the saddle, dropped it in the mud. That would not fit the real Stormfleet! "This spell reverses instantly. Ready?"

"Ready."

Gom looked into the watery eyes and pulled the spell he'd practiced these many months past. Power surged from the crystal, like a snake uncoiling. It twisted in lines of fire, looping around the cito's old gray body, until the horse was encircled by a mesh of spinning whorls. Gom held them steady, until the lines flared and fused. Somewhere behind him, he heard Hevron's soft whuffle, yet Gom did not turn, made no sign, only kept his mind firmly on the task before him.

The light faded, and the old gray hack dissolved into tenuous mist, hanging in the air. Gom felt a surge of joy. Stormfleet to be his own matchless self again! He pictured Stormfleet as he had been: tall, with black coat and shining silver ringmark, and the proud, unbreakable spirit of an immortal cito.

The mist sparkled, began to shimmer. A young colt's body began to form high above the ground. Four long, fine legs sprouted from it, neck, head, then mane and tail, blowing in the wind. Bright fierce eyes looked upon him.

"Stormfleet!" Gom cried out in exultation.

The colt shape twisted, contorted; the head stretched, eye and mouth pulled down into a hideous grimace. Hevron started in alarm, and Keke flew up with a terrified shriek. Gom stared in horror. He'd lost control! Quickly, he recovered, directed the mass back to its proper pattern.

The colt reemerged, took firmer shape, became solid and rounded. And then, at last, the glossy black form of the cito colt stood before them; proud, beautiful. Gom slipped the crystal back under his shirt, letting it fall against his chest. Stormfleet, stirred, reared in triumph, neighing loudly. Hevron, too, rose up, joining in.

"Stormfleet." As Gom had first seen him in the moonlight on the High Vargue. He reached out, touched the sleek, glossy body. "It *is* you."

"Who do you think it would be?" The cito came down on all fours. "Now let us get on!"

The Spinrathe saluted from Hevron's back. *You are truly a mage, and fully deserving of the starstone. Would that I had brought it.*

Gom eyed him in dismay. "What do you mean?"

At great risk to life and limb I found its hiding place. But not the stone.

"I don't understand."

The niche was empty. No stone. Nothing.

"Then . . ." Gom's face fell. "Why did you come?"

The Spinrathe raised his sword. *I pledged you in your hour of need. I had to bring you something.* He glanced around. *And lucky I came, or you'd be singing another song.*

True. Gom was instantly ashamed. But talk of the

stone had brought back thought of Katak. "He's some-where close." Gom pointed down. "Beneath this fen, as I guess."

Why? It is far from the stair.

"There's a gemstone hoard under Sundborg. But don't worry, it's locked away, and the mountain is sinking. I don't think—"

Trumpets sounded over the field, drums beat loud tattoo.

"The mountain sinks! Flee for your lives!"

Chaos struck the lines, figures ran in all directions, some into the marsh. Then bugles sounded once more, and Galt's criers called across the field: "In the name of the king! The enemy tricks us! Back to arms!"

But the damage was done, the war had become a rout. And Galt?

From his vantage point, Gom spotted the king making for the Causeway. Even as Gom watched, Galt wheeled his horse and set off back toward the mountain.

Keke flew in, crying loudly. "Galt escapes, see! But he'll not get far! I shall peck out his eyes!"

"Wait, Keke! He's going for the stones!" Gom turned to the warrior. "To rescue them before Sundborg sinks."

I shall stop him, the warrior nudged Hevron forward. *Cut him down as he goes!* Even now when they were side by side, the warrior did not speak aloud.

"No." Gom scrambled for Stormfleet's high, glossy back, slipped, tried again. "We must follow him. Let him unlock the stones—if he can reach them—and we shall simply step in and take them."

Is it worth the risk?

"There is one stone," Gom said, scrambling to get onto Stormfleet's back. "The emerald Seal of the Lakes. If I can return it to its owner—it would do much good—not least to me." Gom finally made it onto the wide and slippery firmness of Stormfleet's back. He tightened his knees into the colt's flanks, remembering a perilous flight across the Vargue. He'd have to learn to ride all over again.

Very well, came the gruff reply. *Let us move along.*

The Sundor king was pulling ahead along the Causeway, cutting a swath through the fleeing hordes. Gritting his teeth, Gom set off after him with the Spinrathe, Keke sweeping overhead, urging them on.

"I'm slipping," Gom complained, tightening his grip on Stormfleet's mane.

"Lie along my back as I told you before," Stormfleet cried. "Here, I'll change to rack, how's that?" The cito's stride smoothed out some, and Gom felt more secure. The horses raced neck and neck, keeping the king in sight, until at last the mountain hove into view. The Causeway before the Gate was already under water, forcing the horses to swim under the portcullis arch, in the king's wake.

Like a mouth, this Gate, Gom thought, an open maw, swallowing them up.

The warrior glanced his way. *The waters are rising fast. Another hour and we'd not have gotten in.*

Oh? Gom thought, as Stormfleet swam through into the hall. And in another hour? Shall we get out again? But he kept it to himself.

Water swirled up the staircase leading to the higher

levels. Gom nudged the cito forward. The horses went slowly, feeling for footholds on the stair. They clopped up, out of the water, but around the next bend wet already glistened under them: Galt's trail.

A sudden flurry, and Galt's horse came rushing down, past them and on, going for its life.

They clattered up to the second level, the third, the fourth, the horses' hooves striking hollow in the stairwell. Keke flew on a way, came back again, never going too far ahead. The whole mountain was deserted—save for them, and Galt. Gom rode down the hallway to Galt's chambers, following wet hoofprints, coming and going, through the door, across the outer chamber where the king had sat with his advisors, and on through to the inner room.

The king was standing before his open vault, scooping gemstones by the handful into a large bag.

"Hold!" Gom nudged Stormfleet forward. "Drop those stones!"

The king turned about. "Stay away. You shan't stop me." He closed the bag, fastened the strap. As he did so, Gom caught sight of something lying beside the king, half hidden by a chair. The body of an armored man, bare-headed. The face was turned toward him. Gom sucked in his breath.

Galt.

He looked up, and met the eyes of the other. Cold hit him, numbing his flesh. Not Galt, but Katak, Spohr, shape-changer—the Lake Lord's emerald Seal glittering in his hands!

Beside Gom, the Spinrathe raised his sword, and froze, weapon in midair.

The false Galt laughed, and dropped the Seal into the bag with the other stones.

Gom's anger surged. These years of work, of learning—were they all to come to naught in the space of a breath? He fought to raise his hand, to reach for his crystal. Even as the cold drained his will, he forced his hand inside his shirt and clutched the stone, striving to focus his thought, to draw on all the remaining tiny points of light, spells still unspent, to fuse them into one bright ball of power.

The Spohr's eyes went to Gom's chest. "How? What have we here?"

Gom found himself lifting the crystal from under his shirt to dangle it high on its chain. As it flashed in the lamplight, the Spinrathe cried out aloud.

"Well!" Katak smiled. "Here I scratch for pebbles—while you hold the one true key."

Key? Gom looked down at his crystal, shaking his head. "You mistake. This was Harga's."

Katak laughed again, and over his laughter came a high, anguished voice that sounded quite unlike the warrior's: "Gom—the crystal you hold: it is the star-stone!"

Still clutching the bag of gemstones, the false Galt leaped high, and, reaching for the crystal, closed his free hand over Gom's.

Gom cried out, tried to pull away, but his fist was numb. His fingers began to uncurl. "No!" Gom summoned the last of his power. Released, the warrior seized Gom's free arm, while, with a flutter of wings, Keke locked her talons in the false king's hair.

"Fool!" Katak cried in Galt's harsh tones. "You have

the stone, yet you know not how to use it—but I do: see!" The cold hand tightened on Gom's.

The walls dissolved, and mist swirled; familiar mist, pearly gray and luminous. And through it something curved toward the sky; glassy, delicate:

The crystal stair.

Chapter Twenty-three

GOM LOOKED about warily. Beside him, the warrior sat, unmoving. Hevron snuffled softly. "Where are we?"

Stormfleet sniffed the misty air. "East of the Vargue, or my nose tells false. And that must be the crystal stair."

Gom was still holding his stone. *Starstone!* He closed his fist about it, and turned uneasily in the saddle. No sign of "Galt," or of Keke, either. He dismounted, walked forward and touched the stair. It felt real. But then it had last time. He looked back. "Are we really here, do you know?"

The warrior stirred, lowered his arm. *We are, by the crystal's power.* The gruffness was back. He sheathed his sword, slid heavily to the ground.

Gom opened his fist, looking down. "Harga never said. I never knew."

The warrior said nothing.

"Katak has disappeared." Gom looked around, into the mist.

He'll be back, the grim thought came.

Gom gazed up at the visored head. "What am I to do?"

The warrior stepped forward, set a mailed foot upon the bottom stair.

We shall make a stand together.

In a sudden whir of feathers, Keke swept into view and landed unsteadily on Hevron's saddle. "Where are we? How did we get here?"

Gom's spirits rose to see her still alive. "The man you attacked—where is he?"

"Ke-ke-ke? Man? What man?" She ruffled her feathers crossly.

The journey has shaken the creature, the warrior said. He raised his head, listening, and drew his sword. *Katak is near.*

They waited, silent, while the mist swirled about them, wrapping them together. Now, thought Gom, now it was the time. At any moment Katak would come out of that mist—and Gom would face him before the crystal stair. He held out his crystal. "What am I to do?" he cried. "No one has told me!"

You must destroy the Spohr.

"But how?"

I know not. The answer lies in you, somewhere.

Gom sank onto the step. "I don't even know where the gate begins. Is it the bottom step?" He patted the stair beneath him. "Or the top one? Or the doorway to the hall?"

You have seen the Tamarith.

Gom nodded shortly. "Aye. Alamar."

Did you try to reach it, to touch it?

"I did, but something stopped me."

That is the gate. That is what Katak must breach by the crystal's power.

"How? How will he do that?"

Through you. He'll make you work for him, the way he made you bring us here.

"I don't understand."

His gift is to bend others to his use.

"How?"

Many different ways. Greed, ambition—

"But that won't work for me."

So he'll find some other way. That is his gift. What is your weakness, Gom Gobblechuck? Speak out, do not stop to think.

"I—I'm afraid. Of this stair. I nearly fell last time, and then I was here only alamar. I'm afraid for Harga. And for Ulm. Oh, skies—" They were within a hair of its destruction!

We have found your weakness, I think, the warrior said gravely. *Beware, or he will use it. As he used it to get us here.*

"But this was the last thing I wanted!"

Exactly. Fear can pull a thing to you as surely as desire.

"You're saying that my very fear of his coming here actually brought us?"

The warrior nodded. *As it will get him up the stair if you do not take heed.*

Gom leapt up angrily. "I shall not let it." He slipped the crystal's thong around his neck, still holding the stone in his hand. It gleamed so brightly under the misty light, and yet . . . "I had pictured something . . . larger." Like the stone at Jastra's brow.

Oh? The thought was wry. *Larger is more powerful, is that it? I would disag—* The warrior broke off, and Gom felt the cold even before the horses shied and Keke sounded warning.

The false king strode out of the mist, past the horses, to the foot of the stair. He gestured upward with the bag of stones. "Do you go first, keybearer," he said. "Lead the way."

Gom grasped the crystal firmly. "Nay," he said. "I have your measure. I'm not afraid." Oh—he'd given himself away first draw!

Their eyes met. Gom's spirits dropped. He of no sense and little learning—how could he hope to prevail against a Spohr when even the Spinrathe could not? He backed up a step, then halted angrily. "I'll go no farther!" he shouted.

The lip curled. "We shall see."

Cold twisted up through Gom, probing, exploring. Fear flowered within him, fear of anything, everything. Fear, anxiety, curling him up, all the fears he'd ever known, like a nebulous fog below the level of his thought. To Gom's horror, he found himself backing up the steps.

The warrior called warning. *Think, don't feel: stand fast.*

"I'm trying! You must help me!"

I cannot stir a foot! came the reply.

Gom was losing ground. Katak was winning, using fear to breed fear. How to break the cycle? Gom ordered himself to stand fast, but his mind wouldn't obey. They moved steadily up the glassy spiral, Katak keeping even distance. The ground disappeared into the mist.

Please—help me! Gom sent out the anguished thought.

There came the sound of foot upon the stair, the warrior appeared, his arm raised, his sword gleaming in the pearly light. "Murderer!" he called aloud, and his voice rang high and clear. He swung his sword.

The false king dropped the bag of gems and disappeared, and the warrior tumbled down. Gom closed his eyes at the thud of body hitting the ground. When he reopened them, a shape had begun to form in the air before him. Katak—in well-remembered guise! The death's-head floated, hollow sockets staring, seeing all: the fear, the worry, the insecurity. Gom shivered. He was alone on the high stair.

How brave the mage now? Katak mocked.

Gom tried to rally, but his will began to crumble. He could stand for an hour, for a day. But he could not hold on forever! It was only a matter of time before Katak prevailed. He stepped up backward, reached to steady himself. No rail, of course. And this time if he fell . . .

He thought of the warrior lying below, a moveless heap on the earth.

Laughter issued from the hollow skull, derisive, cold.

Step by step, Gom continued up the twisting stair, until his head began to spin. But there was no thought of falling; there was no thought at all. Suddenly, his back foot encountered level floor. His eyes fixed on Katak, he retreated down the passage, and into the sky hall where soared the Tamarith, star-gate, shining crystal pillar ringed by twelve pools of bright blue fire.

As in a dream, he backed toward the center of the floor. A single thought—a *feeling,* fleeting: a few more breaths and Ulm would be no more. Sweat pricked his brow and trickled down his face, like tears.

There came a sudden shout. "Gom! He rules your thought through fear!"

Gom wrenched his eyes away, and felt release. The warrior was advancing, his whirling sword blade a shining disk of light above his helmet.

Gom shook his head clear, rubbed his eyes, his strength of mind returning. He looked about, saw with a shock where he was, the skull hanging before him—and the warrior, swinging back his sword to strike.

Now, mage! Think! Destroy the Spohr!

Think? Destroy? How could he possibly do that! What could he use against this alien thing, this shape-changer, this consummate master of transformations . . . .

Transformations!

Gom almost laughed aloud. Master of transformations? Why, he could play that game! As the warrior cut the air with his sword, Gom reached for the hum. The whirling blade passed through the ghostly skull as if through air, then flashed, enveloping the warrior's arm in flickering light.

With a loud cry, the warrior fell, rolled, and lay still.

The skull, unchanged, turned its hollow eyes on Gom once more, but Gom was ready. The starstone raised high, he pulled the transformation spell.

A thin laugh echoed out, and the skull, advancing, sent out its cold force, but as it reached Gom, his spell's power surged, enveloping the death's-head in coils of light. As the lines of fire twisted about it, the thin laughter turned to a snarl, then a wail. The lines of light flared, and fused, and the skull began to dissolve. Gom felt a surge of elation, checked it fast, holding his mind steady. Now was the greatest danger: a fine gray mist still hung in the air, essence of Katak, Spohr. Gom didn't have long!

The mist began to shimmer.

As the skull started to reform, Gom pulled the polarity spell, then reversed it. The mist flared—and vanished.

Gom waited. Nothing. Katak was gone—forever!

The visored warrior lay, unmoving, his sword beside him, a strange, spent thing—no light-blade, only the hilt, studded with crystals like so many buttons. Gom knelt, looking down at the still, warlike figure, recalling how he'd cupped its image in his hands, this figure and all it represented.

His life's companion.

He bent down. This grim, gruff warrior had saved him, had given him—and Ulm—that precious second chance: had it cost the man his life? Gom grasped the helmet with its pale green crest and carefully lifted it off.

Red-gold hair sprang out, thick, shining coils of it, bright as the setting sun. It twisted, spread, to lie in silken waves about the lifeless face. The helmet fell and rolled as Gom cried out.

The warrior was no man at all!

Chapter Twenty-four

A GIRL—AND very fair. Her face was oval, her cheeks, wide and high—pale now. She had golden-brown skin like Jastra's, a wide, strong mouth, full in repose.

Gom touched her temple. Not dead.

A young Spinrathen woman dressed as a warrior—fighting as a warrior, not only here, but on the alien battlefield? The truth rushed upon him; the why, and the how. The gruff thought-voice, sounding like a man's. Times, though, she'd lost control and called out aloud, and the spoken voice had been her own: high and clear, a young woman's!

Her eyes opened, brown eyes, flecked with gold. For a moment, she lay, then she turned her head and saw Gom. *Katak?* she asked gruffly.

He smiled at the incongruity. "Gone. Like your helmet."

The girl's hands flew to her head. She tried to sit, fell back again and closed her eyes.

"Is there anything I can do?"

"I'll be all right." She looked up at him. "Katak's *gone,* you said? What do you mean, gone?"

"Let's say he's scattered to the winds—forever."

She smiled radiantly. "Didn't I say you could? How did you do it?"

"With a teacup."

Laughing, the girl struggled up.

"Here, let me." Gom helped her, conscious of their touching. Strange, she didn't seem so strong now.

She picked up his thought. "The battle suit's a great equalizer." She reached for the helmet, ran her finger around the rim. "When it's off, the circuit's broken, and the suit's inactive." She shot him a look. "And then I am as I really am. I suppose I should tell you. I'm—"

"—Anja."

Her eyes flickered. "You've guessed, of course. Oh, well, now it's out."

"Out?"

"I would have had it thought that I am dead."

"Who's going to tell?"

"You mean you'll say nothing? What of Harga, and Jastra?"

He shrugged. "I'll tell only of the warrior who—"

"No!" Anja cried. "For if you do, I could not come again!"

"Why," Gom said slowly. "Jastra doesn't know—no one knows you came. Come to think—*how* did you come? How did you get through the gate?"

She turned her helmet over, examining it. "With—a teacup."

He grinned. "Why did you come?"

She kept her eyes down. "I told you: I'd promised."

"Anja: when I couldn't reach Harga, why did I reach you instead? And only you?"

She looked up now. "Few of us keep up the old practices. But my mother did, and me. And my—my brother. If this is ever over, perhaps we shall revive the ancient ways, work to make our minds strong again."

She set her helmet aside. *That is how we touched, I in the thick of battle.* The gruff voice of the seasoned warrior was back—quite convincing. "But the next time you called on purpose. 'Kurnyn,' you called—you almost got me killed!"

"I had thought— He's dead, isn't he?"

Anja nodded soberly. "He saved my life. They got Mother, then came for us. He died holding the door while Hujen—he was Kurnyn's retainer—got me out—against my will. There was fire, our palace was totally destroyed. They think we both perished in it, and I'm not disabusing them. Only Hujen knows the truth—and you, now."

"Why do you have them think that you are Kurnyn?"

"In the beginning it was to fight my uncle: to avenge Mother and Kurnyn, and to keep what is ours. Then I heard of the Spohr." She pursed her lips grimly. Gom could not take his eyes off her.

"So you fight as a man." He nodded. "Ulm women don't fight, either."

"You misunderstand, Gom Gobblechuck." She smiled. "It is not my sex that I disguise. Some of our greatest warriors are women. The battle suits provide any physical strength you could possibly need. No, I am underage. I am younger than Kurnyn by some years. So when I'm on the battlefield, I do not speak, and I keep my visor down. And if folk want to think I'm Kurnyn's ghost—" She broke off. "Can you believe what's just happened the way we're sitting here? Think, think what you've just done! Your mother will be so proud!"

Gom swallowed, suddenly overcome. If he could only see Harga's face and feel her embrace when she learned the news! He could almost hear her now: *Gom, son, I knew you could!* He looked up, caught the quick sorrow in Anja's face. Anja also fought alone—but with no mother to urge her on and praise her victories. Gom's heart went out to her. "I could not have succeeded without you." He leaned forward. "Listen, if we can destroy one Spohr this way, what about the rest?"

She shook her head. "It's not so easy, mage."

"I don't see."

She sighed. "The Spohr are . . . connected. Rest assured that the other two knew the moment of Katak's destruction. They'll not let it happen again." She retrieved her helmet and got to her feet.

Gom scrambled up after her. "What shall you do now?"

Anja nodded toward the gate. "Go back, I suppose. Things are bad, you know. And getting worse."

"My mother—"

"—was alive and whole, last I heard. I won't lie to you: she's on Lantyn—my Realm—and she's cut off. Jastra, too. But she's in a safe zone, at least—" She bent, picked up her strange weapon. "I must go."

Gom caught her sleeve. "Let me go with you!"

"You cannot." She disengaged herself. "You still have your work here."

"How shall they know that Katak is destroyed? Who will tell them?"

"The news will travel, I promise you." She began to walk toward the gate.

Gom hurried after her. "They'll not make me a wizard!"

She turned about. "They don't have to. You're one already!"

"You don't understand," he cried. "You cannot practice magery without the Hierarchy's consent. Without their official scroll I'll be hounded from one end of Ulm to the other!"

"What? Have you lost your good common sense? Down below lies that emerald Seal. Restore it to its owner and you have an ally there. Then there're those you saved from the marsh. Yul Kinta? And there have got to be at least a couple of mages on your side. Use your wit, bring them to your cause, and your enemies will have to go along." She leaned forward, kissed him lightly on the cheek. "Until we meet again."

She stepped through the unseen barrier. The beam of light shone down, wires hummed, and the tiny silver bells jingled in their hollow spaces up and down the column's length.

"Anja!"

She smiled, saluted, then lowered her helmet. Her form shimmered, vanished. The beam cut, and Gom was alone.

He stood there, looking after her for a while. Then he turned away and walked toward the stair.

Katak destroyed.

Well, he could say nothing about that.

The battle was over.

Leochtor's emerald Seal was found and soon to be restored.

The Yul Kinta were saved.

He nodded slowly. Anja was right. Time to turn his skills to his own uses. He pictured himself riding up on the cito's back, handing over the Lakeland Seal to Leochtor. How could the Hierarchy deny him, when he'd done what they could not? Oh, they wouldn't make him one of them, hadn't he already known that?

Gom the Brown.

It had a fine ring. Staff, he had, to give him strength in time of need. And rune—such as no other in all Ulm possessed! He lifted the little crystal, held it out toward the Tamarith, like to like. And he had a horse, the envy of all men, that he could ride now openly, hadn't Vala guaranteed it?

He paused in the doorway, looking back. Anja was speeding out to the Realms, but she'd return, and then?

He went along the passage, whistling.

Minstrel's Wedding Song

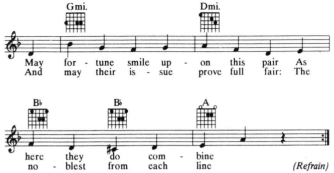

May   for - tune smile up - on this pair As
And   may their is - sue prove full fair: The

here   they   do   com - bine
no - blest from   each   line   *(Refrain)*

Note: First time refrain comes, first word is "Come"; second and third time, "So"; last (fourth) repeat, first word is "Now."

Gom's Song of the Dunderfosse

in the style of a canon

Luck - y the few who tread these ways, and

dwell with - in these bounds   Where

Luck - y the few who tread these ways, and

cool bough shades the sun's bright rays And

dwell with - in these bounds   Where

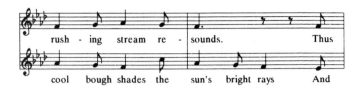

rush - ing stream re - sounds. Thus

cool bough shades the sun's bright rays And

with glad song to Har - ga's lake We

rush - ing stream re - sounds. Thus

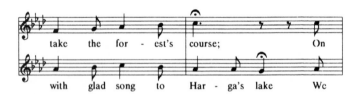

take the for - est's course; On

with glad song to Har - ga's lake We

Har - ga's isle new lives to make, for

take the for - est's course; one

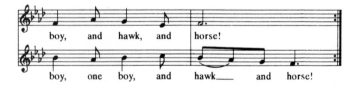

boy, and hawk, and horse!

boy, one boy, and hawk and horse!

Gorfid's Lay

Envoi: follows Stanza III:

Lo! The Slee - per doth a - wake, to bring thee on thy__ way, That curse may now its__ ven - geance take and e - vil mon - arch pay: Gor - fid's Chim - ney is the crux o - ver which you'll kneel; Trace the Wat - ers to the Bung, foul Sund - borg's taint to heal!

See pages 175-176 for the rest of the lyrics.

Grace Chetwin

has been thinking about Gom Gobblechuck and his history for a long time. After graduating from Southampton University in England, she moved to New Zealand where she married Paddy Roberts. During the busy time after their daughters were born, she taught school and also formed her own dance company. Later her family settled on Long Island, New York, the setting for her first two suspense fantasies, *On All Hallows' Eve* and *Out of the Dark World*. Through it all, she continued to be fascinated with thoughts of what had happened to Gom in the land of Ulm. Then she began to write the TALES OF GOM. The first, *Gom on Windy Mountain*, is the prequel to a trilogy that includes *The Riddle and the Rune*, *The Crystal Stair*, and *The Starstone*.